game

JJ ROSE

JJ ROSE

POPCORN PRESS

First published in 2022 by Popcorn Press, a division of Fair Play Publishing
PO Box 4101, Balgowlah Heights, NSW 2093, Australia
www.popcornpress.com.au

ISBN: 978-1-925914-41-2
ISBN: 978-1-925914-42-9 (ePub)
© JJ Rose 2022

Cover design and typesetting by Leslie Priestley
Printed by SOS Media in Sydney

All inquiries should be made to the Publisher via sales@fairplaypublishing.com.au

A catalogue record of this book is available from the National Library of Australia.

CONTENTS

Part I

1   October 2009, Brisbane 1
2   October 2008, New York 8
3   June 1974, Frankfurt 14
4   May 1978, Geneva 19
5   December 2009, Dubai 25
6   February 2010, Doha 34
7   March 2010, Glasgow 44
8   March 2010, Gafsa 47
9   March 2010, Outside Gafsa 72
10 March 2010, London 83
11 April 2010, Glasgow 93
12 April 2010, Nairobi 114
13 April 2010, Gafsa 129
14 April 2010, Hamburg 137
15 May, June, July 2010, Everywhere 144
16 June 2010, Cairo 154
17 June 2010, Gulu 160
18 August 2010, Amsterdam 169

Part II

19   August 2010, Beijing   180
20   September 2010, Dubai   188
21   September 2010, Lhasa   197
22   October 2010, Amsterdam   208
23   October 2010, New York   214
24   November 2010, Kuala Lumpur   221
25   December 2010, Al Khobar   244

Part III

26   December 2021, Brisbane   261
     Acknowledgements   285
     About the Author   287

DEDICATION

This book is dedicated to my brilliant and amazing daughter, Aceda. You were named to be strong, beautiful and extraordinary and you are surpassing even those lofty aspirations. You never cease to inspire me and to motivate me always to be worthy of your eternal gift.

And to all those out there everywhere, on the dusty fields and in the slums, on the streets and in the suburban parks, or on any patch of ground or grabbed space in between, with a ball at your feet and the people's game in your soul, this book is for you.

Part I

1

OCTOBER 2009

Brisbane

A long summer is promising, reaching into spring to grip and clutch at the air. A torpid exhaustion on the streets of post-consumerism. A warm westerly like a smoker's breath along Cavendish Road. Swirling wastepaper slapping at the empty store-fronts. Traffic lights changing and blipping for no-one.

I walk the streets in the night, searching in vain for cool air, and then lay awake on the bed, sweating, heart beating, feeling the blood under the skin. Sleep, as usual, comes as prolix, daily thoughts became sparse, abstract and otherworldly, falling into its alternative universe.

A phone call wakes me.

"Mr Asher Fox?"

The accent is French-Mediterranean, burred and thick. I rub my eyes and see myself in the mirror by the bed, reflected in the blue-grey light, hair askew, face crumpled. Head like the unmade bed I was groggily sitting on.

"Mr Fox. I am Abdulhamid. I am calling from Gafsa in Tunisia."

He waits.

At just past 3am, the mention of this country is like a bucket of cold water. I clutch my ribs. The top of my head lifts off, gently, like I'm not supposed to notice.

I knew enough to know Tunisia right then was not a place for a nice holiday and a few happy snaps with some guys in red fez's.

The man is waiting and I tell him I'm listening.

Sir, he calls me, to bring me into his confidence, assuming I'm informed.

"As you know, we are right now fighting the detested regime and we are winning. The workers' council is now in a position to reach out and utilise its position. We have made a decision upon how a certain portion of our resources can be used to help reach our global vision."

This is not just about Tunisia, not just some Arabs on the other end of the world, he said, with bruises in his voice. This is much bigger than that.

Abdulhamid's solid voice commanded authority more so when it is absent. Despite the crackling line and sense of distance I feel a shiver of something in the silence. I feel his eyes looking into me, through the satellite, across the oceans and deserts. Broken echoes of his accented English hang in the air. Tiny doors opening and closing.

I think into the gap that hangs there, projecting parts of myself, waiting for more, wondering if I have to speak. I have nothing to say.

The mind works fast. Information aligns in my head. Tunisia, revolution, *resources*. His word.

What resources are we talking about?

A fuzzy silence. I don't have to ask him to go on.

"We have money, Mr Fox. Fairly gained but I can tell you no details. It is people's money. *Our* resources, returned to us. You must trust this is so. But we don't need all the money ourselves. This phase of our struggle is almost over, and we are now looking ahead to the future. We are looking to serve our people, but also our faith. This is a faith in our God but also a faith in humanity. It is time we put back what our regime has taken away from us all. This aim is bigger than all of Tunisia. It is time we become who we really are again. To give of who we are. This too is part of what freedom means. The freedom to choose freedom."

His voice and my mind-voice blabbering away. I cut in and ask, "What is it you want from me?"

"Sir, Mr Fox, we want you to use some of this money. We want you to be the…" He pauses. "The point guard, for the interests of those like us and our people."

Basketball term. American educated?

I'm thinking now that they want a consultant, which sounds like the sort of thing I can do.

Seems fair enough and I began mentally drilling down into the details, spraying up words and thoughts like dirt and rocks. The well I am about to drill is deep.

It's pre-dawn. This is hard and my bed is soft. I want to cut to the chase.

"So, you want a consultant?"

"We want you to do a very special job. We want you to manage a very special project. We have a very firm agenda and a very clear place we wish to start our global revolution Mr Fox. Gafsa is just the beginning. We do not see liberation as something that ends at our borders. We do not see freedom as a state of affairs that is only for those who carry Tunisian passports. Liberating Tunisia is only an early phase of our global ambitions. Freedom is about all of us. We cannot be free if someone else is not.

Dr Martin Luther King said that."

I'm silent.

"We have a place we wish to start."

I keep waiting.

"We do not have the ability, nor perhaps the will, to redesign the global political or economic system. These are forces beyond what even our significant resources, now liberated from the dictators, can manage. Perhaps for another day, but not now."

"What are you asking me?"

"We don't want a deal maker or a businessman. We want someone with a proven moral compass. We want someone who has shown he is willing to put values before value. You have shown us that you are that man." He pauses once more. "Our efforts now will be focused on one thing: the football World Cup, and we want you to run that campaign."

I had no reaction. Stunned and confused. The World Cup? Why me?

"Football is the oldest game that is commonly played around the world, sir. Its associate body has more members than the UN, more than the Olympics. There are more football players around the world than any other team or active sport. There are more followers of the game than any other sport, maybe four billion, one of every two people on the planet."

He sounds almost fanatic.

"There are more football fans than members of any one religion. If football fans were a country, it would be the largest and most widely dispersed on earth. This is a very large constituency Mr Fox. This is our target audience to affect a revolution of political, social and economic change throughout the world. It will be the foundation for us to begin to completely restructure the planet to be more in sync with the common man, woman and child."

"I still don't understand what this has to do with me."

"Most, if not all of those followers of football believe the current structure is corrupt and has been overtaken by corporate interests. The people's game has been sold off and the people are well aware of what they are losing. And they don't want to lose it."

I'm nodding along, though I'm not sure why.

"Mr Fox, I would suggest to you that if you were to hold a conference for world peace, you would get a range of officials and politicians, interest groups and activists, and bureaucrats. All would disagree. But, if you take a football to any place on earth where there are people, drop that ball on the ground and let it bounce, I can virtually guarantee you that someone will kick it before it stops bouncing. And a game will commence. Everyone understands a football on the ground. That's power. It beats any conference or global agreement."

I'm taking this in. It sure sounds good. Poetic even.

But…sure I love football. I played it pretty seriously when I was younger, still play sometimes and enjoy it now. Love watching it.

I understand Abdulhamid. After all, I'm one of those billions.

But, world revolution? Global power? Really?

My mind lurches around like a drunk at a fun park. Why me? Seriously. "Why me?" I ask aloud at last

"Well, Mr Fox, let's just say you have been recommended to us by a trustworthy source."

"You're not going to tell me who, are you?"

"It's not so important right now," he says.

Mind still going….

"So, you want me to do what?"

"We want you to get the people's game back. We want you to

win the World Cup."

I broke into a smirk, maybe a laugh.

"Here is a number Mr Fox. One million US dollars."

I blanch. "I don't…I don't understand Mr, er, Abdulhamid. What does this number mean?

"Mr Fox, this is your number. We have set aside $1 million in cash and some million of dollars in assets for you to help us recover our good standing in the world and within our own minds; to use this money, which has been regained from those so corrupt it would be hard for you to imagine I think, for good purpose. This money will begin to restore the balance in our region and in our world through bringing the World Cup back to the people, to gain for the people a victory against politics and big business. We want you to manage this resource, to run it, to represent it as you see fit.

"This $1 million is your budget. Of course, you will need more detail…"

I've stopped listening. Mind-voice is chattering away. Come back, I tell myself. Listen!!

"……arrange for you to be sent funds to come to meet our representatives in Gafsa, where you will be better briefed. If you agree, of course."

*   *   *

Gafsa, central Tunisia, is steeped in history. Romans, Vandals, Muhammaden Arabs are among the raiders that have charged into Gafsa and set up their own versions of history.

The local phosphate mine helps make Tunisia one of the world's leading producers of the commodity. The time-honoured struggle of labour and capital rippled its muscles often here and in 2008, local workers took to the streets. They shut down the mine for months.

The movement was not just about Gafsa, or phosphate, or wages. It was a tilt at the Tunisian government led by Zine el Abidine Ben Ali, and his creaking, malignant government in distant Tunis.

The company backed down and the government in Tunis began its fatal, final wobble. Gafsa was like the detonator to the atomic bomb that the Arab Spring that was soon to become.

Amid all this, the workers had seized a vast hoard of idle money, revenue and other shapes of wealth. This included seized assets from one of the executives and co-owners of the phosphate company, a man who was a notorious government thug and an infamous hard man of the company and the regime. He became collateral. They took possession of his assets in his home after they had taken it over, a marginal moment in a secret revolution.

They found a fortune piled high, pushing against the walls and ceiling of a bunker, deep underground in his vast mansion. There was cash, literally tons of it, mainly $US, but also Euros, Yuan, Riyals and so on, and a little local cash, enough for a nice imported car or two, a city apartment, a functioning business. There were diamonds and gold, jewellery and art works. There were stock certificates, major holdings in well known companies, Swiss bank details.

It took them months to go through all those funds and assets, to count it and to account for it.

History is essentially an objective thing, an artifact of time to be studied and observed at a distance. And here is where the objectivity ends for me. I was about to walk into this forgotten corner of history, like crossing the light throw of a projector and casting your silhouette onto the screen, so that I was part of the story.

2
OCTOBER 2008

New York

A battered soccer ball arcs against the hazy sky of Phnom Penh. It lands with a puff of dust and is spirited away by swift-moving bare feet and flash of brown limbs.

The players move and shape as one, like long grass in a breeze, following the ball as it scurries and flies. Each thud of flesh on beaten, synthetic leather, greyed and logo-less, is like a grunt from this pulsing beast. Voices rise and fall as movement increases. The ball lifts high again.

And lands on a red field in Jabalia, Gaza. Bare feet deftly caress and move the ball, caked in hard-won earth, as blurred bodies focus and fade. It's not a ball at all but a spherical mass of plastic bags and elastic bands, smaller than the standard size, bobbing on the uneven ground and random rubbish. The foot pulls back, and whacks the ball so that it blurs away and hits a makeshift net, hanging feebly from a stripling goal. It is picked up and kicked, high and thwacks against a wall where a soccer goal is painted, white on sad, industrial bricks. On the wall are painted the words 'Take Flight' in street-cred graffiti style. The three upward ticks of the company logo in red are clearly seen. The branding moment is emphasised when an on-trend kid from the Projects, picks up the ball and tucks it under his arm, logo out, and jostles off with his mates and away.

The words 'It's Our Game' lift off the wall and take a bird like form. A booming voice says "Take Flight...The World Cup is about to get real."

Lights flick as the image fades to reveal a large TV screen which still holds the attention of ten men and two women around a large mahogany table. Curtains on the floor to ceiling windows are electronically opened with crooked thumb and the exaggerated point of the remote of the man at the head of the table, basking in filtered daylight and a view across New York from 51 floors up.

Gascoigne Rush stands, gathers, adjusts his suit.

He tells them, "This is for internal use only, and for partners, strictly embargoed, to announce our takeover of the World Cup in 2022. I'll be glad to take your feedback." Looks smugly, inviting conviviality while sending daggers. Quite the trick. Hands splayed on the desk, colonising the space before him. Feedback means compliments.

A polite flurry of queries followed, thought confetti, not meant to be noticed, just some noise and movement to bridge to the next phase.

As the bridge peters outs, a tension builds. A vacuum of facts unacknowledged settles and disperses the idle words, sucks them up with a slow-breathing stealth. The confetti disappears.

It is just an ad. Hell, it was just a draft ad, not even done yet. Just a conceptual meeting, this. But, the reality it conveyed was clear: Sometime in the next few years, the 2022 World Cup venue will be decided. Now 14 years out, the campaign, the internal infrastructure of the world's biggest sportswear brand – Flight – has begun.

Time stands still, the silence is weighted. Everyone here has to sign an affidavit and promise not to divulge the content of the meeting. At risk of sacking. And being sued: "This company's lawyers will be sticking pokers up your arse 24/7 for the rest of your life," as Rush puts it to them with a smile.

As the tension in the room builds, nervous bums shift on seats, a few voices mumbled, Rush ran his eyes along the walls. Posters of Flight's World Cup marketing campaigns past were lined up in dark wood frames, testament to the game's vast reach bouncing around the globe in quadrennial hops: '86 Mexico, '90 Italy, '94 USA, '98 France, '02 Korea/Japan, '06 Germany.

As a locked out non-sponsor, all this guerrilla work costs a lot, sucks up a ton of creative effort and financial resources, and Flight is tired of it. And it was getting more and more expensive while they were kept outside the tent.

2018 is a done deal. Russia will host. It had spent too much time, money and effort, and had frankly scared too many people - Russians scare rivals better than anyone on the planet - to lose.

But 2022 is up for grabs. This one will be different. Has to be. And the decision was just two years away.

Gascoigne's mind drifts back, what, eight months? Back to when he wrote what he calls his Jerry Maguire Letter. "The World Game has been stolen. Big money has slowly but surely reached into the people's game and found ways to make money from it. But we know it isn't a business. It's a game. Our game."

His eyes glint at the memory. Maybe a little over-written and flowery - yes, 'flighty' even. But it was beautiful. And it worked. As his message zinged around company C-suite emails and encrypted chat rooms, his vision became legendary, and the crazy idea took hold.

Flight is actually in a position to grab the World Cup and make it theirs. The game was so badly managed by FIFA, its management so corrupted in the eyes of most, that it could be considered, in investment parlance, a distressed asset. Ripe for a hostile take-over. Yes, Flight could own the World Cup. Why not?

Gascoigne Rush feels that the Game always belonged to the elites, like him, who make it. It is the businessmen and landed families who make the rabble of street football in the poor industrial towns into a proper, elitist game - Association Football - and shape it to be what it is today. Without them, the game would still be a chaotic past-time for thugs and drunks.

But it has fallen into the hands of the wrong elite. God forbid, it may even head downwards, more control devolving to smaller units. The People! Ugh! This has to be fixed. It was theirs - his elite - to own again. It is only just, given their legacy.

And so, Flight's strategy is to hack the world game. Rush, Flight's Corporate Affairs boss, was gaming The Game.

It is an ambush. The ultimate in guerrilla marketing. Rambo Marketing is a term he likes to use.

And this room, right now, is the epicentre of that bomb he had just detonated.

*　　*　　*

They all sit in that big room, with that big window framing the big city and can't escape their own minds.

Rush lets the tension hold, looking at each, searching for character as the walls of the moment slowly close in.

"Qatar," he finally says. "Qatar. 2022. That's our target." He smiles. "Why Qatar?"

He doesn't expect an answer. Looking out the vast window. Someone coughed.

He answers himself. "Look at, say, Chile in '62, Korea in '02, now South Africa coming up in 2010. All embody the growth of the professional game, and a massive increase to the support and consumer base. Qatar is a newly mature oil state in a region where there's a lot of money being spent on the game. Middle Eastern males are among the leading spenders on European football, from buying club shirts to whole fucking clubs."

He stretches out his arms. "You all know the cost of feeding our brand is becoming unsustainable. We need partners with deep pockets. As you also know, we've had a few good years. We're carrying margins in the high 40 percentiles. Times are good. But we know margins are going to narrow. It's getting harder to hide our labour practices in dark corners. Wages are going to increase. The global financial crisis has pissed a lot of people at the bottom off and unrest will grow which, again, will impact on labour and maybe on brand profiling.

"Further, advertising is changing. Online marketing is in its infancy but you all know is that it will soon become very complicated and unpredictable.

"The costs of doing our kind of business, reliant on cheap labour and pushing a simple emotional brand identity is getting higher and more difficult. Workers, consumers, even law-makers, aren't going to keep buying us, product-wise or, conceptually.

"Our social licence to operate is getting more difficult to keep. And more expensive.

"A country like Qatar has to diversify its economy. Consumer brands offer both economic bang for buck - the more you spend the greater can be your domination - and soft power. It's a chance to set agendas, build a global position. Be respected and even loved. A Qatari-founded global sportswear brand ticks a lot of boxes.

"Qatar has plenty of money. But it doesn't have a brand. So, for us, Qatar has a two-fold value as a partner.

"We have to make sure we get Qatar and make that a breakaway World Cup in '22. It's already bidding for the FIFA World Cup. But I don't reckon they have much chance. FIFA won't back them. It's too complicated for them, especially with all the crap they're in. They will be conservative."

He points to the now blank screen. "So, it's *our* game now. Go to work, people. And keep your mouths shut!"

He takes the DVD, the only proof, out of the player and, with it in his hand, walked out of the room.

3
JUNE 1974

Frankfurt

From above, Frankfurt's Main River emerges through the early morning clouds like a blue ribbon. During the day to come, power will be drop from the sky. The BAC-111's and Vickers jets disperse their human cargo, carried from all around the world. Among those people are the 127 members of FIFA, all men, all bound tightly in suits and choked by ties.

Jorge Cordoso looms over the airport rush. His avian limbs and craning neck tense as the throng who have just arrived from Tokyo swept towards the exit. Cordoso, the head of the Brazilian Football Confederation, the former Olympic sprinter, Le Mans driver, owner of banks, pharmacy outlets and oil interests, touched down yesterday from London via Rio de Janeiro.

A long haul, even if it was in First Class seats and lounges, leavened with the best cigars and whisky.

But Cordoso hardly noticed. He spent the entire 43 hours getting to Frankfurt hunched over files, each one topped with a headshot leading to a bio. Each had sub-files: Likes, Dislikes, Important Dates, Family, and one which was untitled which contained all the secret information he could gather on each of the 127 personalities who filled his vast collection of manilla folders and spiral-backed notebooks.

Cordoso slept little his first night in Frankfurt.

It is around 2.45 that afternoon when Sir Cecil Rush drops in and shuffles with his bent gait through the airport and into the Frankfurt air. His polished shoes clacking on the Arrival Hall floor. Not a hair out of place. A lone figure.

Jorge Cordoso is not there to greet him.

Sir Cecil Rush has been the FIFA President for eight years, two World Cups, including the one now taking shape across West Germany. He is part of an enduring and unbroken European dynasty of presidents since FIFA's 1904 establishment. But this cosy cultural monarchy is under threat, and has been since 1958.

The sixth Mondial, held in Sweden had rocked Europe when Brazilian team had won, the first non-European team to do so. Europe's post-war austerity was lost on the Brazilians, whose shimmies and flicks, and outright individualism countered the dour continentals. Didi's back-heels, Garrincha's impossible swerves, and Pelé's nutmegs made stolid Europeans look like practice dummies, their porridgey weight still held by a war that never made it to the barrios of Rio or Sao Paolo.

The victory of the dark-skinned Pelé's Brazilians in the final, in an eviscerating 5-2 defeat of the Swedes at the Rasunda in Solna, was a shrill warning. Pelé's sublime 55th minute goal – a chest down and a balance shift to escape a close marker and an audacious lob over a second defender and then a volley of breath-taking poise and balance – let the world know football was changing.

Watch the video and slow down the footage of those few seconds and you can see the world of football turning.

The emerging nations from South America, like the unbelievable Brazilians, were pressing for better representation. The next World

Cup in 1962 was in Chile as a concession to the Latin lobby.

Journos joked he had been rushed in: *A Rush Job*, or variants thereof, had been the headline trope of the day. Truth was, in the late 1960s, FIFA needed a stern white face to run it. And Cecil Rush's fit. He became President in 1966 as celebrations over England's spectacular if mechanical win at Wembley still echoed around the country.

FIFA's steady, European hand wandered unheralded into West Germany to face a new global order. World Cups would be spread out in the coming years and non-Europeans might lose their domination on the field. But that didn't mean Europe would yield any of the force it could gather off the field.

The product was on the field, but the money was outside the chalk lines.

Back in the present, by the time 56-year-old Cecil Rush arrives in his room at the Hotel Steigenberger, he is tired. His copy of *The Times,* dog-eared and smudged, drops from his arm along with his grey Macintosh. A hidden copy of *The Sun* and its page 3 breasts is folded neatly in his briefcase.

His phone rings. *Let me rest!* But he picks up the receiver. Arthur Bourne, the Associated Press gumshoe looking for a lead. He asks to come up and have a chat. Cecil agrees. Ten minutes.

When Arthur arrives, he and Rush sit in the same formal dance as every time. Cecil is rather used to this rather febrile character and to the florid personalities of many reporters, whom he considers somewhat fluttering and effeminate. He tinkles his full scotch glass with distracted arrogance.

"Well, Sir Cecil, it would appear Mr Cordoso has been very busy indeed. Can we go on the record?"

Ah. Cordoso. Who else?

He is too aware of this stalking, elongation of a man, with the piercing eyes, the set jaw which too easily exploded in a wall of teeth, the cords of blond hair, the plastic smiles and Hollywood laughs. Cecil knows that Cordoso is stalking him, flipping about the world, talking up his candidacy. But he isn't scared. He knows his universe and he knows his people. They aren't for turning.

Sir Cecil isn't even concerned enough to opt for the protection of off-the-record. "On the record is fine, Arthur."

Bourne flips open his pad, clicks his pen, and readies himself. Sir Cecil doesn't stir, staring out the window as Frankfurt busies about in its frame.

Arthur clears his throat. "Sir Cecil, as delegates arrive here in Frankfurt for the four-yearly round of voting for the presidency of FIFA, are you feeling confident your tenure will continue?"

"Well, I can only reflect the feedback I've received," Cecil replies. "I have faith that those holding world football in their hands will take their decisions seriously for the millions of those around the world whom we serve." The FIFA head lights his pipe, puffs, swigs his post-flight Dewars. No wobbling in him.

With a wry smile, Arthur continues. "How do you respond to claims being raised among FIFA board members that times have changed, that you're a dinosaur and that young guns like Jorge Cordoso's time have come?"

"As I say Arthur, I can only stand on my record; eight years, a successful World Cup in Mexico and this one now to come, taking the game into new corners, development in Latin America, and a game that hasn't descended into the ruinous ignoble grab for money that has affected other sports." Cecil shrugs. "If there's a new era Arthur, you better have someone around who knows the ropes. Is Mr Cordoso ready? Does he understand this game, what makes it tick? I'm not sure there's ever been a new era that doesn't need to build on its past."

"Sir Cecil, I've spoken personally to many of the voting members, off the record. Frankly, my numbers have you losing? Is this a concern?"

"No." Word and body language give nothing. Nothing. Cecil fingers the mound of a three-inch scar on the back of his left hand.

"Are you concerned that if you lose, the game of football will change its face?"

"I am concerned only for the future of the game. I think you and I both know what kind of face should be on it, but I'll demur in the interests of respect and not offer any more on that. All I can say is that our game is changing, as it should. Now is not the time to be removing the steady hand we've held there for decades."

Despite his confident words, Sir Cecil notices his knees, poking through his trousers, and wonders about ageing. He sees his hands as he speaks, and they seem frail and unsuited for power. He feels that demon of fear saying, "See? Look at you! You're an old man in this young man's game! Look at you! It's over…"

And suddenly the fight is gone. He knows. Sir Cecil knows and his knees, his hands, his very soul confirm it to him. He knows it is the end. Frankfurt through the window looks like enemy territory.

4
MAY 1978

Geneva

Winter ice nestles and cracks in the grey, chill air. It grips surfaces and holds them, twists them. A drift of flimsy rain floats and swirls in the autumn morning. On the streets of Geneva, a rich city awakes.

Faces are set not only against the climate but against the threats of an uncontrolled life, courage defined by a struggle to manage the chaos and the world that contains it, using numbers and straight lines as weapons. Clouds of warm breath offer the only overt sign of humanity. But they hang and float away on the icy air like life extracted.

Inside the warm building, nestled like a fluffy bird, Franco Gallatese holds a fat cigar and feels suitably warmed by its mere presence; a blood-temperature symbol of life. Musty fumes unwind from its glowing end, which reddens like its volume has been turned up as he draws in the toxins. He puffs and his head is helmeted in a changing cloud of cloying smoke.

Gallatese is Cordoso's right hand. He runs Baleno, the only major sportswear company that can compete with Flight. And he runs the marketing company that now has the monopoly on TV rights and sponsorships for each World Cup. Cordoso and Gallatese are a deadly combination since Cordoso won the FIFA Presidency from

Cecil Rush in 1974, a perfect marriage of popular sport and business.

Cordoso hates smoking. Small figures on the streets below offer mute distraction as he sits and turns away from the pollution stack that is his friend and partner. He waits for the haze to clear and speaks to the window, to the minions below. "Franco, the generals are becoming tiresome. We should have charged them more."

Puff. Puff. Gallatese's face is hidden as he speaks. "C'mon Jorge. This is a process. We can't charge too much straight away, even for those morons. What do they want? It's our first World Cup and we're only a month away from kick-off. Let's just get through it and then we'll ratchet up the next cycle to Spain."

"I'm uncomfortable with Argentina, Franco. It's not good what they're doing. I'm all for the money, but do we need to work so closely with dictators?"

"Show me a country that has no dictators," says Franco, puffing.

In the thoughtful, taut silence, Cordoso stares and Gallatese puffs. The sound of his lips enfolding the cigar, the wheezy inhale-exhale sickens Cordoso a little. But he knows that Gallatese is right. He knows that next month's 12th Mundial in the stricken, oppressed country was already underway, decided before his presidency.

But the Argentinian president Videla and his mad friends are not stopping at hosting the world event.

"You know he rang me yesterday. Videla." Cordoso looks up as he speaks and sees that Gallatese stops puffing, although the haze still hangs in the air. Cigar exhaust nestles like a ceiling just above them.

Videla, the Generalissimo. The Butcher of Buenos Aires, his name loitering malevolently in the air with the cigar smoke.

Gallatese stubs his stogie. "Mmmm. Anything special?"

"He wants to win the thing," says Cordoso, an incredulous lilt on the 'win'.

"Sure he does. Who doesn't? Be good for his regime. Politically. Why would he tell you that?"

"No. He wants me to make *sure* they win. He wants me to round up some friendly members and touch them up to get the right results."

Gallatese's eyes widen, white behind the dissipating darkness of the smoke. "Throw matches? No! Who would you touch up anyway? And how could we guarantee it would work? Not easy to fix a game and not make it look like it, you know. The man doesn't understand the game." He shakily draws on his cigar and continues. "The group matches are out of bounds even for me and you. Italy? Not even with my influence and even if, the price would be too high. France? No way! Hungary maybe, but they're going to lose anyway. And we don't know who they're playing in the knock-outs. So, what's he getting at?"

Cordoso shrugs. "I don't know, and I don't really care. It's the fact that he thinks he can just get me on the phone and line up results for him like that. Who does he think he is? Who the hell does he think *I* am?!" Cordoso's face has gone a shade of puce. His cabled neck is straining. "This sort of thing bothers me. It isn't right. The money's great and as it should be. But, the game is still the game. If we start pulling it around like this, we'll lose what we've already built. Greasing palms, back-handers, doing deals – that's what we do. That's the business we run and we run it well. But the game has to stay. The product has to be what it is. We can't screw around with that."

Cordoso's eyes punctuates his final statement. Crazy eyes, brow creasing in on them.

Gallatese taps his cigar. "Ok. Let's take a look at what you have built, Jorge. First, we're taking on the Olympics as the world's premiere sporting event. Second, we've delivered on our promise to the developing world: eight more teams in Spain in four years, a special quota for Africa. All those votes behind us. And, third, most important, we're looking after our family; we're ensuring those on the inner circle were made even richer through moving the TV rights and everything else." He sounds triumphant.

"We've changed the world, Jorge, our world. This is the revolution football had been crying out for since the Second World War, that people like Cecil Rush were fighting against. It is the World Cup after all!. And we've done it! And we've made us all very, very rich! Why bother about shits like Videla?!"

Cordoso looks out and down as his friend speaks, down on the people on the streets, and he knows, even as Gallatese says it, something in them both can't really believe it.

*　　*　　*

Buenos Aires

One month later in Buenos Aires, a brutish-looking Argentinian, all body hair and muscles and wearing the blue and white stripes of the national team and a number 10 on his back, shimmers like mercury between the orange-shirted Dutch defence. Mario Kempes scores his second goal in the World Cup final at the vast and throbbing Estadio Monumental.

It is the 15th minute of extra-time and the gallant, taciturn Dutch – minus the sanguine genius of Johan Cruyff – are done. Crushed by the bruising style of the home team – and by its delaying tactics at the start of the game as well as the almost physical weight of the 70,000 crowd – one of the great teams in football history is robbed of its chance to consummate its reinvention of modern football with its biggest prize.

*　　*　　*

High in the corporate boxes at the stadium, behind dark, shatter-proof glass, Franco Gallatese and Jorge Cordoso lord it up with the generals as the celebrations go on below. There was smoked salmon, foie gras, Moet, and prime local beef cheeks. Sexy, willing girls and cigars like fence posts. Kissinger is there. The Dulles brothers. Backs all turned to the vast window where the game was playing, the match already long forgotten, the brief, tenuous connection with the population already severed.

Even as the crowd parties with deafening screams and tons of confetti, players lap the field and the nation asks itself if it could believe what had just happened, the game is already gone. The pitch upon which millions gazed only minutes before is a vacuum in history. The Moment has passed. The world is already won. The cup is just a piece of metal. The hunched back of the junta has turned away from the people again and re-acquainted itself with itself.

Jorge Cardoso turns to one of the Generals, his medals tinkling as he faced him, cigar dripping ash on the carpeted floor, stains of red wine around his lips. "The people could turn on you. Right now. Don't you think?"

It is part gallows jest, part genuine inquiry into the minds of such men he couldn't quite fathom.

"You know," replies the General, "We brought people to the stadiums in '76 when we staged the coup, to round them up, pick out the scum and start cleansing the body politic. They stood right there, on that very ground. And we killed them right here." He waved his finger, pointing everywhere. "But they forget. Give them a ball. Give them a game, good players, a victory, a distraction and they will forget everything. You can do whatever you want with them.

Look at them! Insects!"

He curled his reptilian lips to receive the wine and into that moist maw he wetly dipped his cigar.

5
DECEMBER 2009

Dubai

It's me, Asher. Who is this person I'm becoming? Business class tickets. Emirates. An airline chauffeur to the airport. On the way to Tunisia via Dubai. A room at the Dubai Fairmont for a night. They booked it. They paid for it. Honoured guest, they said. It was the only way to play the game, they said. Not football, but the bigger game of football politics. World politics. Same thing.

I have 30-something hours in Dubai and, being jet-lagged and wired with too much sleep, I go walking at 2am.

The city is lit like an open fridge, a 4000 km2 light bulb, fronting an ocean sparkling with evening jewels and backed by a desert of fine, bisque sand.

The yawing wide streets and boulevards largely empty now. Everything is closed - the best parties have moved indoors, private, where alcohol can be discreetly consumed - but a dome of white spotlights in the distance, outshining even the streets lit up like a stadium, promises life.

A huge, 24/7 construction site, ringed by a ten-foot fence with viewing squares cut in it at intervals. Everything roars and shudders and beeps with vehicles and machine action.

I stand for moments. Wondering. The lights are so bright that they pool over the fence and land in wan patches on the surrounding desert, chipped and dappled by the sand waves. I see movement in the half-light and approach.

A group of maybe 20 men, all dressed in blue work clothes, are moving about. I notice a neat pile of hard hats and rows of work boots, and a scattered pile of hi-vis vests. The men take shape. Grunts and shouts. And a ball. Playing football. Pants rolled up. Bare feet. Bright yellow hard hats for goals.

I stand and watch. I ask one close to me where they are from.

"Pakistan," he tells me. "Mostly. A couple of Afghans, Bangladeshis and an Indonesian." He looks around. "If he's here tonight." The man grins. "Our team is one short. You can play?"

I can play.

I lose myself among dark, eyeless, faces, unconnected in everything but this. Speaking the same language. Bare foot and sweaty, running around in the sand chasing a game, trying to impress, and bewitched by it all, like I am eight years old again.

Pre-dawn breakfast, just a few hours later, and I sit here in a fancy suit, stewardesses in their Arab-Anglo finery calling me sir and Mr Fox, on the way to Tunis. I'm on no sleep but freshly rested, smelling lovely, shaved and fed at the elegant, blue-lit restaurant of the hotel, where everyone bows and nods and calls you Mister or Honoured Guest.

A private jet. Lift-off at 7am from somewhere behind the main Dubai airport, tiny customs desk and only a cursory glance at my papers. VIPs don't do passports.

Despite myself, I feel an air of arrogance, destiny, smugness, importance. I'm told I'll need all the attitude, all the carry. It's an act but I'm warming to it and that worries me. So soon. So easy.

Already, I demand the artificial respect that money buys. I walk taller, gaze straighter, like I must act the part of money. The assumption that money betters me, strengthens me, improves me. I don't meet people's eyes, like they are beneath me. I stride. Things become important. I pose. I strut. I assume I am being watched, photographed even, Vogue shoots, Philipe Patek and Bulgari ads, Absolut face, Fortune 500 eyes.

Maybe it's just the game.

I have certainly struggled and fallen in the past. I have refused to play the game. I have smelled wealth, been near it, but never worn it. Money does things and I can feel it. Feel it changing me, submerging me.

My career has been seat-of-the-pants, broke and often broken. Bills unpaid, budgets non-existent, failure looming at every move, defeat like falling arrows piercing my flesh from cold, cold skies, killing me each day, bloodying my soul until there's nothing left of it to give.

But money. Money to take on the vested interests of the Beautiful Game. Money to be heard. Money to be seen. Money to play with power. And more. More of which I was about to learn.

Touchdown in Tunis. Quick transfer and private flight to Gafsa.

I arrive. All is khaki or dirt coloured.

*　　*　　*

The smell of fear greets me as I alight from the Citation Mustang jet. Steps gleam incongruously new against the pocked and cracked tarmac. Shoes crunch sharply on the gravelly surface. It's mid-morning, yet here it seems like late afternoon. A pall of smoke from sources unknown hovers and hangs, moving slowly in the no-breeze air. The heat is thick with power in motion, history in the air.

Gafsa isn't meant to be a warzone. The protests here are supposed to be done, problem solved, everybody happy and gone home. That's what the media says. But there is no peace here. This is a contested, unresolved space.

I hear a flutter, a manic flock of birds, and turn to see a cloud of paper documents riding a breeze, pages dropping like exhausted pigeons, falling into the dust to be ignored and ground into dust. Unimportant here. They flutter on.

A man waits some 50 metres away. Near him is a van, battered and scratched with grimy, cracked windows, looking nasty. Around his shoulders hangs an automatic rifle. A barrel chest turns towards me, brute hands finger the weapon.

His khaki bandanna ripples as a warm breeze steals around his large hulking shape. He motions to me, looks around, motions again, more impatiently. I move in my sharp suit and two stiff, new Gucci bags, one slung seat belt style around my shoulder, the other held tightly in my left hand. Crunch. Crunch. New shoes on old, old ground. Wealth striding across the crippling stasis of civil war.

Closer now. Eyes lock. No formalities. The van door is loudly opened, its rails screeching. I feel a presence inside and, sure enough, two human shapes materialise as my pupils dilate, both with weapons, one with what looks like an RPG launcher. Loaded, its nib-like grenade propped recklessly on the window ledge, window just ajar enough to accommodate it. A warning perhaps.

A smell of dry sweat and large men overwhelms my ritzy, if fake, wealthy-guy smell. Sweat forms in crevices of my new rich man body. Money can't stop sweat. Eyes peer through the gloom and quickly dart away, summing me up in mere moments which, it appears immediately to me, is the only time frame these guys can comprehend. I hope to Christ these are the right people.

"Asher, my friend. Surely you're not afraid of the dark?"

A face looms out of the darkness of which, yes, at this point, I am probably overly conscious. Accompanied with a grunt and a squeak of his chair. Windsor. We shake hands.

I joke. "You should have smiled so I could see you there."

A chesty laugh, like a warlord or a king, appreciative of the mildly racist ribbing that often passed between us. But it was just Windsor with his big face, black as night. "Ah, Mr Glow Worm...The darker the skin, the richer the culture."

Windsor was with me during the Virus adventure, where we exposed some of the darker arts of the pharmaceutical industry. He is like a brother to me. Like me, he had received, and probably still receives, groin-tightening threats likely coming from the US administration and/or African governments and/or Big Pharma due to the involvement of the then US President, Lleyton Trumbull, in the whole shady saga.

Trumbull's henchmen have been active and the story, while making headlines only a few years ago, has largely disappeared. People have been rubbed out or paid off and the spinmeisters have shifted the media's ADD-gaze on to other bright lights and shiny baubles.

"Can't argue that, brother," I reply.

I contacted Windsor to see if he could help out again. I emphasised that unlike last time, he would be paid, and would have an expense account.

"I'm no soccer fan," he had said. "I am uninterested in the sport angle, but am indignant at the corruption."

I wasn't sure if that meant he was in or out. A frequent quoter of Shakespeare, Windsor often gives the impression of running through the bard's volumes, seeking guidance, as if a Bible. Sometimes when he speaks like this, it is like he is talking to the man himself, asking for the right passage to come to him, be delivered, so he can move ahead.

I waited.

"The King must go to war, even though his heart is unsure," he said, creating his own couplet to introduce the prolix response I sought. "Yes, I will join you Asher."

Holed up in Kampala, running his impoverished and underwhelming NGO, doing his civil work to break the back of corruption in his own country, he jumped at the chance to take it all global; take it large as he put it with an odd and incongruous Americanism.

"I trust you with my life," I told him, adding I had done so more than once already. "I will need your calmness in the face of danger, your stoic refusal to be put off and your acceptance of the chaos that constantly surrounds us – your ability to manage rather than seek to control. And I will look forward to your Shakespearean quotes, which always give context to a tense moment. And confuse the fuck out of me…"

He snorted, but I wasn't done.

"I need you in Gafsa, Thursday, and I will put funds in your account to cover the trip and payment."

Now he comments, "The money is more than I have earned in three years. It isn't my motivation, you know that, but I have new shoes."

Indeed, he's replaced the old car-tire sandals that had been his constant companions. These new brown brogues remain in the light from the just-open window as he slumps back into his seat, still chuckling.

"Let's go," I say, motioning with a chopping hand and raised eyebrows into the darkness. The van rattles dangerously off, with

Windsor chuckling as he sees my poor attempt at authority among these men who recognise far deeper powers.

*   *   *

New York

"It's Gascoigne to see you," breathes Gemma, Hector Aronsen's libidinous PA.

Being head of Flight provides such privileges, think Gascoigne as he stands and waits, eyeing Gemma like a hawk eyes a mouse.

His mind wanders over Gemma's firm looking body when she looks at him as she stands near the double doors and directs him into the inner sanctum of Flight's global empire.

The late, winter afternoon is pulling shadows down Park Row, traffic signals, brake lights and the twinkling illuminations of capitalism are beginning to pierce through the dusk.

The corner office is more of an apartment. It's got two rooms adjoining, one bedroom, one media room. There's an ensuite with a circular bath and spa looking out over the city, towering buildings making a bar graph against the screen of glass.

Bathtub. Gascoigne thinks of Gemma, skin glowing, wet and warm and dressed only in soap suds against the New York skyline.

Aronsen is avuncular. "Gaz, wanna drink?"

"Na," says Gascoigne, liking the discipline, the saying-no, for Aronsen already has one, a swig of Lagavulin.

With a nod, Aronsen gets straight to business." Ok, how are we doing on the World Cup? Vote's in what, 12 months? Qatar locked in for us yet?"

"One federation, Oceania, is saying they are ready to jump and go with us."

"One?!" Aronsen looks up at Rush. "No-one from Europe or Latin

America?. Africans? Oceania is the easy stuff. Thought you might be a little further along than this."

"Well, Hec, I hear what you're saying, but we've still got a way to go until the vote. The coup."

Aronsen's tone drops, the eyes penetrate. "Only 12 months Gaz. We need the Europeans, the Americans, and the big Africans like Nigeria, Ghana or Cameroon. We've got a pretty sorry looking World Cup coup so far. What's the projection?"

The city moves below them like a flickering snake, the quickening darkness by now virtually all-encompassing. Gascoigne doesn't like being belittled like this. He hates the fact he isn't king. A few steps off the top is not much different from a million steps at a moment like this.

He prepares the lines that will prevent Aronsen putting some external consultants on the case, to look over his shoulder and get in his way. "The Africans will jump soon enough, Hec, and with them, the Continentals will have to look at us again."

"You mean you've already got rejections from UEFA Associations?"

"Of course, we contacted all the associations straight away. They said Qatar was on the nose even for them. Money can't buy a Qatar World Cup. But it will."

Aronsen narrows his eyes. "Better be so, Gaz, 'cause we got to get Qatar a World Cup, with our name on it, by next December. Since those FIFA buffoons sniffed what we were up to and rushed up the vote for '22 to be next year, we've been on the back foot. We need some momentum. Qatar is our battlefield. Lot at stake here. You've had over a year…jeez, it's your idea!"

30 seconds silence. Gascoigne speaks. "There's another issue which has just come up."

Aronsen looks up.

"I've been given some intel that there's a ginger group emerging on the margins of all this. Someone who is looking to block Qatar. Apparently connected to the rebels in Tunisia."

"Tunisia?! What the fuck are they playing at?" Aronsen's eyes intensified as his brow sharpened.

Gascoigne grimaces. "Well, the rebels have got wind of our moves and, for some reason, have got their turbans in a knot. Beyond that, I don't know. But, it's significant from what I'm hearing. They've filled up a pretty big war chest with money recaptured from phosphate mines in Gafsa."

With a curse, Aronsen replies. "Well shit. Didn't see that coming. Here's me thinking we've just got a good old corporate war going on here. Us versus FIFA. Nice and neat. This fucks us up. You better set up a bed in your office, 'cause I reckon you're going to be spending a bit of time here. Find out what the hell this is all about."

Gascoigne turns to leave. But before he does, Aronsen speaks. "Gaz, you know, I've told you before: this can't fail. There's too much at stake here. We're on the line here. It's us or them. You better have some fucking solutions."

Feeling pinpricks of panic, Gascoigne has nothing to say, and offers a contrite, confirming nod.

He winks at Gemma on the way out.

6

FEBRUARY 2010

Doha

Like a digitised version of a brain, the city and its electric ganglions loom sharp and quiet in the still desert night beneath Gascoigne Rush's jet. The arc lights of its airport shine for no-one. The small city sleeps while lonely bitumen contracted in the night air and unwavering street lights light urban spaces that 40 years ago were not more than simple dwellings and sand dunes.

The pools of spot-lit spaces, the pushed back darkness and the sense of people present but not seen has the feel of a prison. Dark patches outside the lights breath in the silence of the night, like they hold something or hide someone. Towering high-rises on the coast shine like spaceships, throwing speckled light on the water, creating an impressionist's image on the undulating sea. But many are largely empty. In Doha, the "build it" part was underway. The "they will come" bit was still being played out.

One of the phones on Gascoigne's cluttered desk buzzes.

"Gaz? It's Raphael. We may have Sudan for low six figures. But we need to negotiate something with the Ghanaians."

Gascoigne breathes out. "Ok, that's good, Rafa. We'll head to Khartoum to seal that, then to Accra after Doha and sort something out. Where are you now?"

"Right now I'm on my way to Senegal. The new government is meddling in the sporting federations and the old government's guys are digging in. I am thinking some assistance from us may be useful and beneficial for us."

"Good. Keep me posted."

Fifty-four African associations to win over. Would have to visit every fucking one? Another 154 in Asia, Europe, the Americas, Oceania. In, what 10, 11 weeks? Carrying bags of money, offers of real estate, exclusive university and school entries, and yes, the occasional sexual favour.

His small jet curves into the prevailing winds, pointing into its landing course into Doha's desolate airport. They will soon descend and another trip will begin.

Gascoigne bunches the papers on his desk and sighs. He buzzes through to his pilot and tells her to refuel and prep a flight path for Khartoum while here in Doha. He lights another Don Pepe and looks out over the oil black sky where the Doha lights don't sparkle, oddly familiar, through the smoky veil of heady incense that coil up from between his fingers.

Air-con interiors are the prevailing climate in Doha. As Gascoigne sits and waits, he takes in the chilled air, the early morning light that quadrangles across the floor, and the designs that give the space character. It is all baubles and fuss, overly crowded and pseudo-elegant, and for classical art lover Gascoigne, it is nothing but puerile and not a little embarrassing.

He slips off his loafers and reached for the crackling Don Pepe, his third in a row, its blue smoke loitering in the still air.

The Emir wafts in, trailing an aide, both in flowing thobes and immaculate black bishts. He is short and a little bent, looked older that his 58 years, but all has been done to allay the obvious with black dyed hair sprouting from his head dress and nestling on his chin, above his eyes and under his nose, like his face has been doctored by a child with a heavy hand and a thick black texta.

The aide arranges the cushions on the seat while the Emir stands and stares into the middle distance, then the aide places a tea service on the small round table and pours. When this is done, the old man sits, gathers his clothes and himself, and waves the aide away.

Then, only then, does the Emir acknowledge the presence of Gascoigne. "Tea, Mr Rush?"

Gascoigne is not phased. "Yes, thank you, Your Highness. Always good after a long flight."

The aide shuffles forward, pours, and stealthily places a small smoking cup at Gascoigne's side.

The old man asks him about his flight; whether he is comfortable in Doha; if he needs anything. He wishes him well, *Insha'Allah*, rises, and leaves without saying more. The tea is still breathing, both untouched. The Emir is up and away, swishing off with his aide, and Gascoigne waits.

It may be a while. Schedules often don't align.

The Emir and his executives, all family members, zip in and out of rooms all throughout the palace like this, guests waiting until the Emir waltzes into and out of each meeting, saying the same things, asking the same questions and never drinking the tea.

With the imprimatur from the highest earthly level – each important meeting could begin.

And so, Gascoigne waited.

Fifteen minutes later, another thobe and bisht. The same aide whisks in, bearing Qatar's Minister for Interior Planning, the young, immaculate, svelte looking 44 year-old nephew of the Emir, introduced himself with a flurry of Arab names, which ended with

"...but please, you can call me Abdul-Aziz", which Gascoigne already knew.

A few minutes of formalities. Then Abdul-Aziz prompts: "So, a World Cup?"

"An opportunity that you, even you sir, could never buy," responded Gascoigne. "We will do anything to get Qatar to get the World Cup. Further, sir, we will partner with selected Qatari companies to develop a global sportswear brand which will compete globally.

Abdul-Aziz waits.

Gascoigne lets the silence build for a moment, then continues, handing a dossier to the minister "This is, of course, highly confidential. We cannot be an official partner to the bid."

Abdul-Aziz flips through the dossier on reflex, not reading a word. "You understand we are well advanced in our own bid, without you, already," said the Minister. "We have many resources in play. Our Achieve sports academy has been running already six years now. We expect to have professionals who have gone through our system in the '22 World Cup, playing, starring, for numerous countries. Why do we need you? And, I would have to add, what price are we paying for this? Lastly, is this for us? Or for you?"

Gascoigne is prepared for this. "With us, you get a guarantee that all those resources, and all that face, will not be in vain. I personally guarantee you will win the bid. This offer doesn't even have to leave this room. You, sir, can have all the glory."

He has the Minister's attention – so he doubles down.

"You will be getting everything you need from us to establish Qatar's own sportswear brand, a global brand which will move you out of the oil economy and into the consumer brand market where the money and the influence is unbeatable. We are already setting up votes for your nomination in December as we speak. Once you let me know for sure you're in, we'll ramp it up. There's a lot going on with regard to how the World Cup will be run, and we want you to be there. With us, because that's where we are."

Abdul-Aziz taps his chin, his words slow and measured. "So, if I am to understand, this is *not* to be a FIFA World Cup. It is a Flight World Cup, correct?"

"Correct."

The Minister motions to the dossier. "I assume that this outlines what is expected of us?"

"It does. But I can summarize that for you. All you need to do is to agree to host our World Cup, to reap its financial and global profile rewards. You need to ensure your national team has a good coach and maybe a couple of ring-ins, because they'll be in it – and the first time is always the best. All you need to do is bathe in the glow. And to make Flight your partner and the exclusive World Cup sportswear presence. And drop FIFA. That's all you need to do."

The Minister smiles. "Big plans, Mr Rush." He glances again at the dossier. "I'll get back to you soon. Thank you for visiting us. Please enjoy your stay in Qatar, and if there's anything you need, do not hesitate to let me know. Anything at all."

With this, the aide steps forward and holds out a gift-wrapped box.

"Something small to recall your visit to Qatar with fondness," says the Minister. He is up to shake hands and then out the door before the gift can even be opened.

Gascoigne opens the ornate box. It contains a dozen Don Pepe's. The bands are gold, each inlaid with a ruby-coloured gem.

As Gascoigne is admiring this providence, the Minister turns sharp right outside the door. Down the corridor, his slip-on shoes sinking into the thick carpet, topped by even thicker rugs. His aide at his side, he speaks quietly. "The Gaza Room."

Both turn left into the room and sit down opposite his next meeting.

Horst Leverbruck, Cordoso's successor and current FIFA President, rises to greet him.

*   *   *

Glasgow

It sits with him, a weight in his mind as he trots around the luscious grass of the Lennoxtown training ground. Boot sprigs gripping the turf, each footstep a statement on the earth. Banter among the players, fitness trainer barking sounds no-one hears.

He is apart from the group, even as he moves within it. His coach back in Tibet always says he knows a team is in the zone by how quickly their steps fall into a beat as they warm up around the field. Today, his are out. Left to their right. Up to their down.

This Thing intensified after a phone call just a week ago.

"Mr Lampa. Hello Sir. My name is Hussein. I am calling you from Tunisia, a place you may have heard of."

He had listened because his mentor had told him to. "You will receive a call from a man in Tunisia. Hear him, Chodak. You must hear him. Who you are now. You must hear him."

So he stayed silent.

Hussein told him things he didn't want to know. This surprisingly gentle voice fading in and out down a scratchy line from somewhere in that troubled country, told him that the World Cup was rotten like the fruit on the olive trees in his country today.

He told Chodak about the World Cup venue vote coming up, that Russia would win 2018 and that 2022 was a 'corrupted process'.

He told him that Flight and FIFA were slugging it out, seeking dominance over the world game, to get Qatar to win the '22 bid.

Flight and FIFA would destroy the world game.

"This is no longer our game," said Hussein. "This is not a game for the many people that make it what it is. It is not a game for oppressed people like you and me. It is a game which has the potential to unite. But it is being used to divide and conquer."

The bribes that are in play are not just money and power. They are working with the most depraved and, as Hussein put it, "the most unique needs", of those who make the decisions.

He told Chodak there was evidence of children being kidnapped, kids from various countries, Tunisia being one of them, and packaged and wrapped like living sweets, fearful eyes like dark cherries, tiny bodies presented as gifts to be abused by the monsters running the game.

He painted Chodak a picture of their broken and ripped-up little bodies dumped in landfill like bags of rubbish.

"This is an atrocity on many levels," he concluded.

Chodak heard it all. And he felt the guilt rising.

He had come from a background of poverty and isolation. Born in the tiny south-central Tibetan town of Oiga, population 836, he had felt the earth paste on his face day after day for want of water to wash with, had known the ache of hunger, and had watched perplexed as various cabals from the Buddhist hierarchy had moved past on the way to use the special, health-giving springs near-by.

He recalls their rich, embroidered robes pooling like brocade puddles at their feet while the dry wind breathed life into the tattered and faded prayer flags winging out from his home's doorway, framing his view in movement and hope.

Yet, his childhood had been pure in its love, firm in its discipline and extraordinarily rich in spirit. The soul of the universe moved through his life like a ribbon, a constant theme upon which to grip in tough times, admire in the good and something on which to base a life. A life on a ribbon. So fragile and delicate, made miraculous by its very existence.

Driven by a force he knew little of, Chodak had journeyed to Lhasa at 16 years old, made the crossing into India, to Dharamsala. Inexplicably spotted in a dusty regional football tournament down Highway 17 in Palampur by a Celtic talent scout delayed by the peccadilloes of Himalayan weather on his way to Delhi on holidays, to watch England in a cricket match.

A youth contract and a shared flat with other hopefuls in Glasgow just a month later. Immediately, this elegant midfielder, with a sweet left foot, an ability to slide and drop passes on a blade of grass, to ghost through defenders like they weren't there, to think five or six steps ahead, almost ahead of many of his own team-mates, cemented a reputation. His reading of the game left the staff with a dilemma: he was too far ahead of most players and a team would have to be built around him. Even at such a young age.

"Give him the ball and let him move you around", was the instruction to the youth team squad.

He was the sun that drew ten other planets, in green and white hoops around him, pulled by the gravity of his power between the chalk potentially to swing games, tournaments and lives with the caress with the outside of that left foot that landed and gripped on the grass like a sand wedge, or by a mental shift that left all around him in the vacuum of the new spaces he created, a re-wiring of the game even as it fizzed around him at break-neck speed.

At 18, Chodak is considered peerless for his age in Europe and his team is considered potential world-beaters, orbiting his genius, pulsing to his heartbeat.

But the journey is edged in guilt. His family still rots back in Oiga, very likely unaware of the extent of his wealth and fame. Indeed, they may have been punished for his escape from the clutches of the Beijing colonialist warlords. He spoke out on Tibetan independence and had been seen with the Dalai Lama. He understood oppression and he sought out its victims.

His fellow Tibetans crushed in the grip of China's obsession with the ancient land and the massive riches it promised underground, the spaces it offered, the billions all over the world who suffered under the boot of oppression and dictatorship, each had a voice in his mind. For every fan that vocalised his brilliance, for every kid who wore his #66 shirt, there was a tiny point of pain, digging deep into his soul.

This was The Thing.

The lives of those in Tunisia, in Gafsa, appeared not only lost in violence and loss, fear and longing, but had been stripped of its very core, ripped out by the forces that could not accept freedom or dissent in their midst.

And the role of football, its bridging value in this world of hierarchies and politics, barriers and obstacles, and his place at its very pinnacle, bears deep into him.

*   *   *

Chodak's jade green 2008 model Alfa Romeo 1 Generation coupe crackles on the asphalt of the players' carpark at Lennoxtown. Up the B822 it had come, roughly half an hour away from its garage in Hillhead, flashing its racing alloys like a gangster's metal smile through Glasgow's grey streets.

Its driver, no gangster, rests a weary back against the leather seats, expensive feet working the pedals. Shifting up and down gears with a growl and now a purr as it slows to a halt in the spot marked with a number 66. Stops.

He sits amid the ticks and crackles of the settling engine. The sweeping roof of Celtic's training facility seems to touch the low clouds as the Scottish chill refused to dissipate. A gentle ripple of breeze combs the longish grass on the warm-up field. Another day.

Despite the relatively modest vehicle, the driver will earn around 500,000 British pounds this year, as he will every other for the next three years as long as he doesn't go to another club for even more.

But anxiety grips his chest. How can he feel this way when his world is so abundant, so golden? He can have anything he wants. He is surrounded by expensive everything's, by fawning people who treat his every move with awe, every word like the sayings of a prophet, every waking moment gilded by shiny, luscious wealth at every turn. How can depression even scratch the surface of a life that most people would kill for? How can being paid a fortune every week to do what most people would – and no small number could – do for free?

But, it does. He knows where it comes from. No-one should have this much. Guilt and Gilt.

Because of where he comes from, because he is grounded in the culture of the word, he knows it as karma. His life is the force of a spirit too big for him to deny. He has seen what he wished he hadn't. He knows what he wished he didn't. All this money raining upon him is filthy, like acid rain, burning his skin.

What is his karma? Is he being punished or rewarded?

And now, what he is about to do…

Chodak Lampa, one of the leading young guns in European football, Tibet's first - only - world class athlete, looks down. Feels the blood pooling in his feet clad in red, blue and yellow sneakers. Tibetan flag colours.

7
MARCH 2010

Parkhead Stadium, Glasgow

The crowd rise in expectation. The strike from the new golden boy is about to put Rangers to Celtic's sword. The air in Parkhead holds and gathers. The final moments of an epic. 2-2. The winner. Surely.

The ball is just a millimetre away, its roll just a millionth of a cycle too much. The strike is just a whisker's breadth off perfect. The keeper's fingers find the ball's edge, tip it around the waiting net.

The air sucks out of the stadium like the world had ended. Celtic and Rangers fans alike are stunned.

No-one swears as well as a Glaswegian.

Around 60,000 bums hang in disbelief and then sit down again. Hands hold heads. Faces stare at the ground. The game suspended for a moment, two, in that split second of disappointment. A vacuum of unreality.

As he waddles down the tunnel, a few jeer. Chodak doesn't hear them.

It is hard enough playing games like this week in week out, without any other voices adding to those already crowding his mind. Millions of expectant souls riding you like their lives depend on you.

This game is not won or lost between the goals. It's won or lost between the ears. Hadn't he heard that somewhere?

Sitting in his Hillhead apartment later that night, avoiding Match of the Day and endless repeats of his miss, Chodak mixes two soda waters with a little lemon juice.

Outside, night-time Glasgow seeks attention, lights glimmering, weather shaping, but Chodak ignores it.

He sits in his armchair, his face distracted and unreadable, and hands a soda water to his manager.

Dorje has been with Chodak from the early days. He was at the game in India where Chodak was discovered and happened to be on hand to act as an interpreter when the Englishman sought to engage the boy after the game.

He told the Englishman that he knew Chodak even though he had never seen him before in his life. Said he was well known as a young star in Tibet and in this corner for exiles in India, when he wasn't. Now he has one of the game's biggest rising names.

Dorje knows little of the game, seeks no fees from his client and lives in one room of an adjacent three-bedroom apartment bought by Chodak to house him. He sleeps on the floor, never quite able to let go of his refugee ways.

His weary Tibetan face shatters like a smashed windscreen as it shapes to drink. Tiny slit eyes disappear into the folds of brown leathery skin.

He waits until Chodak is ready. When he finally speaks, Dorje put down his drink with a cool clink to listen.

"It's never going to be the same," Chodak tells his manager.

Dorje watches him and drinks. "A river changes every instant."

Chodak groans. "What should I do?"

"What your heart tells you."

There are tears in Chodak's eyes, now, tears of sorrow, frustration, something else he can't identify. "I can't hear my heart. It isn't talking."

"Then stop listening." Dorje speaks as though it is the clearest thing in the world. "Just hear. You'll know what. When."

Chodak looks over at the crusty face which looks right back. Wonders whether Dorje really was as wise as he sounds, as he tries to appear, just answering a question with his enigmatic aphorisms.

Chodak realises he never really knew him. Probably never will. Should he trust this man who is helping him get rich, making him famous, to advise on something far more important; the destination of his soul?

8
MARCH 2010

Gafsa, Tunisia

Dun buildings, spewing dust and innards onto desolate, debris strewn streets. Alleys dark and mysterious, betraying no movement, no life that remains. Electric wires hang listless in heavy air. Skeletons of homes, broken and exposed, window sockets like a battered boxer's eyes, scarred and dented, doorways like screaming mouths, homes and offices shaped into surreal abstracts of order and life.

We stop.

Is there a more crushing silence than this? Not even our breath penetrates this veil of horror that hangs here, obliterating all senses until it's all a universe of unyielding pain and a wonder at the ability of humanity to build all this then to tear it all down. It's a negative awe. A frightening realisation of who and what we are, of what world we have made, of the evil we create in our own names. Silence like a wall of industrial noise. Silence that hurts. Silence that doesn't shut up.

Somewhere here brave, exhausted but unbroken men and women met in basements, weary faces peering through the smoke and war-breath. This tiny peoples' movement, deciding, debating, playing at leadership and hoping for a future to govern. Here it's supposed to be safe. Not today.

The first landed about 100 metres to my left, where a faded sign in red Arabic hung from a hoarding, seen as we drove past it just seconds before. I felt it. Never actually saw it. It was a hot wind, a rushing wall of a billion tiny noises mugging me from behind, muscular arms pushing me down, a battalion of feet charging over me. Then a second. A third. A fourth. A fifth. Maybe less than 10 seconds.

All is dark. Senses have been killed. Don't know where, who, why, when.

Somewhere, a rational brain is working away. What to do? What's the protocol for being bombed? But that little part of my brain is being kicked and bashed into some tiny, hidden corner of the skull. Can't be heard. Gives up.

I am rolling in some kind of direction, crawling through the cloud. My lungs are so contracted by fear that I could find no breath. I am suffocating here in this street, like I was under a tsunami of dirt and flying city.

Then I hit something. A wall. I'm not rolling or crawling. I was flying. Right scapula punches the bricks which yield under the force and crumble like stale bread, raining pieces of crumbed concrete and built life. Something roars past and another massive jolt of energy shudders the world.

I have no sense of where I am or whether I am safe. I can't see more than an arm's length in front of me. My skin is numb, like I have a cloak of lead about me. Faintly through the haze, I note, almost idly, blood splashed across the palm of one hand, lines of red, torn flesh - mine or someone else's - powdered with dust.

I am aware of the human shape next to me reaching out to me as the haze lifts and grabbing my collar. I run with him as he holds me by the belt, pulling me like a horse through another layer of bombed out detritus. My ears are ignorant of the stopping as they are still crackling and throbbing pneumatically. I don't even realize that it isn't my belt but the elastic of my underpants that he holds as we run, my pants gone. I certainly don't know that I am wet with my own warm piss.

We are huddled over a gas flame, holding up a coffee pot which sends up the sweet, incongruous aroma of coffee, clove and cinnamon. My eyes adjust to focus on a tableau of six figures, three from the van I came in and two unknown. And Windsor.

Windsor stares back at me. Gesturing to where I had just come from, he stands and, looking at me, says, "You are alive." Looking away, he asks, "You know the saying, 'To Hell and back'? Well, it is wrong. There is no going back once you've seen Hell. The world has gone from you now. You can't get out of here. You never will. This is a horror that you can never escape, Asher. War is the cancer of humanity."

He thinks he's deep, but his pretentiousness is giving me a headache right now. We were just *bombed*. "Jeezus, when do you stop living in books Windsor? Give me that fucking coffee..."

I swear when I'm stressed. When my life has almost been taken from me, I swear.

Windsor's eyes dance as he hands me a steaming cup.

Coffee is blood. Drunk at roughly the same temperature as the fluid that moves through us, it is life giving and affirming. Through cracked cups and cracked lips, nothing that has tumbled down my throat has ever felt as good as that Tunisian coffee, made Middle Eastern 'mud' style and sweet as mother's milk.

As the aural and visual haze of the latest bombing raid fades and life returns to the air and to the bones, we squat amid debris, fingers of sustenance uncurling from our broken mugs.

Around us, tentacles of wire hang from blasted ceilings, foundation bars bent and twisted from inside shattered walls, reaching like claws into space. Something drips, echoes, forming pools of water coated with shimmering skins of dust. Something like dried blood stains a smashed window, lying in glinting pieces on the floor. A TV guide and a child's toy car lie in a shallow crater in the middle of the beige-dirtied floor. A shoe. A packet of cigarettes. A destroyed laptop.

The building feels alive because I can feel it dying. A construction site in reverse; a de-construction site where everything is being pulled apart piece by piece, atom by atom.

The five men offer names – each presumably a Nom de Guerre – and tell us it was the Russians. They have changed their bombing pattern of late, hence we were caught in it. "The Saudis are here too," they say. "The Iranians, the Syrians, the Emirates, and more. All here. Under the radar. Something's building."

Windsor and I are given our own aliases. I am Abu Ashraf Salim. Windsor is Abu Walid al-Latif. While here and in the company of these men and their colleagues, we are never to use our real names in case anyone falls into torturer's hands. Their eyes tell of the likelihood of such an eventuality. Dark eye rings, red rims and sagging under-pillows belied their age. Twenty becomes fifty here overnight. Days become years. Faces hung and collapsed like the architecture around them, broken and scarred, damaged, enervated.

They are filthy and smelly. Sweat, piss, blood, spit and who knows whatever else stiffens their clothes into shapes that resemble their wearers, but they are like shells. The bodies inside are trembling and scared, pasty skinned, youthful chests forced to expand to the results of old men's decisions, corrugated rib cages like fingers gripped around them, trapping them to be forever young even as they died of old age here within days in the time-eating savagery of organised violence.

One of the men approaches me. "We have business," he says. "Come." He gestures to my unclad legs and the disgusting stained underpants I still wear and adds, "You will find something there. Pants. Let's go!"

A warren of destruction winds ahead of us. We follow the man, known to us as Muhamed al-Islam, through a nightmare of broken lives, our feet crunching on the debris of urban existence.

Daylight breaks in on the hitherto interior rooms of the apartments we pass through, casting odd, incongruous images. This is not the world. This is somewhere else. Rain begins to fall, and I have the instinct to move the exposed furniture under cover even though none is salvageable.

We leave the building and scurry down alleys, accompanied all the while by the eerie silence. An even, shadow-melting half-light bleeds through a grey sky. Rain? Or the pall of war?

Dead, perhaps. But people still live here.

A small house, crammed in among others but remarkable because it looks more or less intact. Muhamed writes something in Arabic on a scrap of paper, slips it under the door, knocks, and waits.

A moment.

The door opens to a hubbub of lights, computers, TV screens and cables. And people. It's hard to imagine how so many things and bodies can cram into this tiny space. All is busy and purposeful. An upward-barrelled cone of rifles near the door like kindling. Screen light casting a soft, full-moon glow over faces and walls.

Muhamed, Windsor and I sit on a cluster of milk crates piled near the left side wall of the dwelling, presumably in what was once the family lounge area.

I look to Muhamed with a questioning face. He returns with an assuring hand and a nod. His hands looked soft, long slender fingers. His eyes are hooded by fatigue, but they hold a spark of intelligence and humanity. I wonder about his story.

"Now," I ask, "What about some pants?"

I was sitting in my undies still, although no-one seemed to notice. I was self-conscious and not exactly in a powerful state to deal with this odd and stressful situation.

"Oh," says Muhamed, and he disappears to find a crusty, almost solid pair of jeans which looked roughly my size. "Ok?"

I put them on. They are too big. But there is no belt, and it seems a little precious to ask for one, so I sit down and tell myself to remember to hold up my pants when I stand up. Unneeded distraction, for sure.

"How long have you been fighting?" I ask.

"I think maybe one month. Not sure."

"This, er, struggle is supposed to be over, is it not?" asked Windsor.

There was no answer, only an inscrutable look.

"Where are you from?" I say after a pause.

"South, near the border." He twisted a smile across his face, like it had been so long since those muscles were used, it was almost painful. "I miss my sax."

My friend perks up. "Your sax? You play sax?" Windsor is always willing to engage with fellow creative types.

"Ha, my friend...I am not getting enough sax." A sheepish look, a smirk. An old joke used often to impress English speakers. "I play in a jazz band on weekends. It is my, er, lobby."

Hobby.

"Are you a musician?" I ask.

He shakes his head. "No. I am teacher. Enough. Come, let's go."

We stood and my pants dropped to my ankles.

The buzz went on around me, all serious, oblivious to this moment of arch humour in the room. Windsor didn't miss it and his face smiled and winked. I hitched up my pants and scurried to catch up.

We are directed into a back room, stepping over and through the multi-coloured spaghetti of cables and cords, edging past jutting furniture and hunched backs. We shape ourselves through a doorway into a small bedroom with a window, like all the others here, boarded up and taped. This one has various notes and post-its scattered across it like pinned butterflies. Some are stapled into the wood, some nailed, some just taped. I wondered if this reflects a hierarchy of sorts; the permanence of the fixation, a comment on the value and tenure of the message.

The only lights are those of two humming desktop computers and a TV which is silent running the BBC. It is hard to see him at first, but a man sits on the floor in the corner, knees pointed upwards, head leaning into a sheaf of documents held before bespectacled eyes. He looks up. Eyes down. Kept reading.

We stand and wait. Maybe five minutes. The man gets up at last, puts down his sheaf of papers, and approaches Muhamed. He speaks to him in short grabs of Arabic and, patting him on the shoulder, says "*shukran*". With that, he sends Muhamed the sax playing teacher back to the front lines, only minutes away.

It's our turn. "Ok," the man says in a southern English accent, looking at us and smiling openly, "I'm glad to tell you both you are my hostages."

Windsor and I look slowly at each other. Windsor grinned, incongruously. He makes a face, eyes popping and a downturned smile, mocking everything in all ways.

The man is talking again, looking straight at both of us like he was interviewing us. Face still retaining something of the youth that resided behind the tired and stressed eyes. Black, corded hair flopped over his collar and a thickening beard, something like what a five o'clock shadow looks like by around 10.30, darkens his face.

Lights still on in him. Screen-lit head emitting intelligence and calmness. The eyes make contact and speak through them. The humanity has not yet been blasted out of his character. He wears grimy jeans and an open-necked blue shirt. His wrist is wound by an expensive-looking watch. Two rings on his slender fingers.

"Let me explain. It's not as bad as you think." He opens his hands to us. "My name is Abu Hamid. I am the regional operations commander of the People's Union of Gafsa and Tunisia. You may have noticed we have a small war on at the moment, so things are a little, er, unusual."

I bite back my sarcastic reply.

"You have come to me because you are doing some important work for us at the international level, I believe. I don't have details, but I expect you know what you are doing. I don't need to know. I have access to the funds and assets liberated from the regime, some of which will be signed over to you to do your work. You and I will be the only ones who will know of the codes and passwords attached to these monies. If we die, the money is signed over to the PUGT after you sign. Here."

I do.

He continues. "But, we're going to kidnap you and hold you hostage so no-one knows about your movements subsequent to our meeting. Your Australian authorities have no reputation for rescuing revolutionaries, and so we don't fear any retribution. As for you Abu Walid Al-Latif, well Uganda will yawn with the news. Nothing personal."

Windsor shrugs. He knows who he is.

The man says, "We will announce your incarceration at the hands of an obscure pro-regime group no-one has ever heard of – war does rather offer opportunities for twisting the truth – and call for an impossible ransom. If any authorities do happen to find you with us, we will simply say we have liberated you from said group, and will perhaps receive a reward for handing you over. You may even buy us some of our own captured men and women. It's one of the games we play here. You foreigners who stumble in here are like currency to be traded."

I nod. A grim human chess game, where there are no rooks or knights, just kings and queens and pawns.

He seems pleased that I understand. "It does take you both out of circulation so that no-one knows where you actually are. It also helps ensure you are not linked to us. Kidnapping you also allows you – and us to some extent – some breathing space to establish your position and set our foundations for our work together. You won't have to stay here by the way. Once we're done here we'll get you away and release you."

He smiles like all good kidnappers should, then moves back to his piles of paper. Windsor and I exchange furtive glances. I stood, holding my pants up, and wait while he flips and shuffles, at one stage removing a semi-automatic rifle desk to better get at a file. He speaks into what I assume is a satellite phone. Hangs up.

He then motions for us to follow him.

"Come with me. I have someone for you to meet."

We walked for maybe five minutes, through the broken buildings and rubble of Gafsa.

Down a tight alley, three of us single file with the walls almost touching our shoulders, shadows stealing scant warmth from the winter sun in the enclosed space. Our breathing disappears in clouds above us.

Desperate voices can be heard ahead. Hoarse yells, grunts, inarticulate expletives, a sense of movement and effort bouncing off the walls and funnelling down the alley.

I envisage, in my naive and movie-influenced mind, a pocket of rebel fighters, huddled around a mortar stand, or a scuffle between rebels and government troops, or perhaps with the shady internationals dropped in. Why are we being brought here?

We emerge into an open area, a square, ringed by dishevelled buildings and held by the cold air and weak sun. I don't see it at first -- but then I see them.

Men in fatigues, bandanas, army boots or sneakers, running, stopping, running again. Some walking. Others stand still and watching. Feet scuffles and shouts echoing around the crumbling walls. And that sound. Unmistakable. Instantly recognisable.

A football. Fired off a boot and hitting with a gun-like smack against a wall where a goal shape had been painted in white. Maybe 15 guys playing. Another 20 or 30 watching.

Muhamad stops us and points. "Those blond guys there are Russians. The guys in that uniform are Syrians. That's our guy, and there, and there." He continues to indicate players. "That guy there–" he points out a short, stocky fellow in shorts and a long sleeve sweater "-is a government official from Tunis. That guy with the sunglasses is Iranian."

The game rumbles on.

Windsor and I look at each other. He is as confused as me.

"Aren't these guys, er, fighting against each other?" asks Windsor.

With a laugh, Muhamad says, "Yes. But this is football. Every afternoon around this time, we stop and play. Anyone is allowed, after handing in your weapons and undergoing a body search."

He turns to look at us. "Football is football."

His eyes return to the game, and he points out a shortish man in the midst of the game, dressed in army cargoes, a black t-shirt and sneakers. He stands in a centre forward position and as the ball approached him, neck-high, "And that is Haykel Sassi, who you must meet."

Sassi's touch was sure; the ball stops by the chest, drops to foot. He turns and moves, head up, passes through the defence line to a wide player. Clean and swift. After the pass, he moves, props, holds a space behind the lines. Sharp and knowing. The wide player, blinkered, ignores him and fizzes a shot from a poor angle which hits the wall well outside the painted goal.

All stop and awaited a restart. Muhamad takes the opportunity to call Sassi, who approaches us. He walks a footballer's walk, legs loose and sprung, jaunty stride, body rocking with a walk-off-the-field walk. He is a man used to being watched.

Muhamad introduces us. "Haykel is the main man on the World Cup project. You should talk."

We go to a nearby café that is miraculously intact amid the ruins. Its civilising atmosphere is a comforting haven from the destruction all around. Men's voices and the smell of coffee, a reminder of a world that seems light years away.

Haykel exchanges *Ahlans*, *Salaams*, and *HaBibis* with the patrons and the tired looking proprietor at the counter. Hugs and slapping handshakes filling the small space.

We sit.

There is something distinctly delicate about Haykel, aided by the soft latte skin, the black pupils in his eyes, the finely coiffed hair. In comparison, it seems everyone here is one step from Neanderthal, us included.

When Haykel tells us his story in excellent English, I feel safe and engaged, despite the cold winter light and the dust of civil war.

He was born into a simple family of phosphate miners in Gafsa and from there, in one of the many often unlikely stories within world football, became a professional player. From growing up breathing in phosphate dust every day, he played in Tunisia until he was spotted as a 15-year-old by German club Hertha Berlin. He stayed at Hertha until he was 19, when he was transferred to Bayern Munich. Then, after six seasons there, he spent four years at Galatasaray.

It was a more than impressive career. He made a lot of money, enough to ensure his family didn't have to spend any time in the phosphate mines anymore and he won some silverware.

"I have been very, very fortunate," he tells us. "I owe football a lot. But, for all the fame and fortune, the most memorable moment of my career was sitting alone in a hotel room in Budapest. Nobody else knows about this – only my close family."

Windsor and I lean forward. The weight of the secret hangs in the air as Haykel continues.

"I was with Bayern, and we had just played a UEFA Cup game against Honved in Budapest. I had played off the bench and did well, got an assist for our equaliser. 1995. I was 21 and my career was just getting started. I was good talent and people were starting to notice. That night, I got a call from the France Football Federation. 'Will you play for France?' he asks me."

Haykel pauses as our drinks arrive. He swirls his tea in the cup before taking a sip. When he puts the cup back on the table, something new is in his eyes.

"I hadn't played international at adult level, only for Tunisia at Under-21. I was still, you might say, up for grabs. My first thought is,

I am not French, why would you even ask?"

He stopped and glances outside, then turns and meets our eyes.

"You see, I speak French – but that's only because Tunisia was a French colony. They asked me because they thought – they still think – that they own us and that we will always want to be part of the boss's team."

His lip curls, a harsh look on the pretty face.

"We are supposed to forget what they did to Bourguiba? We're supposed to say, oh the Red Hand and Hauteclocque didn't exist?!" He slams his hand on the table, making the cup shake. "Oh yes, we will play to help and glorify the same people that killed my brothers and sisters for their own narrow ends! Yes, we will forget this!"

He takes a moment. I say nothing. There's no contribution I can make.

Haykel starts again with a darkness in his voice. "Maybe they believe that because we play football we are not very intelligent, that we have amnesia or maybe we are stupid from heading the ball too much. I remember Mekhloufi and the Algerian FLN Team. An Algerian national team before there was even a nation called Algeria. They refused to play for France, or for French league teams. My Dad told me about when they came to Tunis in 1958 to organise after they had all fled from France, in secret."

He stares down at his cup, but does not drink again, then continues.

"Those guys travelled the world and played anyone who would play the Algerian anthem and raise the Algerian flag. That was even before Algeria existed! Ya, what a team. Zitouni and Mekhloufu were supposed to play for France in the '58 World Cup, but they refused. I rang my family and they all said, 'no', And so, it wasn't hard. I called the Federation back and said 'No, thank you.' And I hung up. And I never spoke to them again."

I suck a breath through my teeth as the enormity of the story hits me. "That's…" I don't know how to continue.

Haykel smiles at me, though it doesn't reach his eyes. "Think about that 1998 France team, the one that won the World Cup. You know that team? Desailly, Thuram, Karembeu, Viera. All born outside France. All sons of colonised parents, playing for the oppressor. Like I was supposed to do."

"They all got that same phone call, huh?" Windsor observes.

Haykel nods. "Why did they say yes? Well, I don't know their politics but I know they must have known, their families must have known, that you won't win any World Cups in 1998 with Ghana or Senegal or Guadeloupe or New Caledonia. You probably won't even play any World Cups. At all. No one has heard of you. You don't play World Cups, and you're not George Best or Ryan Giggs, your value goes down. Look where those guys played: Juventus, Chelsea, Arsenal, Milan, Real. Do they play for those clubs if they don't play for France, if they don't win World Cups? I think maybe not."

There's a pit forming in my stomach. None of this is news, and yet his words are like acid rain, like a thousand tiny bombs that dust the war-torn air.

"And then there's Henry, Zidane," Haykel continues. "First generation French. Parents are Bumidom immigrants. Born French. French for sure. But how much French and how much Martiniquean or Algerian? Their feet in France, yes. But where is their heart? Where is their soul?" He looks up at me, earnest now. "You know who else is from Martinique, like Henry? Franz Fanon. Yep, Fanon. The guru of anti-imperialist thinkers. You think Henry doesn't know about Fanon? Martinique is not that big a place. Maybe his parents bumped into him in the street. You think Henry hasn't read Fanon?

But he plays for France. Self interest or maybe family over culture and heritage. It's a kind of spiritual choice none should have to make, young men especially."

Freedom is about all of us. We cannot be free if someone else is not. Isn't that what Abdulhamid said on the phone that night? This is what he meant.

"I know Zidane," Haykel tells us. "Not well, not like a good friend. But we spoke many times. I know he asked himself this question many, many times. Where is my soul? He's a born revolutionary, Zidane. He knows his history alright. He knows about the FLN and the 1950s. He's Algerian! But he had to swallow his heart for bigger agendas. I guess. I never really understood him. I know he was bound by the FIFA rules, but, ya, maybe, maybe he could have fought them. He was such a big player..."

"And you?" Windsor prompts.

"Ha, me. My choices probably ruined my career. I played for Tunisia but never played in a World Cup. I was injured in 2006 when we made it for Germany. I kept playing a while in Europe but never really made it as a regular first team player. Ended up in Egypt and then back here at home. Big name here but that's not worth a lot really. My career might have been bigger if I'd played for France, I think that's for sure."

We're interrupted as passers-by approach, more than once, to fawn over Haykel. He's polite in the face of his fame. When our drinks are done, the small, stained cups are collected by a sad looking waiter. Haykel orders more. He wasn't finished yet.

I'm sure Windsor feels that, like me, this guy could talk all day and we will be happy to hear him.

"Anyway, I could go on," continues Haykel, "But we have limited time. Maybe another day we can chat more freely. *Insha'Allah.* I have many stories to tell. Bottom line, I chose to play for Tunisia for a reason. I am Tunisian. I relate to Tunisia. I feel Tunisian. My heart and soul are here. Which is why I am now here, in dusty Gafsa, living like a wolf, not in my very comfortable villa in Gouvernorat de Medenine with my family. And my aim is not just our political story, not just about Tunisia."

He catches my eye, and I shiver. Abdulhamid's voice is in my head again as Haykel speaks, their words mixing in a chaos of sense.

"FIFA has been taken over by the corporates. It has lost its way and become too commercialised and too political, which is kind of the same thing I would say. Flight- you know the company Flight, yes? - is trying to take over the world cup, take it away from FIFA and make it its own. We know, and I think you know, Qatar should not get the 2022 World Cup. Qatar is not a bad country, certainly not compared to many in our region. But, we think it has allowed itself to become a bone to be fought over by the war dogs at Flight and FIFA. Our game is not a, a, er, *biens meubles*."

He consults his phone for the translation.

"Chattel. Our game is not a chattel."

The word makes me shiver. Men and women in chains. Bought and sold. Figures, not people.

Haykel's voice softens. "I know you are helping us to block the Qatar bid. But I am concerned. The bid will just go somewhere else and that somewhere else will be politicised and corporatized too. We don't have the time or resources to put together our own bid, or to devise another one before December."

"What do you propose we do?" I ask. The waiter returns, leaves our drinks, vanishes again.

Haykel spreads out his hands, palms open. "I don't have any idea. But we have to find a way to get the game back to the people. Those of us fighting here in Gafsa - and believe me this is just the beginning; this region is about to blow apart - are reacting to the theft of our souls, a fire sale of the things that make us human, giving up the things that make us human and bring us together as a species. We can all see how hollow this system is and how the system needs to be changed."

This is heavy stuff and Haykel's words weigh in the air, wrapping around the aromas of coffee, men, and violence that surround us.

We drink our new coffees silently, each in our own bubbles of thought, as the cafe exists around us. The urban destruction visible from our seats mocks the conceit of our strategies, flimsy as they are.

With a quiet, almost reverent tone, Haykel speaks up. "You know, I remember that phone call. I remember that feeling. No-one should have to make that choice. Football is the world game. We call ourselves the football family. So, why do we limit who can participate in the central event, The World Cup, to nations, to politically manufactured constructions that don't reflect the people that live there?"

"Politics," Windsor says, and it's almost like a curse.

Grimly, Haykel nods. "The World Cup as it is is like the kind of democracy that only elects those the government itself has picked. That kind of democracy is called a dictatorship. The world is not just nations. There are those who have no nation or who have no allegiance to that they've been born into. We in Gafsa have seen that. We feel it and we know this is a powerful force and a powerful moment. There is an imbalance that must be righted. How can we fix this? What can we do?"

"Sure, it's only a game and we are just some unknown and unheralded workers in a north African backwater," Haykel says, "But it's a game that symbolises so much for all of us, even those who don't play or support it. This game stands for something very human. How can the World Cup actually represent the world?" He looks at us both. His tired, dark eyes pulling us towards him. "You see what this game can do? You saw us playing, enemies joined by the game. We can actually do something here. This is important, don't you agree?"

Like a hook, the question mark hangs above us on a rafter, swinging over our heads. Like a noose.

*　　*　　*

Gunshots in the distance. *Ratatatatat...* silence... *ratatatatat...* silence.

Nobody seems to notice.

Haykel long gone, Windsor and I are following Muhamad. Windsor hands me a note, Shakespeare scribbled on it while Haykel was speaking. 'There hath been many great men that have flattered the people who ne'er loved them.'

What does this one mean? Great men? Big name footballers? Those that never loved them. Is that their former colonial overseers? Windsor's eccentric approach just confuses me further.

Back at the 'office', Muhamad says, "You should maybe sit down." Bracing himself against the desk as he speaks. Perplexed, we sit.

Within seconds a large explosion rocks the room, shuddering the wood panels on the windows, swaying the light bulb hanging from a thread and shimmering the cobwebs hanging from the ceiling.

Muhamad gives an apologetic glance. "The time of day..." He looks away again, keeps looking through his papers.

After a moment, he brandishes a thin, dun-coloured folder, covered in grime and handprints, and flips it open before us. "Ok," he says with surprising freshness, "Here's your papers."

An inch of bulging pages, interspersed with coloured folders, post-its and marker stickers. Inside, stock certificates and legal letters to authorise me as proxy, bank account details, research and data. A file of photos, paperclipped together. Names on the back, some stapled to bios.

"Who's the woman?" I ask.

"That's Ebaa. She will help you. Maybe."

I study the image. The glamorous shape she places next to various men of power. A picture of her in a crowd of alpha men. Foreground, background, arms taking ownership, drawing her in. Her letting them, with guarded eyes.

*   *   *

We are shepherded into a waiting van, parked at the end of two lines the tyres had made through the dust and rubble. The van looked like a pre-Cambrian relic, with no windows or windscreen, bald tyres, dings and dents, and a skin of dark rust, blotched with a map of the remaining paint. Beige. Everything here is beige.

Its idling engine rumbled in the narrow street. Its waiting driver's head turned as we entered, checking out the moving cargo. Us.

"The trip is dangerous," Muhamad has told us. "You cannot fly out now as the airways are closed. You will be shot down. This is the only way and we cannot delay as we are on the move soon. You cannot come with us."

He hopes we would be across the border and into relative safety in 12 hours.

"Abu Salim is our best man," he had said.

We look in to see the hunched back of the best driver in Tunisia from the back of the van. He twists back from its cursory glance and curves around the wheel again, never to let go for the next few hours.

Windsor and I sit on the busted seats. Fear is not a thing I often see in Windsor, but it flickers there in the flare of his wide nostrils.

"Would you rather walk?"

He shoots me one of his looks. "We have to drive through the battlelines, Asher."

I sigh. "Yeh, I know mate, I know. I'm scared too."

He's automatically riled up at my words. "Scared? Who's scared?! This is an experience to be savoured. We are to be tested today but these men and women are being tested every day. I want to know that. I want to know the testing Asher. Scared…"

I'm too used to his eccentricities to be impatient with him. "Well, I'm shit scared then. I think I can live without the experience of war."

Windsor claps his hand on my shoulder. "It's a generation like you who have lived without war that will ensure another is coming, brother. You don't know how bad this is and so you wont fight hard enough for peace."

"If you have to fight for peace, is it peace?"

"Everything has to be fought for." He looks out the open back, through the absent window, towards the fruits of that truth. The cityscape in the distance is mainly rubble.

We lurch off in a haze of dust and debris.

Before long, the fumes coming in through the back window space made us nauseous and dizzy. The rumble of the aged and battered engine and the discomfort of the decomposed seats makes for a journey I am keen to end.

What scenery we can see is surprisingly unwarlike. It is deserted. We are soon out of the city, or what is left of it. The small urban clusters that race by seem utterly unpeopled. Hungry-looking dogs hang around, looking for food and companionship, sniffing every surface like coke addicts.

Camels stand in stately cabals at a distance, assessing the lay of the land and pondering Armageddon, as camels always seem to.

"Did you see the look in their eyes?" asks Windsor, "You know, the guys back there?"

"What do you mean?"

His voice is serious, earnest. "The lights had gone out, I think is how you might put it. These people are fighting for life but they are already dead."

A chill runs through me, but I say what it is – "Understandable."

Windsor disagrees. "I would have thought fighting for your beliefs would be energising. Why do those who have won at life, who have cheated the odds and survived, look so depleted and devoid of life? I had expected more fire, more charisma if you like. They just look like shattered bodies inside human shaped husks."

I shake my head, slowly. "I think you've got a skewed view on war and fighting, mate. I don't think it's ever meant to be life-giving. Not for those doing it. "

Windsor stares at me, but his focus is directed inwards. Thinking, questioning his mind, observing its motion. "It's such a cliché: no-one wins. It's not true though is it? Someone always wins. Usually it's those who stand aside. Those who can fight, but don't; who chose where and when to battle, or not to battle at all. Those who have a choice, win."

"Those guys have a choice. They could have left."

"They could have left physically, Asher, but not mentally. They could never leave, because their heart and soul is here. The winners have no such investment, maybe they don't have the material... no heart or soul."

I ponder his words. "Are we winners, Windsor?"

"We've got more chance than they have. Choosing to fight is one thing. To have to fight is something else. You never recover from that. Even the winners in that case lose. Even if they don't know it. Maybe you should get in fast and choose to fight before the fight chooses you. Maybe that's the secret of life."

*　　*　　*

We've been travelling for some hours and have gotten used to the rattling of the van, the dust, the fumes. Suddenly, Windsor looks up, a finger aloft, eyes staring at nothing, brow wrinkled in effort. The din of the van makes, it hard, but I hear it too. A screech. It came from a distance and quickly, frighteningly quickly, approaches and then became deafening, rattling the metal of the van and piercing our ears like spikes.

There is silence for a minute or two, then the howling screech in the air grips at the stomach before receding, shifting the horizon with its decibels as it goes. The dinosaur van slows and stops as the trailing veil of smoke and dust catches up and tumbles around us.

We pull into a deserted-looking roadside village. It's hard to see much in the darkening light. A few stores gape open to the relentless, empty landscape and the almost invisible road that traverses it. It is almost night. With our little pocket torches, we spot an old white Mercedes, rusted, wheelless on three sides and up-hooded, resting in the foreground. A clutch of ever-present camels looked on from a dark distance, etching against the sandy dusk of desert.

"Russians! Russians!" shouted our driver, unpanicking as he points upwards, hurriedly motioning for us to take shelter in one of the empty shops. We fall out of the back and sharply head for cover. "Bag! The bag!"

The shoulder bag that carries all the papers Muhamad had given us, the bank account details, the bios and research data, the stock certificates and proxies, laying in a pillow of fine sand.

"Shit! The fucking bag!" I turn to go back.

Windsor pushes me. "No, Asher, keep moving." We struggle. Windsor is a big man. He wins, and we fall into a rickety stall that looks like zero protection against the looming threat.

We can see it now through the open side, bulleting across the almost dark, disembodied from the wail it produces, well in front of the banshee roar of horror it pushes out of itself.

The van driver, Abu Salim, is still in the open. He starts running. No athlete, and heavy steps, unbending knees, stout torso and stumpy arms fought against each other to push him forward. stumbling as the sound avalanche rolled towards us. The fighter jet appears to be aiming straight at him, at us.

The eerie disconnect between the inhuman noise and its trajectory across the sky makes it seem surreal, and its malevolent targeting of our little enclave seems too odd to comprehend.

"The bag!" I yell, pointing and throwing my arm in an arc to alert his understandably overstimulated senses.

Abu Salim falls over it. His large frame seems pinned to the ground. The fighter jet bears down on him, dipping and pointing at his prone form, his black clothes against the earth. Hard to say how far away now but growing closer every half-second, the rumbling sky seemingly driving it on.

The driver gets up, grabs the bag, and shuffles towards a stall. His fear seemed to suck him of movement. His limbs flail, and, as if in a nightmare, he seems to struggle to co-ordinate his bulky shape in the simple act of getting away.

The roar is now rattling the frame of our deserted shop and the sand dances on the ground like it was on a struck drum skin. The bonnet of the Mercedes outside slams shut with the activated air, but we don't hear anything over the ever-approaching wave of horrible noise.

Abu Salim makes it under shelter as the thing levels and flattens its trajectory, now perhaps a hundred metres off the ground. It sweeps straight over us, the sound rolling behind it like a tsunami. Windsor and I cower behind and under the shop counter with the roaring beast's scream tearing at our ears, at our stomachs.

The noise decreases and drops. We breathe. But just as fast it grows again. It's coming back!

A sound of screeching gets closer. Something whizzes past a moment before the van blows up in a flash of diabolical light and noise, throwing debris into the air and onto the roofs of the stalls and shops.

The sound decreases and is soon gone.

We wait, hard to say how long. Then Abu Salim rushes in, shouting "Hallo!" "Hallo!".

We pop our heads over the counter. He makes motions in the dots of light we can muster, telling us that, as we already know, the van is no more.

We shuffle outside to a black rosette of burnt desert where our vehicle once stood. Pieces of it have rained down all around. Windsor grabs my arm and points to one of the van doors, its bottom corner stuck into the wooden corner post of the shop we were hiding in, projecting from it like a wing. Inches from it is plastic sheeting. Inches from that, until moments ago, was us.

The roar of the Russian fighter jet can still be heard in the distance, trailing its source like a cloak. We are emboldened to approach the ex-van to investigate whether there is anything to salvage. Metal innards, my black jacket oddly intact, sand burnt like black glass. Desert art.

Moments pass as we stand there The horizon, lit by something big, a facility, is attached to grey smoke brains attached by darker cerebral cortexes. Disaster's thought bubbles. Someone's loss. Someone's gain.

What now?

The driver, devoid of English, points to the stall in which we had hidden.

It's home for now.

"*Parlez vous Français*?" asks Windsor.

He grunted. A negative.

"That's all our languages then," said Windsor.

9
MARCH 2010
Outside Gafsa, Tunisia

"What are you looking at?" Windsor's question broke a long silence.

Sitting in the little stall. Gaping sides – best we could find – letting cold night air seep in, stealthily and without the assistance of a breeze. Just being cold. Windsor wrapped in a canvas tarp he had found.

My gaze came back into focus, saw Windsor in more detail. "Oh, nothing. Just thinking."

"What about, man?"

A deep weariness fills my bones as I answer. "Stuff. Why are we here? That kind of thing."

He eyes me. "Why are we here, reasons...or we talking more existentially why are we here?"

"Um, somewhere in between I think. Prosaic and poetic question."

Windsor turned his head and we fell into a shared thinking space. "I'm not sure we need an answer, Asher. I mean, we're here because we're here aren't we?"

"Yeah, but we've made choices to be here. We think we're trying to do something. What is that? Why are we trying to do anything when none of it, even if we're successful and even if we do something, there's no guarantee it actually means anything? It's like we're trapped in our story and can't see who's writing it."

With a sigh, Windsor replies, "As I said Asher, I'm not sure these are questions we can answer."

"Is love an answer?"

Windsor ponders an answer. We can hear the screeching of distant planes, searing terror across the landscape. The darkness only emphasises their malevolence. We sit in the jumping orb of light cast by a scanty candle we have found. Its edges moving like a borderless nation, and we, held by its unfaithful sense of hope, its cynical warmth.

We listen to people dying in the distance. Small arms fire. Armies clashing. History writing itself in chattering clacks across the crisp air.

Windsor doesn't answer so I offer my thoughts.

"I'm not sure I've ever loved someone that much that I feel they are living in my landscape, that they know my story and I am willing to let them behind the narrative."

"What about Cal?" Windsor looks up.

Cal. The name stole my breath for a moment.

"She betrayed you." Not a question.

My heart clenches. "Lovers can do that. You let them do that."

"You still love her, Asher?"

I consider the question. "I'd like to see her again and find out. I am in love with something I call Cal. But I'm not sure it's the same Cal."

"You've seen her since then?"

With a frown, I answer. "Spoken once or twice. Not really satisfactory, She's corporate. They pretty much own her. She's sold herself for six figures, a pension plan, dental and a promise of a place in the C Suite in a few years."

"She's not for you Ash. Why don't you trust me on that? I would make the analogy of a welder's shop."

"Oh?"

"People, like metal, can join together in a shower of sparks and in the heat of the fire. But then, after the fireworks are no more, they realise the welder has joined them back-to-back. I think this is you and Cal, my friend."

I shift the focus. "How 'bout you Shakespeare boy? You ever found your Anne Hathaway?"

He chuckles. "Brief as a woman's love, all too briefly. I lost the woman I loved most long ago. And I have been looking for myself ever since. She took something with her that I can't replace."

"What's that?"

"The will to live."

I didn't know how to answer.

I'm saved by Abu Salim. "We Go! Go!" He pushes through the canopy that offers our only shelter. He has been on the satellite phone he had miraculously hung onto, hooked onto his belt no less, trying to contact freedom fighter units close by. It looks like he's found one.

Candle out and blackness, like a fridge door closing. Eyes adjust to complete blindness. Not a shard of light to latch onto. Dyspeptic war sounds rumble and coughing nearby.

Over the din, the sound of an engine, closer, fast approaching.

Outside. Nothing to see. Hear a vehicle approaching but see nothing.

"Lights blacked," whispers Windsor.

Almost upon us now. Stopping. A tsunami of fine dust rolls into my face, cool and gritty.

Engine idles and Arabic voices. A torch points downwards, maybe a foot from the ground to give orientation. Lighting the base of the wheel, then running to our feet. Path. All the while whispered Arabic, strained English. Urgent.

"Now. Go."

The driver pushes me into Windsor, and we move along the path, now dark again without the torchlight. Hands out front and touching the warm bonnet, sliding along to feel an open door. No door. Just a gap. A hand guides me further to another gap. Our door?

I enter and felt a seat. Windsor too. A muffled sound, a sniff, and a presence next to us. Our former driver, Abu Salim. Passenger now. And off we go.

"Border," says the new driver from the front with his desert night accent. "No war there. Lot of trouble. But no war. Safe for you."

"How long?" Windsor asks.

No answer.

Black but for a small screen held in the driver's hand. A GPS. Driving blind along a road.

*　　*　　*

Cairo

In silence and in some shock, sitting in a cafe in Cairo's old quarter. Hookahs around us bubbling like our minds, emitting aromas of apple, cinnamon and ash. Tobacco smoke tails lashed upwards in slow motion. Faces mysterious behind impenetrably dark glasses. Age and history, vast unknowns and a cavernous knowing-everything energy hung about like the stench of mummy flesh. All and nothing. Here and Somewhere Else. Dead and alive. Cairo.

The border crossing was smooth, taking around two days. Slept in the car. We hugged the coast of north Africa, quite stunning in parts, crossing northern Libya and into Cairo.

So many crossing points in this geography, so many boundaries scarring the ground. But the grains of sand in Tunisia and in Egypt look just the same. The redundancy of states written across the dry earth.

At some point the bald tyres and rusted metal passed over an imaginary line, but it remained unmarked and unheralded, and Windsor and I remained numb and ignorant of our fate.

Wadis and wells, deliveries of fuel from gruff and weary functionaries along the way, while the camels congressed and the sun arc'd and faded against the sky in oil painting blobs of thick, harsh colour.

Mystery tour but no magic, in Windsor speak.

The city appears as light through the van windows at around 8pm. Near midnight we are unloaded in front of a residence and sleep without either food or the faces of our hosts being known on a bed of trust for ten hours.

*　　*　　*

We are meeting them at 11.30am. Our hosts gave us some wrinkled Egyptian cash and shuffled us into a waiting cab.

Traffic weighs on Cairo. It clogs every avenue and esplanade. Only the alleys, and there are many, allow a human scale. Alleys so narrow, two people must breathe in to pass, Walls wearing centuries of body smudge. Sun never seen in some.

One of our hosts leans in and speaks to the driver. He gives him an address, written in swirling Arabic. We drive off. He stops after a few minutes. We wait while he went into a pharmacy and comes out, not making eye contact, and continues without a word. Not a sound the whole way.

We could be swallowed by this place and never be seen again.

My fingers coil around the door handle.

When we arrive, it is probably a neighbourhood. But it's sometimes hard to tell in this city. Urban surfaces coated with grime and grit, dark tattoos of ancient history. A shop of some sort nearby which looks to be selling dust, the bellied proprietor standing sleepily in the door, modelling it.

Few people. Quiet and feeling abandoned. Our building at the end of the cab driver's index finger. "Yes, Yes," he says, and points back to the note I had given him.

No signs or suggestions of where we were. It seems a normal looking terrace house, concrete with few embellishments. Cold looking. Hard. Unwelcoming.

A man at the door watches us and opens the door as we approach. Expecting a tall, white guy and a portly black guy and there are not many versions of us around to make a mistake. Double doors open, and inside there is a concrete lobby of sorts. Our eyes adjust from the powerful light outside. There's a smell of damp rising on one wall like something from beneath the bowels of Cairo, reaching up, gripping.

Only one door, thick, metal, and we enter. No-one. We can hear voices behind walls, feel humanity's presence, but no actual sign of life. Small glass of coffee on a desk, furling caffeine cloud fractals towards the low ceiling.

A conversation getting closer. Voices, their language indefinable, more vibrations through the furniture than words.

Slight movement of the walls and floor as they approach, their weight and gravity announcing their closeness. Two men and two women now seen rounding from a corridor, turning, faces.

Windsor let out an uncontrolled "Ohhh" as he sees their faces. He turns his head away and looks again to make sure.

It's Cal.

"Welcome to the kidnappers' lair," she says as she approaches, hugging us both simultaneously. "You've been released." She pulls back and keeps smiling as she says this. Looking at us both, taking us in. Formalities delivered with informal humour in her eyes and a what-the-fuck-are-we-doing-here-again face.

We sit around a small desk, knees squeezed against the sides in odd rickety chairs and under a dim light hanging above. Cal, Windsor, someone called Massoud, and me.

"Welcome to freedom," says Cal, smiling, stretching the joke.

"You're not who we expected to meet here," replies Windsor.

"Yeah? Same to you," she responds. "Just over 48 hours ago, I was having a tortilla at Canary Wharf with some drones from Barclays and I get a call. Someone says, you're booked on the Emirates Cairo flight in three hours…"

Massoud's phone buzzed. He grabbed it and started talking in Arabic. He gets up and walks away, leaving the three of us alone.

"What the fuck?" I say to Cal as if there has been no interruption.

"And who called you?" adds Windsor.

Loud whispers, more in shock than conspiracy.

"Well, I'm in corporate affairs for Retero-Varsey. We do financial services, transactions, credit, trades listed in London, do all our work there, but actually HQ'd in Yerevan, owned by two Armenian brothers. We've just got some serious Chinese money to start raising dollars for green-field gas projects in Tunisia, hooked in with these guys…" She indicates Massoud's empty seat "…and got our hands dirty a bit."

I only just manage not to scoff. "What is about you and shady corporates? "

My first meeting with Cal West was in a Starbucks in London. She was defecting from her role as PA to Wonder Zap-Mills, CEO of healthcare company BioHorizons, to join Windsor and I as we sought to blow open a case of unethical HIV vaccine testing in eastern Africa. She was a trusted colleague. Or so I thought.

Cal is a flipper, a shape shifter. She about-faced and fell back into the embrace of those on the wrong side of the story.

But she is lovely still. She is conservatively dressed for her; jeans and buttoned-up shirt. She is usually showier. Maybe she's overcompensating on the Islamic country dress code for women – kind of unnecessary here in Cairo. but you never know, I guess, with Mubarak simultaneously skirting and embracing extremists.

"What's shady?" She speaks as she usually does, breezy and humoured, southern English accent, clipped and always seeming to be prepping for punchline. A smirk not of arrogance but of comfort with her context, confident amusement, seeming off-guard but never, never switched off. Mind like an algorithm.

"Well, the Tunisians are fighting for freedom, fairness, maybe a change of government, aren't they? Getting into bed with the Chinese and the regime in Tunis and snuggling up to their petrodollars smells a lot like exploitation, doesn't it?"

"You said it yourself; getting your hands dirty", adds Windsor, who seemed to reserve his most cynical air for Cal. "Maybe that may explain something." He sits forward, elbows on thighs.

"This looks like an interrogation from where I'm sitting." Cal, looks a little flushed.

"Just looking for a story," I say. "To pin you on."

She frowns. "Look, we make our living where we can. We draw our moral landscapes with our heads and our hearts. We've had these debates before, you guys. I am not a bad person. I'm not doing bad work. If you want to make change you have to get close to those who need to change. Then you change them. You don't know the full picture and there's no time now to fill you in. And anyway, you know, you might be a little more grateful. If it wasn't for me..."

We all jump before she can finish. Something, a picture, fell off the wall. Unseen but heard. A sharp and heavy noise.

Windsor speaks. "What happened to Wonder and the charity? What was it, The Albert West er..."

"...Traditional Medicine Research Institute," Cal completes. "I'm still with them, working on natural remedies for mainstream ailments. Still going well. We're onto something called Cistanche Tubulosa, or Broomrape, Desert Ginseng, which is grown in Xinjiang and really interesting to the Chinese—"

Windsor cuts in. "Xinjiang?!"

Cal throws a glance at him. "Xinjiang," she repeats, firmly, defiantly.

Windsor looks pointedly out the window.

"So, what's your plan?" I ask after a moment of tense silence.

"Here's not the place. Or the time. Trust me, guys."

I know the score. I'm well aware the Chinese have likely cozied up with the Tunisian phosphate barons and the country's political leaders. I know that the Chinese like to see Arab nations as the Europeans did in the 19th century – as a workforce, source of materials and, eventually as markets.

Cal was playing a finely balanced game if she's in the thick of that. Xinjiang, home of the Uyghur people and site of some of the most pointed and stealthy, ethnic-based repression seen this side of the Holocaust. It was no place to be doing business.

For me, and I think for Windsor too, the mention of Xinjiang gives shivers and a sense that Cal's role in Tunisia might be against our cause. But I know Cal enough to know that things were never quite what they seem.

Cal offers an explanation. "There's freedom going on in Tunisia, starting with Gafsa. So if we can find a way to help that process and to benefit from it, where's the problem?"

"Who's *we*?" asks Windsor.

"The Chinese. But good Chinese. They do exist, you know. And others. And it's not what it looks like. Please trust me on this. I know where you're going, and I know what you're thinking. I'm asking you to trust me."

I raise my eyebrows, but indicate she should go on.

"It's all numbers and spreadsheets for these guys. If you don't have a slideshow, you don't have a strategy. You don't have a voice. The battlefield is on a board room table. You've got to play that game. That doesn't mean I don't have a moral investment in this."

"Are you truly sure about what you're doing?" I ask.

"I'm never sure." She is looking at her feet. Looks up. "Are you?"

Those eyes.

"What about the whole World Cup thing?" I ask. "You know that's why we're here, that the Tunisians have hired us to get it away from the corporates."

"Flight has taken on FIFA and that the World Cup has become a money ball being kicked around by FIFA and Flight, and others," Windsor chimes in.

She folds her arms. "I'm just here to help get you guys out. Get the credit for Retero-Varsey, being the good guys, get the pats on the back, do some happy snaps and leave, bugger off."

Her mood seems to darken.

I feel Windsor's energy. Something just happened. Didn't know what though. Whatever it is keeps crackling through the silence, complete with cries from outside and the occasional vehicle, a phone ringing, and muffled voices from inside. Uneasy.

Windsor starts doodling on a notepad left on the desk. An eye.

Massoud returns. He limps. Thin and wiry. Hardened face, etched and focussed. He doesn't look at us. Sits. Shuffles papers in a folder and pulls a sheet out.

"Here are details of your – our – holdings in Flight," he says, speaking English with a French accent. "We have been able to oblige the owner of these holdings to sign them over to this company - he dropped an index finger on the name - which you now represent."

We all know what *oblige* means. No prisoners in revolution. Even peaceniks sometimes need a loaded gun in the back pocket.

"Cal here, and Retero-Varsey, have also identified various interests with large holdings in Flight shares. We feel, as do they, that there are possibilities for developing a shareholder coalition at each company to pressure each to drop the Qatar campaign and to democratise the World Cup."

Massoud continues. "And we feel you can work to develop public awareness campaigns around Flight and FIFA to better inform all stakeholders about their intentions and their agendas. You have your budget."

And with that he leaves.

Next day, so do we.

10
MARCH 2010

London

"It has to be done, Asher. It's their funds, and they say it has to be done." Windsor sits sitting astride a plush leather couch in the centre of The Emporio Armani. The soft lighting forming shapes on his bare head. His battered sneakers and bedraggled clothing oddly chic in this temple of now.

Now I stand and ponder the presence of the credit card in my pocket which seems too hot to touch. This card, so it was explained to me amid the rubble in Gafsa, is the "shopping card".

"Buy everything on this so we can easily track your purchases."

The credit limit is $US2 million. I could live off this for years. It is overwhelming and my brain explodes gently inside my head as these vast sums are handed over to me.

The London excess outside provides a shifting tableau across the shop front window from our inside perspective.

"How do I drop into a secret, civil war zone, where people are starving, no access to healthcare, can't escape, and then leave loaded down with money that's been stolen from them to spend on making myself look nice?"

I can't wrap my head around it.

"I'll tell you how," says Windsor. "Because they want you to.

Do you know how much those thieving murderers stole from the Tunisians, just in Gafsa alone?! What you're about to spend is a pittance. And what you can do with that spend is limitless."

He leans forward to pat my arm.

"You have to see this as an investment. That's how the Tunisians are seeing it. You're the investment. See yourself as a property. A walking stock certificate. And all the money in the world is worthless right now in Tunisia. What they need can't be bought. That's all this is. You're expected to provide a return. If you don't, it's a loss for sure. But the investment had to be made."

"What if I fail? How many lives does that cost?"

The shop attendant, who is far too well dressed and presumably far too well paid to be called by such a relatively lowly title, approaches. I wave him away and hold up five fingers as minutes to return.

"Asher, you are making the mistake of seeing this as a revolution. A revolution, if the term is taken correctly, is simply a movement to get back to where you started. Many regime shifts have been just that and the new leaders are just as bad as the old. But this is no revolution. This is an *evolution*. It is a new system, a new structure. Something entirely new is being built here and although the world doesn't understand it yet, it is about to be shown how a country can be run by its people and how something that is owned by the people can be run by them too. And to do that, the structure outside needs to change too."

The words make sense. "But the money…"

"Money is simply a vehicle. These guys are trying to change the road rules so that it isn't the only vehicle. But right now, it is, and that's the system now. And that's where you come in. You are the avant garde for changing that system, Asher. It can only be changed from inside. You have to play the game to win it. And you have to win before you can discard it, know the rules before you can break them. There's not many who can carry that discipline and you are someone who can. I know it."

"Are you?" I ask him.

That Windsor smile. "What do you think?"

I think yes. I tell him so.

He drops a heavy hand on my shoulder and we fall silent.

After a moment, he says, "Anyway, who else can they pick? This is not an insider's job. An insider would not have the objectivity, to see the bigger picture. By definition. You need to be an outsider to get this done. They don't have anyone else. We're a pretty rare breed. They have chosen very well, my friend. Trust me. And trust yourself."

"Do you trust me?"

"With my life, brother."

He looks around him at the style and the wealth, the steady, silent hum of sharp lights finely focused. The glow of power accessories and wealth in their well-lit, glass boxes, like dead icons on show. The elegant attendant, the power of being inside while the majority world passed by outside, looking in.

And, for a change, I'm being looked at. I'm the guy inside the fancy store.

"And all this stuff is just the means to the end," adds Windsor, waving his hands at the air. "It's like football boots for the player, or skis for the racer. That's all."

The attendant returns and I tell him what I need. Basically a wardrobe.

He asks, very discreetly and politely, to check my card. I hand it over and he disappears, presumably to check its limit, its validity.

After a few moments, he is back and asking about colours.

"I'll take your advice on that."

He nods politely. He brings us chilled champagne – for which we were charged, I notice later - and we get started.

An hour later, Windsor and I are in the store's black-tiled bathroom, each standing at a urinal, giggling like school kids at the absurdity of our situation, the dizzying speed of our journey to here.

"What are we doing here?" I ask him.

"We're starting at the top, my friend..."

We laughed some more.

*   *   *

Amsterdam

"All this money has to buy *something*." Windsor says as he looks through the pile of papers the Tunisians had handed over to us. "We can't just leave it here idle. Clearly we have a duty to put it to work."

I look at the papers. A surprisingly small sheaf given the grunt they carried and the money they represented.

The credit card details were huge enough. Six figures each on multiple cards. Breath-taking and creepy somehow. Oddly abstract numbers. But, the stock certificates blew my mind. Laid in front of me are ownership slabs of major companies, global brands, multinational giants. Coca-Cola, Microsoft, Google, Morgan Stanley. And more. Not enough to make a racket, but enough to make some noise.

I hold the formal proxy documents that gave me the right to action these shares. These letters and forms signed over those rights to me. I have the right to vote with these shares, to make resolutions, to generate movement.

Signed over to the Tunisian revolution. All counter signed and proper. My name all over them.

I have taken a furnished apartment in Amsterdam, with a view of the Keizersgracht Canal and in earshot of the fun and games in the red light district. It is tiny, the bedroom like a closet and the bathroom barely with enough room to dry yourself without bumping a limb on a wall or fixture. Euro luxury though. I am paying 200 Euro a night and have paid 3 months in advance.

Documents are scattered across the dark wood coffee table, and I sit looking out onto the postage stamp courtyard which is pulsing with alternating light, from overcast dullness to strobe-bright sunshine, the light seemingly caught and thrown by the hand of a stiff breeze.

Amsterdam is an easy place to hide. No-one asks a lot of questions, even in officialdom, and few are bothered about who you are. Liberty translates to privacy.

And this is Cruyff's home town. The best ever. A brilliant player and an even more brilliant mind. A man of action and heart. A democrat. A rebel. A leader and an inspiration. The nearby suburb of Betondorp is Cruyff central. Where better to base a project like this, who better as our symbol?

Windsor is here too, soaking up the culture. And, thinking, always thinking.

Within 24 hours of us arriving here from London, we both begin researching, phoning, emailing, writing.

During our first dinner, we started planning.

"We need to *work* all these guys," I say, pondering the paperwork.

I continue. "Are we a give campaign or a take campaign? Adversarial or aspirational? We need to work out what is our best strategy to get corporates on board for our bid. Should we focus on those we want to deny or those we want to anoint? Who do we target?" I look up.

"Whom," corrects Windsor.

We both sit and ponder this vast wealth at our fingertips and the very limited clout even this sum allows us, especially given how widely dispersed it actually is.

"What are our needs? What is our purpose?" asks Windsor, as the numbers float surreally around us.

Time folds around the moment. It sounds simple enough, but we can't grasp the complex details, the alchemist's world of global equity investment and financial transactions.

I look at Windsor, searching for an answer, and he replies with a similar look.

We seek words to help guide us through the landscape and start circling the topics again.

"Our starting point is we need to get some kind of control over Flight and over FIFA," I say.

"Actually, we need to weaken them all," counters Windsor, "In order to allow a third force to arise. We don't really need any of them, do we?"

We let the thought hang.

"There's potential to go whistleblower and play the market on Flight. We could gain some momentum that could help us."

Windsor shakes his head. "We don't have time for anything complicated. "His voice breaks the whooshing sound of passing traffic. "Let's work on Flight first."

"But we can't afford to buy up their shares, even if they're dumped, to get to a significant enough chunk. Even the Tunisians don't have that much."

"Yes, but as fellow shareholders, we can pressure other stockholders on the looming business case crisis Flight is getting itself into by trying to take over the World Cup. They start dumping shares, the price goes down and we can buy them and more to gain a larger stake in Flight. Make a take-over even. Then we can start getting at them from within and break down the Qatar bid."

I drum my fingers. "That's a lot to do in, what, eight months?"

"But, right now it's maybe the best we got."

He sighs and reaches for a full glass of water on the small table near the couch. He over-balances on his elbow and his hand jerks sideways, bumping the glass which spills its contents over the paperwork.

The moment is loud and abrasive and we both react sharply. I leap to my feet and Windsor swears and reaches for the glass, uselessly setting the now empty vessel upright.

We hang the papers up in the bathroom, drooping them over the curtain rod and towel racks in a desperate big to get them to dry. We cannot afford to lose them.

Outside, I noticed the light show had ceased. It had evened to a uniform blandness. The canal bubbles and the streets becomes shiny. Lights becomes blurry. Amsterdam has begun to rain.

I look out the glass doors into the streets. Puddles of neon light scatter like jigsaw pieces on rain-wet pavements. The air is chilled now, and I shiver from cold or fear. Or both.

Windsor leaves for London the next day. I stay behind to start planning our assault on the world's investors.

*   *   *

London

A few days later, I meet Windsor at a cafe in Chelsea. He has hit the suit stores and picked up a couple of off the rack efforts, even descending, as he put it, to buying a few ties which he couldn't guarantee he would ever wear.

"My mother should see me now," he says, as he prepares to lift off on his morning flight to New York and his first meeting with Morgan Stanley later that same day. Charcoal suit, crisp white shirt, shiny black leather shoes. A tie is folded menacingly in his hand luggage, threatening to be worn by this man who vowed that they were no more than fancy nooses.

He models his recent purchases, looking elegant despite his bulky frame challenging the seams of the apparel.

"Good luck," he says as we leave the cafe. "Let's do this job well."

And he was gone and flying. Like dust.

And so, for us both, the world becomes an airport with channels running to hotels and boardrooms.

Munich. New York. Tokyo. Sydney. Paris. Jo'burg. Jakarta. Beijing.

Big cities and shifting time zones. No sleep and too much sleep. Days and nights like lights turned randomly on and off by malevolent children.

And odd, hard to get to, places, counter-intuitive places for corporate dealings: The Cook Islands. Montego Bay, Newport Beach.

Money like water goes anywhere. Like bacteria, lives anywhere.

Flash suits and fancy hotels. Individuals and companies. Meals in outrageous restaurants. Back of limo meetings and embraced by lush arm chairs in massive homes in spectacular settings. Swish offices with nosebleed views. Scotches and cigars. Meals of dead things sacrificed for the pleasure of these already lost and emptied souls. Money everywhere. And us spending big to look competitive and of their world with sickening regularity, totting up horrifying amounts spent to parley with these machines masquerading as people.

Faces and places. No glamour, just grind. Humankind blurring into one amorphous lump. Dispiriting and enervating, each face attached to a hand that wants something, that seals a gain, a benefit, generally one which can be plotted on a screen, worked into a spreadsheet, numbers that had currency notations next to them was the lexicon we used. It is all numbers. Damned, numbers.

So much time lost, time that can't be regained, following lost dollars down dark holes, finding light in amounts to be spent or saved, listing goals in strings of numerical gibbering's, marks like bird footprints running across pages, punctuating the demise of our species, encoding our defeat.

A man who runs a hedge fund in Barbados tells me, "You can't waste my time with this stuff. Where's your numbers? You talk morality, sure, I love morals, they market really well, but where's your numbers?! How can you prove to me what Flight is doing is wrong, that this will cost us? They might win!"

In truth, I can't argue.

These are dark, desperate days, weeks. Windsor and I both feel our moral compass spinning dizzyingly, unable to fix on a point at which anything made any sense.

We catch up as often as we can, when crazy schedules allow our paths to cross, like corpuscles in the veins of a vast, breathing body.

He is losing weight.

I am losing my mind.

We get nowhere and the figures we run past each other confirm that the world's money was controlled by more shits than we have thought. Arseholes who can simply out-arsehole everyone else. And profit from it.

"It's a wash out," I say as Windsor pours over the cloud-based documents we have shared along our travels, seeking to leech meaning beyond the dismay.

We have spent a lot of Tunisian money. Ponced about the world in our fancy kit. Travelled and stayed at fancy hotels, dined in luxury and met the world's movers and shakers, laying our arguments with our stock certificates across hundreds of tables.

We've told them, "If, when, Qatar wins, and people find out how, the share price will go down. We will go public with our reasons for dropping the stock. It will damage the brand of Flight, FIFA, put a bear claw in its share price."

But few bought our line. And we have come up with a duck egg. A doughnut. A big nothing.

Our - the Tunisians' - paltry stake in Flight plus a bit more we have picked up from supporters won't make a dent in the company. We can rant all we want. We have lost.

I have been in touch with Haykel throughout. I now sit in a hotel in Tokyo or maybe Singapore or maybe Hong Kong - Asia anyway - and put through another call.

"I have to tell you Haykel, I don't know that we can do anymore. We haven't got anywhere and I can't see that we will. I don't know what to do."

He's silent for a long time. "Get to Glasgow," he finally says. "You need to meet Chodak."

11
APRIL 2010

Glasgow

Sometimes, Glasgow might be pretty. Today it isn't. Grey heavy clouds shift mournfully across a low ceiling sky. Although without rain, the light is layered onto buildings. Things seem heavier, more difficult.

But in this land of rotten weather, elements of modern football are born. There has to be a reason for that. And perhaps the reason is right here, in the back streets of the city as an army of joyful, expectant faces makes its way to The Game. Green and white dominates the apparel, from shirts to hats, to flags and scarves, from backpacks to shoes. Celtic Bhoys.

Their energy dissipates the weather like a heat ray. The mood is uplifted and excited. Expectation of victory is perhaps the sweetest, and most effective, anecdote to foul conditions and the fact that the game is played outside, almost without fail, even in the most appalling conditions, only emphasises the ability of football to overcome the constraints of its setting.

And because of that, because of its character, football once was and had always been a working-class game, born in mills and factories and on boggy communal fields. It is the game of the masses. People stand throughout a match, packed against each other like cigars in a box. Huddling for warmth in the long winter months, breathing each other's stink.

But no more. Now it's a toff's game, a game for the Hooray Henrys, the Made Men who have moved in and flashed about their gaudy rings, their money, and bought the game. They have taken it away from its base. Russian crooks who won in the economic lottery of the post-Soviet era. IT parvenus. The dilettantes of Wall Street and London money bags. They packed the corporate boxes, and they funded the dreams for others, the upper middle classes who could afford the season tickets or the hundreds of pounds it took to score a ticket on the street. All partook of the wafting aroma of ill-gotten gains and allowed the shapes on the field to set the patterns of their own agendas. The compact field, its players, its rules, its winners and losers. The game now epitomises their view of the world and those who won, its players, its managers, became projections of them. And all are paid accordingly for such a valuable role.

Victory seems distant for me however, and I feel heavy with defeat. Even Windsor's optimism has waned.

We are given a corporate box at the Celtic home ground, Parkhead, and we are to meet Chodak Lampa and his manager after today's match. Being an actual Celtic player, Chodak has some sway.

Windsor and I are in our sharp suits – Windsor is rather disappointed with his, as he said it swished as he walked. I tell him it is his chunky thighs mate, not the cheap bag of fruit he was wearing. He laughs and we ride the elevator up to the box. It feels for a moment like we belong.

But the fraught nature of our quest lingers, pressing on our shoulders. Maybe it is just that we are getting used to the pressure we are under, feeling comfortable with discomfort.

Massive feature windows open onto a breath-taking scene, lush green grass, untrampled and pristine, lined with the snow-white lines and green and white-netted goals at either end. There was something majestic about this view, like the field is a battlefield or some exalted plain upon which history is made. The ghostly cries of crowds past, the emotions that have been expended here in this space as all gaze upon this rectangle of dreams, like a slice of heaven had fallen down here among us, and was fit to be trod by only the Gods of our world.

There are few people inside yet. The only real movement, apart from a few groundsmen and staff, is the LED advertising hoardings running around the perimeter of the pitch. Emirates Airlines, Visit Spain, Amazon, Jaguar cars, iPhones. And Mr Fox.

It flashed. Mr Fox. Mr Fox. Mr Fox.

I whack Windsor with the back of my hand and point to the screen below us.

A and W

Hi (Smiley face emoji)

We know you.

We know what you're doing.

You can't win.

You won't win.

You should stop what you're doing.

Now (Flashing)

Goodbye.

(Dead face emoji)

And then an ad for Celtic's next home game.

It took maybe 45 seconds in all.

Windsor and I sit in silent panic. My instinct in the face of fear is, I'm sorry to say, to hide and disappear to safety.

My heart lifts to my throat. My head pounds with heavy thoughts. I feel nauseous.

I know what we are doing has always been likely to be making some very powerful enemies. But the distance between concept and realisation, in such matters, is one I actively cultivated. It is inevitable, with such a strategy, that worlds will collide. It is a horrible shock when they do. It's horrible when fear wins.

I looked to Windsor, but he won't look at me. His eyes are in that half distance where thinking takes place. I can feel him cooking up a relevant Shakespeare moment, to be delivered with the usual combination of timing, gravitas and gallows wit.

A knock on the open door breaks the tension. We turn to see a guy, cameras hanging off him, who quickly, without asking, takes some photos of us.

He says, "It is a complimentary memento, provided by your hosts."

He gives us a URL and a password where we can download the shots in a few days. And leaves.

Windsor finally speaks. "Don't touch that URL."

"I know." I bin it.

We say no more and allow the movement around us, the stadium filling, the building anticipation, to distract us from what has just happened.

Soon before kick-off, as we are about to settle in with a scotch and canapes, brought to us by a liveried waiter, I notice my hand is shaking.

A message is delivered by the same waiter. Chodak Lampa wants to see us and has invited us down to the changing rooms.

"Surely no-one's going to try and do something in a stadium with random people everywhere?" I say.

Lots of dark places in a stadium, I mentally answer myself.

Down in the bowels of the stadium, lots of empty spaces and corners. Eventually we are directed to a surprisingly dark and oppressive corridor which leads to three doors, one marked 'Home', another 'Away', and a third 'Officials'.

The assistant leads us to a hulking man in a tracksuit on the door, like a bouncer at a nightclub, who glances at us and motions us into the inner sanctum.

The changing room is largely empty. Empty Celtic shirts, emerald green and white hoops, hang like slabs of meat on a butcher's rack, alive yet disembodied, with coat hangers emerging from the shirt necks like thin birds' heads. Large black numbers and names across the shoulders. I count 17 shirts. One yellow one with patches on the long sleeves. Goalkeeper's.

A man emerges from around a corner and approaches. Diminutive, with a furrowed brow and small features etched with a fine brush across a cat-like skull. His head mainly bald save for a skerrick of hair that clings to the back half, like his forehead had grown through. Lugubrious eyes gaze downwards by default and a slight hunch in the gait seems to discourage looking straight or upwards. His tan suit and white shirt with blue tie have clearly not been purchased from where we have recently bought our fancy threads. He looked like he was dressed by his mother, who lives in the 1950s and has poor vision and no money. His tie has stains on it.

He looks up from his hunched space, eyes held upwards for brief glances before flicking downwards again, almost like he is afraid we are going to beat him up. His head only reaches my solar plexus. His voice is tight, high-pitched, raspy. I felt like the 12th Century is speaking to us.

"Hello. You must be Mr Fox. And Mr Obili. Good to meet you. I am Dorje, Chodak's assistant. I am glad you could come. Do you want to join us for warm up?"

Eyes moved upwards and held. Held. No handshake.

"Warm up?" Windsor pops the silence. "I didn't bring my boots..."

Dorje suggests we follow him as he beetles off into another room.

It is a huge space, with various random-seeming lines painted on the walls and floor, circles and rectangles. Netted goals are set up at either end. There is no-one here. Or so it appears at first. Windsor alerts me to a figure, lying on his back, arms spread out, with his legs straight up against the wall. His feet are straightened, ankles flush to the wall and soles facing upwards. On them, a football rested. His eyes are closed. He wears a t-shirt and shorts. No shoes.

"Warming up," whispers Dorje. "Please. Join."

With this, he assumes the same position as the other man, legs up, bum to the wall, soles to the ceiling, arms out. Eyes closed.

So do we. Ridiculously. Windsor struggles to straighten his legs and ends up with his feet against the wall, knees bent. All is silent, apart from distant voices and shouts, locker room shuffling echoing in the other rooms.

I keep my eyes open and watch the man who holds the ball on his feet. Without moving any other part of his body, he flips his feet quickly, so the toes are now pointing upwards. The ball, miraculously, stays balanced under the toes of one foot. The other stretches over his shoulder. The remaining foot and leg shift in tiny movements to hold the ball in place. The foot which was taken away returns and slides under the ball allowing the other foot to be taken away and flexed.

Then, the ball flips off and, landing on his prone chest, is clutched. He stands, places the ball in front of him, pushes it forward with the sole of his foot before kicking it and sending the ball swishing into the goal at the other end of the room, where it hits the net with a satisfying sigh, coiling gently into the folds and landing softly.

Then, he opens his eyes.

He sees the three of us lined against the wall, L-shaped, incongruous and utterly foolish in our suits. The pants legs of mine has slid up my legs, revealing in this order from sole to above-knee: expensive shoes, expensive socks, and hairy legs of limited value. Such threads are surely not made for this.

Chodak Lampa - I know the face from photos - looks at us shyly. We stand and he shakes hands without speaking.

He turns to a woman who we had not noticed sitting silently in the room. She looks a little older than him, Middle Eastern dark eyes and olive skin. Gorgeous and compelling. A kiss, a hug. Affection, but not outrageous. Respectful lovers. A real relationship.

Without another word, Dorje gestures for us to leave.

*   *   *

Back in the money seats in the corporate box, the two teams emerge at precisely 2:45pm.

The stadium now seems to balloon with the sound of the energy it contains. The sides must be bulged like too-full tyres as the teams took the field. Today, the home team plays Aberdeen, way down the celestial pecking order, although they are only a few places below Celtic on the table.

Chodak Lampa comes out last, almost as if he was an after-thought. Colours explode onto the lush, soulful green of the pitch in crisp shapes and fluid movements. The air crackles with intensity and excitement, charging the space and etching the players on the pitch with sharp edges. The green and white of Celtic and Aberdeen's red, like spinning blooms in a dream-like spring park, blaring with life, transfixing and mesmerising.

A whistle screeches across the held silence. The game starts.

The woman that Lampa had been with before sits near us. Do I know her?

Then I remember the picture in the file given to me by the Tunisians. The woman I was told might help us. Maybe. Her name is Ebaa.

*　　*　　*

After a home game, and often after any game in Glasgow or nearby, it is customary for Celtic players to head for the fancy, outrageously priced upstairs private room of a bar owned by a former player. But Chodak says there will be too many eyes there. "Too crazy," he says, face becoming uncharacteristically comic for a moment.

We drive to a neat, busy Lebanese restaurant near Glasgow Cathedral, park, and go in through the back entrance and into the kitchen. It smells spicy and burnt and has greasy walls. There is one closed, yellowed window. It is hazy and fetid, cloying. The sounds of a busy night out dent the air regularly. Pots. Stirring. Sizzles. Splashes. Shouts.

Windsor. Chodak. Dorje. Me.

A small, paint chipped table and four unmatched chairs just off the kitchen. A mute TV in the corner – playing Match of the Day – and a faded poster of a past Scotland team; Gemmill, McQueen, Macari, Dalglish, Rioch, Jordan. Signed by some.

"We own this place," says Chodak, almost apologetically.

"Lebanese?" I ask.

"Well, a good friend of mine is from Lebanon," replies Chodak. "Her idea."

He has a way of talking that draws you in. The eyes are warm and dark, couched in soft wrinkles less of age than of heritage. The cheek bones are widely set, the forehead generous. The mouth seems capable of both great harshness and touching intimacy.

It is a face produced by countless questions erupting behind it, struggling to hold the enquiries. It is a busy space.

His body is well wrapped in stylish if not overly lavish taste. Chinos, V-neck sweater, scarf, loafers. A body, strong tea coloured, small and nuggety. Legs seem on springs and of remarkable torsion, long arms and compressed torso. Low centre of gravity. Balance.

"Would you like to eat?" asks Chodak.

"Sure," Windsor and I more or less say at the same time.

Dorje gets up and disappears to order some food.

"We enjoyed the game today", I say. "We both really appreciate your invitation. But, we had a…moment."

I tell him about the threatening ground advertisement that spoke directly to us.

"Oh," he says. "Who would do this?"

"That's what we would like to know."

"We can find out who paid for it, check with the office," offered Chodak.

"Thank you. Certainly scared us."

Windsor shot me a look as if to say *speak for yourself.*

"Yes. Yes. We are moving in dangerous waters," says Chodak. "We must make courage." Windsor starts to say something, but Chodak, maybe not hearing or seeing him, cuts him off. "But this was not the real game. Isn't that why we must talk?"

Windsor finally gets to speak. "You have heard from our mutual friends in Tunisia?"

Chodak nods, distracted. "Of course. Of course. Yes. We must work to help those who need us. We have money and this means a lot. But what are we to do with it? I am not a diplomat. I am worth more to my people wearing a number on my back and a ball at my feet. What can I do?"

"What do you know?" I ask Chodak.

Chodak sucks air through his teeth. Folds his mouth around them and smiles, eyebrows taking flight, eyes widening. "I know that we have World Cup going to Qatar that we need to block. I know we are supposed to work together but we have no plan. I know we are being trusted to do something very big and very important. I know that I have been asked to enlist the football family, allies, to help with this task. I know I am thinking more about this than about my football."

We are all sitting forward, held by the tale we are making. We feel it unspooling around us, entwining us with every moment and searching for threads of context and meaning. It is like we all stop breathing.

Dorje returns, placing numerous plates before us. Round breads and bean dishes. Salads. Chips. A neat ring of beige humous frosted with russet coloured paprika and indented with a button of oil was soon violated as we dip into this that, hungrily pasting each mouthful before throwing it into our unconscious mouths.

Chodak continues. "The Tunisians have make contact with me and you to try and ensure their freedom fight is not in vain. They wish to ensure that their victory is a people's victory. They have choose the World Cup to make this point. It is ambitious and surprising to say the least. But this is world in which we live, yes?"

We nod.

He continues. "So, both Flight and FIFA want Qatar to have the World Cup. Flight want Qatar because it sees a business future there. FIFA want Qatar because Flight does. Qatar is, by population, maybe the world's richest country. But it is built on oil, which is losing value. It makes good business sense, the World Cup. We can agree this is a war between FIFA and Flight, for the dominant position in the sports brands world."

We eat in silence.

"What else do you know?" I push Chodak.

"Well, I know the Tunisians have trusted you with significant funds liberated from the phosphate robbers. You are to use these funds and your experience as a, er, whistleblower?"

I nod, more to continue than to agree, and he went on.

"You will expose the corruption and restore World Cup to people. This brings honour to Tunisian people. They make…" He looks at Dorje.

Doeje says, quietly, "Democratisation."

"Yes, democratisation of the world game."

We eat some more.

"Ok," I say. "What's your role here? What have the Tunisians signed you up for?"

"Ah, yes, we have been signed by the Tunisians! Free transfer!" replies Chodak.

Dorje and Chodak exchange smiles. Some kind of joke between a pro football player and his manager.

"You want to know what position I am playing?" He laughs. "Ok. I think you are centre midfield." He moves some plates and puts a broken chip down. "You. And I am maybe centre forward." He takes another piece of chip and placed it in position in front of the other chip. "Me."

"Not much of a team is it?" says Windsor, surveying the table of half eaten food and two desolate chips in the middle. "Only two players."

"Ah, yes, but a good team can be made around few good players. Some teams only need one good player and rest just not bad players who know what to do. But those players have to work well together, have to understand each other. Very well. That what we must do."

Chodak continues. "I am a man who is very aware of my place, my opportunity. I come from a simple place. Very poor in money but very rich in humanity. People don't get gifts I have been given for no reason. I am a believer in karma. I am obliged, *compelled* to do something with it. That is my journey. The Tunisians are moving many things. They are not simple revolutionaries. These are men and women with a vision for the world and the future. They understand the value of the game. They see a partnership of the oppressed as a powerful thing, most powerful thing."

His eyes stare. The face set. "Tibet is a most oppressed nation and the Tunisians see our liberty as helpful to theirs. They see all oppressed people as same team. In this game, like any game, there are winners and losers. No-one plays a game to lose. I don't play to lose."

We allow Chodak's bravado - seemingly out of character, yet still devoid of ego, more a statement of an accepted fact – to linger and waft on the shouts and banging steel, the clashing personalities and stormy weather brewing in the hectic kitchen pouring in hot, pungent clouds through the open door.

"Ok, so here's you over here," I say, pointing to his chip. "What are you supposed to be doing there? What's your game plan?"

"Yes. Yes. I am the most famous Asian player. Maybe, right now, most famous Asian player in the world. Young Scottish Player of the Year. Already very famous. EPL, Serie A, La Liga want me. Big clubs. I am now 19. So, if I play in the World Cup this year, in South Africa, I have maybe four or five World Cups to play. But, I will not play in South Africa because Tibet will not qualify. Actually, Tibet has no team. FIFA does not recognise us."

Chodak stops, frowns. Starts again. "So, maybe I say, I want to play World Cup. I want to play for China. China want me very much. Pay me much. They will give me many things. Make me big man in China. It will be good for me. But why would I play for China?! I am not Chinese! Many, many players have this problem. They have no country. Someone says your country is not real. But the player knows it's real. They were born there. They make life there. They have family there. Or maybe they come from a small country. It may be a real country, but a big country says you play with us, you play with our big country."

This sounds familiar. Haykel. *"They still think that they own us and that we will always want to be part of the boss's team."*

"It's a very bad situation," Chodak concludes. "What can a player do? He is a young man. His family maybe says 'play for our little country'. The player thinks it's good for the family because they live in a small country. But he also knows the country is shit, the government shit, football people shit. He thinks, I want a big career. But my family helped when me when I little boy, he thinks. His parents worked hard for him. He would not play without his family. I must repay them. It is very difficult."

He looks down, like he is reliving those troubled moments.

"What's this got to do with what we're doing, with the Tunisians?" asks Windsor.

Chodak takes a few minutes. He keeps looking down. "Football is a world game. It's a game for the heart. Football not politics.

"The World Cup should be for everybody. Every country. Every people, even if they have no country or their country is so shit they cannot play. World Cup can be everybody. Even men and women, no? Together. Same time. Why not?"

Dorje nods. So do we.

Chodak picks up the sad little chip, holds it aloft. "My role in this team is to score goals. But I need the ball. Your role, I think," he picks up the other chip, "is to get ball to me. My question now is, how are you going to do that? I am here." He shakes his chip, "Calling for ball. I am a very good player. I score goals for our team. Can you give me the ball?"

Windsor takes the cue. "You know we come to this from a different place than you."

Nod from Chodak. "Yes. Yes."

I add: "We have tried to convince investors to pressure Flight to pull out of its World Cup ownership bid. But time is against us and those investors weren't listening to us. We told the Tunisians we have failed and need a new plan. We told them we had no leads on FIFA and weren't sure what to do. They, Haykel, told us to come to you, to speak to you."

Dorje and Chodak look at us. Look at each other. Look away.

"You need to wipe the white board, shift your Xes and Os around, Mr Fox, Mr Obili. Maybe start again," says Chodak. Wise, for just 19 years of age.

"Well, yes," says Windsor, "This plan has failed."

"You have to take stronger action," says Chodak. He slices his hand across his throat.

Something odd is in the air and I need to clear it. "You're saying we need to *eliminate* people?"

"Revolution has its victims, Mr Fox," says Dorje.

"Revolution is a much bigger word than ethics," says Chodak.

*　　*　　*

"What was that!?" Windsor exclaims afterwards,

I just shake my head.

"All this waffle about chips, scoring goals and getting the ball. And now we're assassinating CEOs and whatever. This is *nuts*, Asher."

We are driving through the streets of Glasgow. Late night city lights smear across the windows as we go, not really sure where we were going. We are perplexed and thrown by this turn of events.

I know Windsor and know well enough that his statements are not definitive. He is searching and his verbalisations are his compass, guiding him to the answers he sought. The words that fall from his mouth are just footsteps on his map to himself.

We arrive back in the underground car park of our apartment block. The car holds us in a plush embrace. The silence and stillness after the drama of this night are intense. We sit in the moment, gripped by the vacuum in time and space we had arrived at.

"Honour hath no skill in surgery," utters Windsor, as if the lines are spooling into him from above. "What is honour? A word. What is that word, honour? Air. Honour is a mere scutcheon."

"What's that from? I ask.

"Henry Four. Falstaff."

We get out of the car.

"What's a scutcheon, then?"

He snorts. "You're the honour expert. You tell me." That Windsor laugh booms through the cavernous car park.

*　　*　　*

"Asher! Asher!" Windsor is prodding me gently but, in my slumberous torpor it seems violent and obscene. It is a voice in a dream, heard like an audio backing as some odd chaotic narrative played out in my sleeping head.

I jolt. "Wha' wha'…What is it?"

"Asher. Asher, my friend."

I wake a little more. "Windsor, what is it mate? What the fuck is…"

He looks anxious. "We must talk, my friend. We need a strategy."

"What, now?! "It's," I check my phone, "3am! We really need a strategy, now? Like, right now?" I have awoken sufficiently for indignation but not for logic.

Windsor stands and looks into my eyes. "I'm in the lounge. Coffee is on," he says, walking off.

The room smells sweet and aromatic as the coffee machine chats to itself in the kitchen.

I groan, get up, follow after a bit.

Windsor is pacing when I enter. "Sit down. Let's talk. I have reached some conclusions."

"They couldn't wait until a normal time?" I ask.

"It's a normal time somewhere, Ash. Sit." I do. He goes on. "Of course it was The Man himself."

Shakespeare, he meant.

"I was reading Richard II. This man, this king, who was weak and dangerous, an unworthy ruler of his people and in need of deposing, and those who conspired to save their country from him. Yet how? How to usurp a king?" He looks up now, into my eyes. His voice, soft and barely heard.

"Let's march without the noise of threat'ning drum
That from the castle's totter'd battlements
Our fair appointments may be well perus'd."

I wait.

"This is Bolingbroke," says Windsor, "As he prepares to take on the King in Wales. You see what he's saying: don't announce ourselves so that we may let slip the dogs of war, Asher. Kings are built for war, they create systems around them just for that. Let's not give them one, he's saying. Let's not speak their language."

"I don't really understand," I admit. I am still foggy and airy.

"We've been taking them head on. We've been playing their game, talking their language of investments and money and business and economics…and we've lost."

I rub my eyes. "Yep. You're right. We have. This is the world we have made." I stand and start walking to exercise my mind. "This is what we've got. We have this beautiful game, that is loved by just about everyone, or, if not loved then certainly felt and known by everyone. And what have we done with it? We've allowed it to be sold to the highest bidder. We've allowed it to be taken out of the hands of the very people who have nurtured it. It's like a kidnapping of the world's favourite child."

He's watching me. My words spill out. "These bastards, the ones we've been wasting our time with, hoping for a scintilla of morality, don't get it. We can't get to them because they just don't get it. Because we've entered their world, been trying to speak their language."

Windsor lets me riff, despite being the one who got this conversation going. He disappears to get coffee and places a steaming cup on the table.

"So what are we going to do about it?" he asks.

My mind zooms to my experience in Dubai, about what the game meant to those who didn't own it.

"Real people," is all I can reply.

Not an answer, but a pathway. Perhaps.

*　　*　　*

We both sit on this for the rest of the day, circling ideas like curious birds. Staring, taking notes, staring some more.

Windsor cranks up Ludovico Einaudi on Spotify. "Meditation music," he says.

We both love Einaudi. Kindred spirits, we sit and gently wallow in the deep cello voices, the wafting violins, the tempered structures like steps into a life. *Una Mattina.*

And, amid the minimal cellos and sparse piano notes, it comes to me. It can be done. I know what we had to do.

"Flight and FIFA, two, let's call them both companies. Other World Cup hangers on, sponsors, official suppliers and so; maybe another what 20, 30 companies? Media companies with World Cup rights? Let's be generous and say a few hundred. Hotels and whatever in the host country? Let's be generous and say a thousand. Others, jeez let's go crazy and say, another 5,000 companies or individuals who benefit somehow from the World Cup. Where are we, maybe 10,000 companies? Let's say every company has an average of 100 employees. So, that's a million people."

"Right...?"

I continue. "How many football players worldwide? Maybe 300 million. How many supporters? 3.5 billion. Let's go back to that 1 million. Now not all of them really benefit. Many are just desk jockeys, worker bees, grunts and whatever. It's only really the elites who will see direct benefit from the World Cup. Let's say 20%, 200,000 individuals." I lean forward, emphasising my point. "Two hundred thousand. Versus 300 million. Versus 3.5 billion! What the fuck are we doing wasting our time with these elitist arseholes?"

Windsor's face freezes. His eyes stare. "Why indeed?" he finally says.

*   *   *

I watch a late night replay of the 2009 FA Cup semi-final between Manchester United and Everton while running all those numbers through my head. Windsor is off for a head-clearing walk in the dawn light.

The moment when the idea comes to me is like something reaches out of the TV screen and plunges into my guts. It is exhilarating even before I know what it is.

What are you? What are you telling me?

I force myself to sit with it, grab a notebook and poise my pen, mind open.

As the raw idea darts through like an electric lizard, I search for info on the FA Cup.

I inevitably arrive at one CW Alcock. Before I even begin looking into his role in starting the FA Cup in the 1870s, I note that he organized the first international games for the newly minted Association Football; England v Scotland at The Oval, London, on March 5, 1870.

Old mate Alcock, despite his name, sure had balls. And brains.

The value of the FA Cup concept back then was that it lined up the big wigs, like the amateur toffs from Etonians or Wanderers, with little workers' teams from the grimy, coal dust and factory-floor corners of industrial Britain. Everyone had a shot on the nominally even playing field of football.

How about many thousands of teams, scattered all over the world? A world FA Cup? The idea seems too outrageous to be logical, as good ideas often are.

I have become used to equating football with life, or life with football. The lines between them have merged in these past months, blurring into non-existence. Whenever I think of football, I think of life similes and themes, reflexively and without effort.

A global FA Cup has become a symbol to shatter the political cage that traps the game. How can all those people, all those identities and cultures, ideas, and agendas be captured by a few hundred teams?

It's like holding a global election and inviting a few hundred people to vote, like Haykel said. This is a way everyone can have a shot, and where identities and ethnicities can be represented and celebrated.

A Better World Cup.

It needs work. I need to put it free of opportunities for exploitation by those whom we don't want to encourage, the misanthropes and psychopaths, the fascists and assorted lunatics who rally around a flag or an identity like it is a weapon, not a banner of shared experience.

I'm buzzing with excitement when Windsor returns. We work on as morning widens into day and then afternoon, dusk. Eyes and body waning and sliding but kept awake by minds that won't stop zinging and spinning.

We fall asleep and wake late. My mind is already active even before my eyes open again.

I accost a half-awake and shuffle-walking Windsor on his way to the loo. "Up for an adventure? Us two?"

He yawns, rubs his eyes, chuckles. "When am I not, brother? But now?"

"I made some calls earlier. Contacts from other campaigns."

We are tired but ready for anything. There is something in the shift of focus from corporate dictators to actual people that lifts me. It is like the lights have come on, the air has become clearer; I am surging like The Kop in the old terrace days, and feeling like the world, suddenly, can be won.

"We're going to Kenya. I've booked it. Get packed and let's get going," I say.

Windsor nods and starts packing.

12
APRIL 2010

Nairobi, Kenya

The Jomo Kenyatta International Airport is grimy and broken. The metropolis holds some 3.5 million souls throbbing with that odd combination that only Africa knows, of ancient humanity and too-quick modernity. The ageing planet weighs heavily in Nairobi amid the modern smog and tightly packed civilisation.

"What are we doing?" Windsor has asked me numerous times in the few hours that have passed since we - I - decided to come here.

I haven't told him, perhaps a little afraid of my boldness and courage. "I have an idea, allow me to see if I can bring it to life."

"I'm with you, Asher. But I need to know at some point." My friend.

"You will," I promise.

At last, over a sleep-addled hotel dinner, punctuated with strong local coffee, I lay it out. "I have thought a great deal about our plight, our failure. Our efforts to address the problems in football from the top down..." I sit and pondered my reasoning, looking for words.

Windsor fills in the gap. "I have been playing a game in my mind. Allow me to test if I am right." Without any more preamble, he launches into *The Merchant of Venice*. "It is Portia speaking with Nerissa who says, 'how far that little candle throws his beams!

So shines a good deed.' And Nerissa replies, 'when the moon shone, we did not see the candle.' Is this what you are thinking Asher?"

I blink at him. "Jeez, Windsor, I love you, brother. I love working with you and I love what you do. But I generally have no clue what you are talking about, especially when you're off down the Shakespeare path."

He laughs that easy Windsor laugh. "Asher, my brother, you are smarter than you give yourself credit for. I know you know what I am talking about. But allow me to precis for you, in terms so you can understand: We have lost sight of the candle because we've been blinded by the moon. I think we are here to find the candle. And once we do, we will find millions more."

I look at him blankly, searching for a meaning. Amusing myself by how baffled I am. "I guess..."

He chuckles. "I ache for your dull mind Mr Fox, I will put it this way; we have become enamoured of the big picture, the bright light if you will, and forgotten our actual aim. I suggest that *we* are the candle. Our job is to use this to light other candles, the candles of the grass roots of this universal game. If one candle is strong, imagine the light from many millions. Lighthouses used to be candle power only, you know. Many candles can light up the night, Asher."

He's on a roll – and I let him continue.

"The Tunisians have given us a strong candle to light others. We have been trying to use that candle against the fluorescent lights - the moon - of the world's rich and fatuous. They would never see our single candle, Asher. But they will see many. Am I making sense to your unfortunately illiterate mind?"

I playfully roll my eyes at his grin. "Not how I would have put it," I reply. "But I reckon you've got it. I think we need to remake the world game, bottom up, blade of grass by blade of grass." Groping my way back to normal language.

Windsor looks deep into my eyes. A fraternal intimacy. "This is your value. You stumble about, get lost, struggle with yourself, but when – when - you allow yourself to be free, you see the truth. This is a gift, Asher. This is your superpower. You know how things work. You understand we are living upside down, that everything is the inversion of what I should be. And you see things as if everything was the right way up. You see the world from the bottom up. You have a vision others don't have."

I don't know about all that. "If only I understood it myself," I reply. I have the sudden overwhelming sense that I have wasted whatever gifts I've been given, plunging into the shadows of recrimination that hang about my every moment like a fog.

"No, Asher. If you knew how to control it, you may diminish it. Yours is the force of inspired creativity, the gift of spontaneous genius my friend. This is a thing that must remain unleashed, untamed, unknown even by you. Don't give it shape. Don't give it a name. Just don't ever let yourself ignore it. And don't ever think you aren't needed." He reaches out. Briefly touches the back of my hand before retreating. "Don't ever stop acting on your *what if...* moments. It's where you live, Asher."

My eyes fill with the truth of his words. He is right. What I have is a complex thing. Hard to define. Hard to value. A tumble of myself, a landscape of my fears, anxieties and self-criticisms are laid out before me and, yet I see through it and feel my latent power. And it fills me. It saddens me. It both empowers and enervates me.

Windsor finishes his coffee. "Let's go and do it then," he says.

As he gets up, I grab his arm. "My gift needs you. I need your courage. It's like a bulldozer that ploughs all my shit out of the way. I can't find whatever this gift is without your light, mate."

He smiles broadly, genuinely. "We're a team, brother." Simple as that.

And we clink our empty coffee cups.

*   *   *

Next morning, we hail a taxi. I tell the guy where we want to go.

The driver says, "No, not going there." We complain, but the guy is adamant. "No. Too dangerous."

So, we get out and go back into the hotel. Find the concierge and tell him where we want to go.

The concierge stammers. "Ummm, errrrr, ok. Let me find you a driver…"

In an hour-ish, we're told our driver is here.

He has a dusty black car with darkened windows. The guy standing next to it looks like a boxer, wearing a singlet which holds the kind of wiry, veiny frame that bears the power of a whip - not much to look at, but just hear it crack.

We get in.

One eye black patched, while the other burrows into us from the rear vision mirror. He wears a red bandana, like a comic book pirate. Windsor's face is set and earnest. It feels tense.

"Kayole, here," I say, and hand the driver a hand-written address.

He grunts, and we're underway.

"So, what's in Kayole?" Windsor asks at last.

I am silent for a moment. "It's a slum. It's pretty dangerous."

"Of course." He smiles.

We drive through the shabby streets for maybe an hour, the scenery getting ever drearier and sadder as we go.

We stop at a sort of roadblock, rocks and rubble and a rickety wire fence across the road. The driver reaches into a pocket in his door and pulls out a slightly curved, nine-inch knife and rests it on his lap. Winds his window down as a man saunters up to the van.

We're inside the Kayole 'compound', about half an hour after entering via the guarded perimeter of the slum and the worrying presence of a nine-inch blade glinting on our driver's lap.

"They're volunteers trying to stop criminals getting in. It's very dangerous." Her name is Patricia, a Kayole local I knew from a previous time. She's explaining why we were stopped, and why the driver thought it wise to get his knife out. "You don't know if the roadblocks are to stop criminals, or are set up by criminals. And a knife is better than a gun because, if it's criminals, they will hear a gun and come running. A knife gets you a few more minutes. Your driver knows Kayole."

We glance back. He sits in his car still, waiting for us, glaring with his one eye, and refusing to move.

Patricia is the manager of a childcare centre for kids who have lost or are losing their parents, to the many hazards of dire poverty. In 2010, HIV/AIDS is darkly prevalent, as are a host of other ailments. Drug and alcohol addiction is rife. Domestic violence is normal. Mothers who work the streets often just don't come home. Dads in search of work or better opportunities in rich countries leave before dawn and may never be seen or heard from again.

Parents absent without notice seems to be the most common reason kids here are orphaned.

Yet the kids all smiled and high-fived us.

This place, a small building in an always moving area of cars in tight spaces, and rangy, desperate people wandering the streets. Kids would be living on the streets if not for this place. Some kids have simply been locked out of home when they came home from school or back from playing.

Some come back to a silent, empty home - or one with a dead body in it - and can't get in. Some hadn't been home for months. Some kids do sleep in the streets, some here. Some live here but they can't stay all day and so they amble the laneways, hustling and growing up too quick.

Patricia takes us for a walk, along a red earth road, past rust-coloured buildings and cars. And people. Everything with the hue of dried blood.

And there it is. The focal point of Kayole. A brick-coloured dirt expanse, a just-about football pitch sized. Two goals at either end, wobbly poles lolling about in loose holes in the ground. Sad, limp nets, half on the ground, wrapped around these jerry-rigged goals.

"We call this Wembley," she announces as the wind picks up a little and raises a few wisps of dust, like fingers curling upwards, hands beckoning us.

Something about an empty football pitch; no matter how basic it is, it somehow radiates an energy, the sum total of the exertions and sweat, the dreams and failures, wins and losses that its white-line borders contain. I thought of Parkhead, a universe away.

I repeat the name. "Wembley." As the dry wind whispers like a forgotten crowd, lifting the very ground on which we stood, in a pink cloud, changing us and our world as we watched.

"The children will be here soon?" asks Windsor.

"Yes," says Patricia.

And, on cue, a grey more or less spherical thing thuds onto the ground not 2 metres from where we stand. It raises a small dust-puff as it bounces oddly. Rolls a little, leaving a grooved track across the field.

Dust in the nostrils. From just behind us, the patter of bare feet on raw earth, a soft drum roll, rustling clothes, movement and breathing.

Like a beast. No talking.

We turn to see maybe 20 kids, anywhere between 5 and 15. Mostly boys but a few hardy and serious looking girls too.

And it begins. The enduring dance of The Game. The ball, a knobbly sphere of plastic bags and rubber bands, keeping to its own counter-intuitive shapes across the ground and through the air.

And the kids. Bodies attuned and speaking to each other, voices captured in grunts, points to space, the half-said words, guiding and creating the game. Like a world. Souls moving and shifting, meeting and departing. Energies passing and attracting. The beyond-language universe of the game.

The slums, Nairobi, the very planet dissolves. There is nothing else. This is where they live. Their inchoate fears, their Biblical dramas banished to the edges of this place. Sent to nothingness beyond the wobbly, broken white lines on the ground, to the other side of the nets at either end.

This, a whole world. And we see them live it. See them held by it and nurtured as they cannot be out there. This is their parent. This is their family. Their community. Their heaven.

Palpable and clear as a light in the darkness.

Patricia stands between Windsor and me, watching the game. I look behind her to Windsor who, at that same moment, looks to me. And he winks. And I nod. This is It. Can only be felt.

Inexplicably, a flurry of note papers come fluttering across the field, flapping like dying birds in the breeze. From a distance it looks like snow, circling in this place where snow has surely never been. A few sheets of paper landed on the red ground and the game goes on around and over them, kids stepping on them, oblivious. One flutters up to our feet and on it is a perfect footprint, etched in red dust across the centre of the page.

It looks prehistoric. Like an archaeological relic, a sliver of ancient wall-art fallen down through the eons to this time, this place. Given modernity only by the thin blue lines running evenly across it.

I pick it up. And, careful not to fold it, I reach into my case, remove a clear plastic document sleeve and slide it in.

Afterwards, we sit with Patricia. We make a plan with her, after she had consulted with the local community. I don't think there will be any problems with getting the community's support. Balls and kit. Ten teams from the Kayole neighbourhood for a special league competition. Teams of boys. Teams of girls. Teams of boys and girls. No restrictions on gender mix. A clubhouse. An accountability board from local community members, including children. Transport to and from games. A training schedule for every team week-by-week.

And a pitch refurbishment. New goals. Prizes.

And, finally, after a while, in preparation for some as yet unknown World Cup, a Kayole team, primed and funded, ready to participate in The Better World Cup.

We devise an ethics system for the league, whereby games will be self-refereed.

Windsor, Patricia and I sit in the tiny room of her centre for kids. TV images twitch mutely in the corner. One or two kids wander in or out, occasionally asking Patricia for, or about, something.

One young boy asks who we are - to which Patricia replied, these men are helping us make a football competition.

The kid looks at us, and wanders off, saying nothing. Within minutes, we can hear some commotion from outside. Lots of kids talking. Voices. Excited or angry?

We stop talking. Wait. A minute maybe. Patricia goes outside and comes back in.

"All gone. No-one there," she reports.

We go back to our discussions. Which neighbourhoods the teams will come from. Logistics. And we make the plan. Kayole will be the pilot. From then, well, everywhere. The world.

The afternoon sun angles in through the single grimy window. This eternal continent closing down yet another day.

Tired of talking, the three of us go outside.

We stop in our tracks.

On the ground, spilling over onto the road and on to the other side, maybe 200 kids, sitting cross-legged. Not speaking. Looking at us. Waiting.

"Children are like water," whispers Windsor.

"And water always wins," I reply softly. We looked at each other and felt the glow of something great.

*   *   *

The driver sits forward and speeds up, foot on the pedal, surging in a snarl of dust and debris. Buildings and people blur past.

"Trouble," say the voice in front. "Police car. But maybe not police."

Behind us, a black Land Rover, white roof with the word 'Police' and police check designs across it. Hurtling after us, close behind. No siren.

We careen through the narrow streets, people scurrying out of the way. Two cars. The police car so close now we could have seen the faces inside if the windows weren't darkened.

"If it's police, and they want us, surely they will put on a siren," says Windsor, with convincing logic.

"Not police," says the driver. "Gangs!"

We brace ourselves as we bend around corners and charge through stop-worthy points of the road. We have to shout to be heard and to convey our growing panic.

"They see you!" The driver leans into another tight turn. "They think you rich charity or business. They want to shake you down."

"How many?!" Windsor's voice is urgent.

"Full car maybe. Four. Five men."

A chill shoots through me. "Is this something to do with the message at Parkhead, you think?"

Windsor looks wan. "Could be just dumb thugs. But, yes, I get a feeling too this is connected."

We have now left the slum area and the road widens. The police car surges level to us, and, with a tortured blast of an exhausted engine, wheezes past us. It slows down with a squeeze of brakes and edges us, forces us into the curb and we slow. Have to.

The driver gets his knife at the ready again, sliding it in a flap on the inside of his door. We hold our breaths.

Nothing.

More nothing.

Nairobi seems deserted around us, like we were in an airlock. The police car sits there with its tinted windows like dark glasses, staring at us.

I lean towards the driver. "What should we do?"

Windsor gets out of the car before I can finish.

Oh shit.

"No. No!" the driver exclaims, and the words fall from my lips too.

I have no idea what he is doing. But I can't leave him out there on his own.

So I get out too.

We both approach the police car. We stand at the rear door. So quiet now, like a Western movie, when everyone clears off as a gunfight brews.

Windsor bends down and affects a look in the police car.

The front door violently squawks open, revealing a flurry of limbs, not in police uniform, and an 8-ball head. A flash of gun metal and a click.

Before Windsor can stand upright, the man, a sharp-edged bean pole with yellow malarial eyes and fluid movements, has a pistol up under Windsor's chin.

I have to fight the urge to run. No. Fight doesn't capture the desperation of my struggle. Every sinew is pushing me to run.

Fucking run.

I don't know how I resist. I stand, and my body shakes like a leaf.

The 8-ball's diseased eyes bored into Windsor's, a tongue's flick away from his face.

"What you doing here?" he sneers at Windsor. Then those snake eyes shift to me.

I want to leave. We can't. "This is who we are looking for."

Two other thugs have emerged from the other side of the car and are walking around the front of the car to approach me.

"We'd like you to come with us," says yellow eyes.

"Who are you?" demands Windsor, his courage astonishing the breath out of me. His voice is sonorous and betrays no fear.

"We are those who stand in your way. You have made some very powerful enemies and they have told us. You know? It's just a job for us. You can be our guests."

"They don't want to hurt us, Asher," says Windsor, speaking clearly despite the gun jamming in his voice box. "They are just wanting to scare us, you see."

They're doing pretty well then. I stand in slack jawed horror as I look at Windsor with my eyes like dinner plates and shamefully say nothing.

A stall vendor, pushing a cart and oblivious to the situation, approaches the situation from an angle from which he can't see the gun, and is about to walk in front of the two men coming around to me.

At the point the man's trolley blocks the two men, I heard a harrowing yell, a bellow of pain.

The man with the gun falls to the ground, clutching the back of his leg as Windsor and the driver, holding his bloodied knife, scurry back to the taxi. I react with a mixture of adrenaline and panic, and we all fall into the car and take off in a rumble of changing gears and pieces of the road.

Inexplicably, Windsor holds up his phone and snaps a few pictures as we howls off and away. The streets of Nairobi close around this tiny crisis in this city of human extremes. Just another moment. The dust has settled before we turn the first corner.

*   *   *

"Are we ok?" I shout, probably more to myself than the others.

Windsor is next to me and the pirate driver's back is tensed and sweated as we tear through the streets, clearing a path with our obvious need for speed.

Despite our movement, everything seems slowed, every moment noticed. I'm sure the engine roars and the streets around us hum and scream, but I don't hear anything. My mind has shut down.

"Ok," confirms Windsor. "No damage." He indicates the one-eyed man spinning the wheel in front of us. "He saved our life and put his own at some risk."

"He knifed that guy!"

"He did. Don't know what we would have done otherwise."

Back at the hotel, the three of us sit with a bottle of scotch on a table and three glasses, working their way through its contents. We have arranged a change of clothes for the driver and dumped his bloodied kit. Windsor and I have also changed and gotten rid of our bloodied clothing.

We all three sit in hotel robes, like Lords of the Manor.

The scotch, however, belies our visual appearance, and is cheap and nasty. Perfect.

The driver, whose name he now tells us is Leonard, believes the men were gang members in the employ of either a local leader or a foreigner.

"I think I know who. You think they'll be back?" I ask Leonard.

"No, they will leave you alone. They have done their job. I, however, may be in danger. If they can trace me, say through my car registration plate, they may chase me and cause me trouble. They may find where I live. You did nothing. I used the knife. Those men don't like to let local people get away with that."

I blanche. "I'm sorry to have gotten you involved in this, I said. It's nothing to do with you. We can leave the country…"

He just looks down, like he is a little embarrassed that he has even mentioned it. He seems unwilling to talk about it anymore and ready to accept whatever fate has in store for him. The silence of us sitting and sipping our rotgut scotch provides a veil to pull down on that brief journey into the life and troubles of Leonard in Nairobi.

"We just need to find out who it is," says Leonard.

"This will help," says Windsor, holding up the photo he took of the registration plate of the fake police car.

"You can find details here," adds Leonard, offering an online group on his own phone which will trace plate number details in Nairobi. "It's a common problem. Costs a few hundred shillings."

A few hours and an emptied bottle of scotch later, we have details.

Leonard says he knows people who, with payment, can pay the guy a visit.

"Another gang?" I ask.

He nods.

"Bit like a turd in a washing machine, isn't it?"

"Nairobi," is Leonard's shrugging reply.

*　　*　　*

We fly out of Nairobi next day. As I look down upon the sprawling metropolis, I know that down there, the tough who mugged us and got knifed for the trouble has woken up to his car torched and wasted in the street, and to a picture stuck to his front door of one hooded thug, holding Leonard's still-bloody knife, standing in front of the thug's four year old son leaving school. The back of the picture reads, "No more and no-one gets hurt," and there's an envelope containing $US200 "for medical services."

And Leonard is there too, driving about in a new Land Cruiser we bought for him with a few phone calls, along with fresh registration, that morning. Red, to go with his bandana.

Flying over African clouds, Windsor and I spread ourselves out, laying notebooks across the tiny fold-out tables and sticking post-its on the seats in front of us, around the window, wherever we can find room.

The Better World Cup - the BWC - will become an alternative to the current FIFA/Big Corporation system. We will use it as a vehicle to manifest a wholly different view of what a truly global World Cup will look like.

The concept of the nation state, always a problematic and often dysfunctional addition to global order, is to be challenged as a basis for World Cup participation. We will encourage the participation of "non-state" teams, such as Chodak's Tibet.

Breakfast or lunch or something over the Mediterranean and we are swimming in notes, ideas, and charged with a frisson of energy derived from new things and disruptive action. We wallow in the beautiful exhaustion of creativity.

Of course, all this will be useless if we can't convince the Tunisians.

13
APRIL 2010

Gafsa, Tunisia

I don't take the snazzy threads this time. Not sure what I was thinking before. I guess I was playing a part and I was the intended audience. Belief is the most challenging sport of all.

The place seems a little changed. I can't quite understand how the destruction here perpetrated by the Tunisian government and its monied-up goons is not noticed out there in the big world.

While some parts of the city look more or less normal, and seem to function as you would expect, other areas were destroyed. The buildings razed and the streets rubble-strewn and empty. Whip cracks of sniper bullets or street skirmishes and an occasional explosion are like an abstract beat upon the air.

This northern part of the city is effectively closed off. This is Rebel Central. The authorities have managed to isolate this small section and to trap the rebel units here. Of course, supplies and people get in and out. But it is desperate and dangerous.

No place for a suit.

I manage to make it in on the morning checkpoint dash. Hugging walls and stumbling through broken homes and down dark alleys. Eyes and ears darting. Hoping every second we won't be spotted. The guns of the two rebels with me twitch in their arms and seem themselves to be searching for movement with their muzzles like dull, gaping eyes.

It is a different house. But the atmosphere is the same; exhausted and tense. Broken faces and sagging eyes look into flickering screens, wires like veins in a muscle, papers scattered on odd-angled desks; things thrown onto things, onto things and onto other things, building a mountainous vortex of victory and defeat, constantly fluid and swirling. Action and anxiety, everything always moving, shifting, evolving by the second.

Muhamad is different too. Still Muhamad, but a different person. Where is the other Muhamad, the banker, missing his sax? The twisted grin. Sad eyes. I think to ask, but decided I didn't want to know. Could guess.

I explain the folly of our shareholder campaign. I feel awkward and weak, like I am letting down the cause and failing these extraordinary people risking everything for their values, so that others too may know the same values.

This Muhamad has a bulky frame, bearded. Densely forested arms pushed through rolled up sleeves, legs like hams jammed into his cargoes. Buttons seem ready to fly off like bullets at any moment. I guess he hasn't undressed for days and as he moves, a musk of body odour, motor oil and cordite confirm it.

His face is all hair and grime. His eyes hide beneath a more or less permanent squint, but it is just possible to see, beneath folds of skin, wire brush hair and the marks of battle, pupils constantly darting without end. He looks through me, around me, at my feet and at the wall, face scrunched all the while. I don't believe our eyes ever meet.

He doesn't say much, asks a few bland questions in heavily accented, almost unintelligible English.

I am about to tell him about our new plan, The Better World Cup, and to report on our meeting with Chodak. But he starts talking, telling me Haykel Sassi will be here soon. I think that's what he says.

One or two hours. Bear Muhamad had left the room soon after we spoke and didn't return. I sit. I won't move until someone tells me to. A few people, men, women, come into the room, don't acknowledge me at all, and leave.

My back is starting to ache on the wooden chair, like those I hated at school. I need to pee. The blood is pooling in my ankles. I can't take sitting there a moment more, so I get up and peer outside the room. No one. All quiet. Computer screens still cast a morbid light laying lengthy shadows about the room. But it is eerily silent and still.

Shit.

I go on, peering around corners like I am a fugitive, not knowing who, if anyone is here. After a few empty rooms I hear voices. Go towards them.

Next room. The voices seem pretty happy, chatty, and laughing. I edge my head around, eyes straining. A whack on my shoulder stops my heart. I turn to see a face, smiling.

"Come. Come," it says as the same hand that whacked me pushes me inside.

Maybe ten people are inside. Food. Drink. Bear Muhamad sits in the corner talking with a woman so small it seems he can eat her. I notice he is wearing glasses. And he isn't squinting. He looks up at me, into my eyes now, nods, and looks away.

"Dinner," someone says. "Come. Come." And numerous hands make the same fluttering motion.

Haykel arrives around eleven that night. Or at least, so I am eventually told.

I am fast asleep by then, on the scarred, debris-littered floor sheeted by candlelight and phone screen glow, on a jacket pillow given to me by Bear Muhamad.

*   *   *

Breakfast is the inevitable hummus, bread, coffee, a few bitter, greenish tomatoes. And I am grateful for it.

Haykel emerges around the corner as I bathe in the aroma from the coffee bubbling away behind me.

"What happened to you?!" I exclaim.

He is on crutches and a bloodied bandage is wrapped around his waist and left upper thigh. "Smashed hip," he replies, grunting to sit down on the floor opposite me. "From a bomb. A piece of metal just pretty much mashed it up."

Despite his injury and the obvious pain and discomfort it caused, he looks elegant and composed. His fashionable jeans, the left leg mainly cut away, and a miraculously clean, white V-neck, some bling and sunnies on the top of his head belonged in the south of France, not here. I can imagine him wincing in front of a cracked and pitted war-time mirror, gelling his hair and setting his stud earring in place, spritzing himself with cologne. I wonder if it is an act of bland vanity or the efforts of a man who refuses to be anything but himself, perhaps the most human of obsessions.

Soft eyes and clean-shaven face, wafting of something manly and expensive, he accepts a coffee from someone and looks at me. For a while.

Eventually, he speaks. "How are you? What do you have to tell me?"

I tell him while his dark cow eyes stare and stare. I can't tell if he is angry, shocked, or just bored with my report.

"You know what? I'm not surprised," is all he eventually says.

I tell him about The Better World Cup idea.

He stares. Time passes. "Ok," he finally says. He says ok a few more times, like it is marking the motion of his thoughts progressing, cog wheels ratcheting. "I like this idea. I like it a lot."

I tell him, "This, and I know you know this, is not about football or even about sport. It's about human connection and the power of football. The miracle of connection."

We sit on that nice, rehearsed line for a minute or two. But I figure he wouldn't like the next thing I am about to tell him.

"I don't think we should, or even can, stop the Qatar bid."

Contrary to my prediction of his reaction, he looks at me, thinking, and just says, "Hmm." Then, after a few minutes of silence, he says, "This is actually really amazing. I need you to meet someone. She's here now."

He makes a call.

We wait a little.

"She will come."

We drink coffee while he tells me about his life as a professional footballer. "Too much money," he says. "It makes players too scared, worried that the rainbow will disappear, and too conservative. And too removed. Living in a bubble, like a god, being paid a fortune for, what, a game? Crazy." He laughs into his steaming brew. "Anyway, my career is over," he adds, indicating his blown-out hip. "A different life for me now."

Then she swishes through the door. One of the rebels hanging around sees her and grabbed a grubby cushion, the only one there. We didn't have one. But she. She.

I recognise her instantly. Those eyes. The cool gaze that can burn through metal. She hugs Haykel.

"This is Ebaa," he says.

"Yes, we've met," I reply. "Parkhead."

"I wondered where you got to," she says.

"Can you tell Ebaa what you have just told me, about The Better World Cup?" Haykel asks. He doesn't seem surprised by our exchange.

I go through it all again.

"What do you think?" asks Haykel, looking at Ebaa. "Is this a way we can use Flight?"

Ebaa doesn't reply. She only seems to talk when she has something to say. A fine trait that should be more widely practiced, including by me.

"Let me fill you in," says Haykel, back to me. "We too have become aware that it will be very difficult to block Qatar '22. It is already late April and we have made no headway on our campaign to ensure the big companies and FIFA and corrupt interests don't destroy the world's game any more than it already has been."

He pauses. Continues.

"You can have as much money as you want. But you need to work the channels of power. You need to know where the levers are, who are the gatekeepers. You can't get that kind of insight overnight. So, I see where you are coming from. The Qatar decision will go ahead in 2022. Unless the world ends before then, we won't be able to change it. We can't change the system that quickly unless the world gets turned upside down sometime in the next twelve years."

It's hard to express my relief at this admission. Our runs at money and power have exhausted Windsor and me. I can't do it anymore.

Nevertheless, I feel I have failed. I was given a task, I devised a strategy. And I didn't succeed.

Is it possible to feel relief and shame, on the same topic, simultaneously?

Haykel goes on. "So we need a Plan B. Which we have. And I think it fits with your Better World Cup idea."

While Haykel is talking, Ebaa is on her phone. When Haykel put his hand out she drops the phone in his hand.

"Your idea seems in line with Chodak's intentions," she says. "I expect you know he's been looking for a way to get the World Cup more into the hands of the people, real people. Seems you may be onto something." She looks at me. "I guess that's what they are paying you for. I was wondering…"

She holds my eyes with a smirk and a raffish air. It was an insult, but I don't feel hurt. It is an attack with a feather touch. It is, in fact, an invitation to laugh at myself.

I am drawn into her eyes, deep and dark. Black pupils and mascaraed outline, yet there is a freshness in the shadows of her face, an openness. I feel her humour, her spunk, her courage. Here is someone who looks the world in the eye and laughs at it, dancing away into the light to completely transform the moment and making the world forget it has ever been any different.

So different to Chodak, but the bond between these two is clearly powerful and I recognise it immediately. I can physically feel the presence of Chodak. It is as if they were a single energy. This is a power couple in every sense of the word.

"First, we change the leadership at FIFA," says Haykel.

He shows me Ebaa's phone where I see files of bank accounts. Transactions. Large sums. Names I don't know. Clicking through it all. Lots of data here. Evidence.

"I don't know what this is," I say.

"You don't need to," says Haykel.

"There's a lot you don't know," adds Ebaa. "Best you don't."

"The elites at FIFA have been playing some unfair games,"

continues Haykel. "Once we release this stuff to the media, their time left in power will be limited. Second, we tell Flight they can have their Qatar World Cup. But they must pay a price. To us. To the football family. Now, we own them. If they want Qatar '22, there must be a program for a new world order. And they must support it. Or we will fight until that vote in December and, in the next 12 years, make their World Cup a poisoned chalice. And, in time, we will take that World Cup away from them."

He grins.

"They can have Qatar '22, but they'll be wearing our handcuffs. And Ebaa. Well, let's say Ebaa has a few secrets about Flight and its big bosses."

Ebaa shoots me a kohl-eyed look and winked. Half smile. It is stunning.

"We. Own. Them." Haykel say the three words like each is banging in a nail. "But we don't want to destroy them. We want to use them. How can we do that?"

I give them the outline of an idea starting to form in my mind. We discuss it. Ebaa calls Chodak.

We are interrupted by a gun fight somewhere close. The typewriter-clacks of automatic weapons, the thump of running boots and shouts in Arabic filled the tight space with panic.

We can do nothing but wait and drink coffee while small arms fire scatters outside like pepper from a shaker.

After a couple of hours, despite the interjections of history, as the battle crackles, we have decided upon a plan and a way to best utilise Flight's reach and resources.

Now, I have to tell Gascoigne Rush how we own him.

But first, I have to be in Hamburg.

14
MAY 2010

Hamburg, Germany

The Knust bar is packed with a horde of heaving, sweating Germans. The piquant spices of beer and excited bodies hang in a series of invisible curtains in the toxic, smoke-filled air. Large Saxon bodies surge and subside in a random, off-beat response to the four-piece band churning out something manic and punk-like on the stage. Arms and legs, torsos and heads seem disjointed from each other on the dance floor. Seriously, Germans don't dance, they become missiles. The noise is deafening, the atmosphere rank and the mood intense. I love every bit of it.

All this because FC St. Pauli has been promoted.

The game against Rot-Weiss Oberhausen ended in a stunning 5-3 win for St Pauli and the Millerntor and much of its 19,000 inhabitants is rocking. All around, the working-class suburbs, populated by artists, migrants, refugees and lefties old and young, shakes with the celebration of a team on the way to Bundesliga 1. The old, terraced rows around the stadium must be shaking to their foundations.

Earlier that day I was at what had been an outstanding game. Clad in the brown colours of the team, the St Pauli faithful were like chocolate bars lined up around the stadium, belting out songs in support of human rights and against fascism. Anti-Nazi flags and symbols waved about from the stands, rainbow banners and peace signs. AC/DC's *Hell's Bells* rang in the start of the game. The skull and crossbones symbolism, central to FC St. Pauli's credo, is ubiquitous.

When they had cleared away after the game, with the *WooHoo!* From Blur's *Song 2* and the bouncing reaction of the crowd still echoing around the stadium, the seats in the stand were painted with huge love hearts. The seat I occupied, but barely sat in, had a pro-Palestine sticker on its back.

The St. Pauli faces are often hard and jaded, tough, grizzled occupants of a brutal city. But this is a focal point of what I knew as the Earthy Left. No elites and wafty intellectual bleeding hearts here. These were people who had been thrown all of life's barbed moments and explosive situations, and come out broken perhaps, tired, confused, but ultimately human. These folks back humanity, believe in the human journey. They eschew the instinctive reflex to manufacture divisions between them and their fellow travellers on this rough road and choose instead to build bridges between them.

But there are no bridges here at the Knust. This is the football family in full, exhilarating cry.

Hamburg is grimy and smelly, seemingly in a permanent funk of pollution, poverty, and low clouds. The swampy smells and the energies of the nearby docks reach into every corner and smear on every surface, a salty rankness held in the icy, still air.

My visit here was arranged by Haykel, who had played against the club here a few times in his Bayern days and had admired them for their politics.

He tells me how they took on the big old nasties like Dynamo Dresden and their new right, fascist fanbase and took no shit from them when they came to town and tried to kick a few lefty heads in.

Hamburg's large migrant and mainly African refugee community, victimised by Hamburg's monied elites and rightist burghers, became their cause and their crowd at the Millerntor on any given match day is like a United Nations of colours and languages.

"They put on community events," Haykel tells me, "Like free vocational training for refugee kids, days for the disabled, gay pride marches and anti-fascist rallies. This is a real club. This is where your Better World Cup can maybe find a home."

My contact is Gunther, a squat, paunchy man over 60 with a mop of blond hair, a gold earring, and piercing blue eyes. He seems to be surgically connected to his jeans and leather jacket, like he was born in them and they just grew as he did. When we meet at the entrance to the Millerntor, he wears a chocolate brown St Pauli shirt beneath the jacket and his bear head is enveloped in a cloud of warm breath and cold air.

There is still plenty of chill in the air and the grey Hamburg skies add to the sense of urban gloom. But, not between 3pm and 4.30pm here. Not today.

The match, the crowd, the sense of intimacy felt among thousands, the warm bodies like a giant hug in the cold air, holding off the steely sky, and an atmosphere of what Gunther very poignantly, and rightly, calls 'humanity.'

Indeed, this is humanity. That collective embrace of those in a moment shared. This is what sport does. This is what football is best at.

Here we all are, struggling with the obstacles and barriers of life, searching for its rewards and for rest, and yet, inexplicably, we avoid sharing the load. We compete and hide, lie and cheat, racing to a destination we can't see, following a map that doesn't exist. All alone.

Clearly, we need each other more on this odd journey than we are led to believe. But it's not the talking, the words. It's simply the presence of others. Energies, shapes, sounds, smells. If a football crowd does nothing else, it teaches us that humanity is more than the sum of its parts.

When did we forget that?

Gunther had been told by Haykel about the Better World Cup. He is one of the supporter group leaders and, if his group agrees, it is likely the club would support the initiative.

"This club," he tells me, looking around the stadium full of faces before the game, "is like a universe. We have had the chance here to make our version of life, in a microcosm. A few thousand people - well, tens of thousands - all agreeing on a very basic principle: that we are all in this together and we should help each other where and when we can. This is a sanctuary for our ideals, our beliefs. You know we got rid of Maxim magazine - you know Maxim, all titties and pouting and adolescent fantasies...for men! Ha! Men! Anyway, the fans here banned their ads from here because...you know what, we have more women fans than probably any other German club. They didn't like Maxim. So we all got rid of them. We take an economic hit. But values are more important."

He smiles. It looks good on him.

"We have our Leitlinien - our Basic Principles - and that's that! We were the first club to do that, to make supporters' principles like this. And we stick to them. It's not complicated, is it?" He turns to me, and I feel the intensity of his question.

I agree that it is not. And the hoarse voices and thumping vibe in the Southern Stand at the Millerntor seem to confirm it.

Gunther goes on.

"You see, the really strange thing is though, we need an excuse to do it. Like a football club. Now, this is wonderful and a great way to connect people, of course. And a lot of fun. If we are winning - wink, drag on his smoke - but why don't we just do it anyway, you know, choose morals over economics, without a football club?"

I wait for him to answer his own question. It drifts into an ellipsis floating over the Milerntor, on the spiky drum beat of Acka Dacka.

"Maybe it's because we are ashamed that we need each other. Maybe we can't admit it. Why is that? Do we think this is weak? Silly? Why?!"

Again, intensity, cigarette. I have nothing. I wasn't expecting a philosophy examination here on the terraces of a rebel football club.

He says, "I used to beat people up for a living. I used to attack people in the street and steal from them. Sometimes I would just fight people for the hell of it. Hamburg is a very, very rough place you know. But, hey, we discovered The Beatles..." Crowd noises rise and Gunther pulled more on the inevitable fag. "*Love Love Me Do* in the Indra, or the Kaiserkeller, or the Top 10, or the Star Club is not a million miles from the Hymne de St Pauli here. We are very creative people."

With a grimace, he goes on.

"Fascists, right wing fuckers, are not creative. It is easy to lie and deny others. Any arsehole can win. Any liar and conman can win in this system. Where's the challenge there? Where's the journey? They make out like they are all powerful, but they can't even face themselves. How scared can you be!? But how do you win and remain human? Ah, that needs creative thinking!"

Later that night at the Kunst, the beer flows, and those bucket-sized jugs the Germans scull like they're nip glasses are scattered everywhere. African and Middle Eastern faces - mostly recently arrived asylum seekers and refugees, I am told - mingle with Aryan-looking Germans.

"You see?!" says Gunther as we huddle for a moment in a corner, away from the mini-UN heaving and spinning before us. "You see this, yes?! Fascists don't get this! Racists don't get this! Homophobes don't get this! You see this!? They miss out! They never know this beautiful feeling! Of connection!"

His eyes widen with the last word.

"It's a better world," I agree, unaware I am brand-referencing our initiative.

"And we need a better world cup!" he shouts, and with this, he raises his half full stein and pours it down his throat.

Days later, back at home, I hear from Gunther that St Pauli is in. Our first professional club supporter. They will back the Better World Cup. They will publicise it among their networks. They will promote it at home games. They will open their stadium and training grounds up for matches.

Within weeks and after calls or visits from either Chodak, Windsor, and me, we have similar confirmations from others around the world, each with their Gunther's, each with their living bridges and human ideals.

Celtic, of course, is in

AC Omonia is in.

Standard Liege is in.

Hapoel Tel Aviv is in.

AS Livorno is in.

AEK Athens is in.

Boca is in.

Sleman is in.

Rayo Vallecano is in.

CE Jupiter is in.

Marseille is in.

Baha is in.

Besiktas is in.

Ternana is in.

SV Babelsberg is in.

Partizan Minsk is in.

And so, the Association of Progressive Professional Football Clubs, Apropro FC, is born.

The Better World Cup has truly kicked off.

Having set the BWC into seemingly unstoppable motion, it is now time for Flight and Rush.

They aren't ready. But we are.

15
MAY, JUNE, JULY 2010

Everywhere

From Kayole, it happens quickly.

Tendrils grow, cultivated like a living thing by our work, our passion, and, yes, our love for those we worked for.

We map a global plan, and we become world travellers again. But, this time, we are visiting slums and villages, meeting with ordinary people, living ordinary lives in the extraordinary ways we all take for granted. We shake gnarled and dirty hands. We hug bodies broken by pestilence and poverty, disregarded by the world, yet able still to feel the warmth of a fellow human, the universe between us becoming a mere physical distance, a gap in space that can be broached by a simple act, a touch, an eye smile, a hug.

We see lights shine through the eyes after a lifetime of knockbacks and defeats. We see life emerge like the sun from around a person, like a halo of energy that can be felt and, if you look deeply enough, can be seen in the body language, hear in their words.

"These are our people," says Windsor.

"More importantly, we are theirs," I say.

Windsor is the Arch Hugger. He embraces everyone he can. His big body like a home many don't have. He sows his love of humanity in fields both fallow and abundant.

And the game is always the focal point.

Post-earthquake Islamabad and a drought ravaged village in Tanzania where sad, drooping, very dead maize ringed the dusty pitch. We set up a tournament among Tamil, Muslim and Christian Sri Lankans still feeling the effects of a devastating civil war, which only officially ended a year ago.

We bring together ancient tribes and illegal foresters deep in the Amazon. Bring a children's league to a shapeless shanty town no more than a ball's punt from the brilliant, shiny faces of Silicon Valley. We bring games to countless refugee camps.

And I go back to those migrant workers in Dubai. We build a field for them, provide equipment. I play centre back in a friendly between them and the local customs officials and, as we always do, we put on some food and drinks, invite some musicians, and talk and laugh and lament our poor performances on the pitch well into the hot desert night.

In every place, the game becomes the connection between hitherto disparate groups, effortlessly breaking down barriers. It gives us all permission to overcome the differences between us, to traverse the often artificial islands which were built on the shifting tectonics that vested interests maintained to ensure the system that served them continued.

For Windsor and me, this is a period laced together with extraordinary moments that would have overwhelmed us had we had the luxury of forewarning. That we don't know what to expect is both our curse and our good fortune. As we are making it all up on the run, we get a lot wrong and are faced with innumerable unplanned delays, problems, occasional rip-offs and lies and a general melange of day-to-day chaos that constantly threatens to topple our plans into the dust.

But the high points are many, more than enough to compensate. They are more often small events and almost unnoticeable ticks in the universe's unending respiration, like catches in the throat, where humanity is felt in between the reflexes of existence, in an airlock between the life and slow death of our most conflicted and dishonest of species.

In Phnom Penh, Cambodia, we go to a charity school where children who had been rescued from the nearby municipal rubbish dump are able to get an education and a daily meal. These kids, in their neat, clean white shirts and blue shorts or skirts, had been scavenging for things to sell and scraps of food before they were offered a place at school. In fact, many still live in lean-tos and plastic bag huts in the tip itself.

We are told there are 20,000 people living on the tip site proper. Some of the kids, we hear, have been lost in giant sinkholes of rubbish that simply open up and swallow them, never to be seen again. The stink of the place, the stench of modern civilization, is overwhelming and stays on my skin for days after.

They want to be doctors, computer engineers, teachers, footballers, firemen and astronauts. Much like kids anywhere else. And here they at least have a glimmer of a chance, faint and flickering in the putrid air though it is.

We deliver balls, kit for girls and boys, build a school football pitch, fund a league among the communities on and around the tip, keeping the model we are now perfecting. Local media are invited and a TV crew of well-dressed, professional-looking Cambodians turn up - the men shiny faced and sweating in their sharp clothes, the women looking graceful and cool despite their form-hugging clothing and the baking weather.

The media are lugging flash looking cameras and the kids crowd around, getting into a game, kicking and running, smiling, laughing, and fizzing with excitement. Previously unimaginable for these kids.

A camera is hoisted on a cameraman's shoulder and pans the throng. A sea of faces. He hunches. The young woman presenter with her mic gripped like a baton in a relay race pushes him onwards, through the kids. And one girl, maybe twelve, holding one of the balls we've given out, sort of emerges, needing to be looking, not doing anything special, not looking any different, just standing, football on her hip like it's her child.

The cameraman, directed by the presenter, heads towards her. The woman asks her something, thrusts the mic at her.

The girl's face breaks open, flushes red and she breaks down with the shock and the utter oddness of the moment - if you'd told her this morning that today, at lunchtime, an international TV camera... The camera lens lingers, like a square eye.

The other kids sort of stop, sensing the moment. The universe stops turning. An arc between the extremes of human existence, happening now, to this unknown little girl, a distance that few humans can even comprehend. A journey in a lifetime, between universes of crazy privilege and the direst poverty, is tracked in a moment. And I feel, then, like life is too much. How do you rationalise this? I begin to cry too.

She has been picked out. This child who has never had anything, has never been picked out or selected for anything good, who is always marginal and unseen, was destined to live and die unknown and unheralded, in a wasteland patch of unlit ground on the human map, is found, is noticed, is celebrated. She becomes special. Is seen.

She hugs that ball to her like she would burst it.

The moment moves on and she is surrounded by her friends and other kids.

I look to Windsor and see him rubbing his eyes with his thumb and forefinger beneath his glasses. I put my hand on his shoulder and he covers it with his.

That moment comes to symbolise everything we do and, the fact that Windsor and I share it and understand it becomes one of our strongest bonds.

On the Kenya-Somalia border, famine-withered cattle herders, nomads and tribespeople have gathered for food aid. We accompany the World Food Program people there and as we help them unload rice and other stuff, even before we give anything out, Windsor had picked up a broken and dented plastic bottle nestled in the brick-red dust. Unlike Windsor, not a playful or agile man, he starts trying to play keepy-uppy with it. Horribly unsuccessful.

But, spurred to life, the kids emerge from the torpor of desperation and their parents' depression, and join in. Within minutes a game is underway. With a plastic bottle. Skinny kids are laughing. The etched and broken faces of parents, eyes hooded and dust-crusted, are smiling at their kids laughing. Windsor is making a complete dick of himself and loving it. I join in too. A few WFP people jump in. Our unmarked pitch in the dirt, clouds of fine dust marking where the action is, ringed by thorny bushes blooming with snagged plastic bags, and a couple of tired and dignified Maibous looking on like wizened talent scouts.

The unceasing dry wind coils about us, touching us all.

It is like this. Stories on stories. Moments on moments. Lives shared. Experiences exchanged. A bubbling stream of action and movement that nourished and served those whose often barren lives it splashes upon.

And it brings us to life and nourishes our vision.

And football. Football. This lingua franca on legs, an Esperanto of movement, held every interaction, creates so many frozen memories, and builds networks that were felt in subterranean ways, beneath the skin. In the bones. In the organs. In our very heartbeats.

A bouncing ball that touches us all and is promoted onwards, bouncing further and touching more, gently toppling barriers as it rolls and skits across surfaces, across borders and across lives. Always connecting. Always moving.

We recruit locals. We pick from the community directly, not from the ranks of its leadership or its elites, but from among its grassroots, its doers. Windsor and I interview personally or at least online all of the people we employ to represent us in each location.

Apart from being required to follow the models we are hastily building, we ask nothing of recipients. This is a gift, and we carry no patronising, corrupting obligations as to how they can earn these and more. We give without condition. They only had to play.

We are aware that many charities cannot act so directly. Bound by governance rules and laws, they have to account for everything, count every cent, file every receipt, vet every contact, cost every action. We are private and we have no such restrictions. Our rules are that we will treat everyone with dignity and equality.

A conman can look the same as an honest man on death's doorstep. We make no attempt to discriminate between them, believing that the governance process of aid is often an indignity to those in real need, and an unnecessary burden to put onto people when all they want is to be treated like a human being.

We do this knowing that some of our donations will be lost, on-sold, destroyed, stolen, misused. The human universe is complex and fractured at every level and any attempt to ensure the minority of cadgers are denied at the expense of the genuine majority is not only unfair, it is unsustainable. Gaps in the process are a cost of human transaction; undeniable and unstoppable.

We serve and deliver to communities in sixteen countries across five continents in three exhausting, empowering and impossibly crowded months.

I take control of the message, the narrative, making sure that everyone that can know about this knows about it. I write OpEds, often by-lined by participants in the program. I launch media releases, speak at events, meet with everyone from local community leaders to Nobel Prize winners.

It isn't about publicity for publicity's sake. We are carrying a very real and purposeful message: this is the future. We can all be part of this. This is ours.

Of course, governments don't want to know. Corporations, once they understand they have no ownership here, that their money gains them nothing tangible, withdraw their initial interest.

But we don't need the permission of governments, nor the money of big businesses. We never did. We never have.

Mainstream media, when it can break down its sorry prejudices for stories outside the narrow network news boxes and for the narratives of actual people, soon understands the power of what we are doing. The power of our voice, our momentum, cuts through. The beauty of personal stories, captured against the backdrop of a game that everyone knows, most of us have played, and many truly love, wins.

This is a power that doesn't conform to the word. It is power, but it isn't. It is a force. An entity. A being. A Thing. It is the vast sum of us. There's only so long that can be ignored and held at bay.

We have built a movement and now we cannot stop it. And our movement had a name - The Better World Cup - and a logo - a red footprint created that first day in Kayole - and the magic, transformative energy of money allows us to give it breath, to exercise its muscles, to let it live. In this world of money. This is what having lots of it allows you to do. We build towers of hope on the money that the bastard dictators and crooks in Tunisia had stolen from their people, had ripped from the soul of humanity itself.

Mini-leagues, free for all, administered by us but owned by the communities. From one end of the world to the other. Like a field between two nets.

This is alive.

We feel invincible.

*   *   *

But a sprawling, multi-armed and irresistible force is not what we need. Sure, the very energy of it and the power we have unleashed are potent forces and strong allies in our campaign to democratise the world game - and, by association, the world itself. But it needs a shape, or it might consume the very reason it existed.

Windsor, Chodak, Haykel, Ebaa, Cal – yes, Cal is in on this too - and I pull a plan together over a series of phone, Skype, email, and personal hook-ups. A series of inhuman hours and odd locations finds us at various stages of our inner human cycles, and we never really manage to connect when everyone is in the zone. The cogs of life, with their sharp moving teeth, rarely mesh. Someone is always exhausted, ill, anxious, grumpy or somehow disengaged from the rest of the species and there is always the dark pall of someone's misanthropic mood to deal with in every session.

Knowing we have a very tight deadline and knowing too that opportunities would arise for us in South Africa and the looming World Cup there starting within weeks, we work hard and push on through the sludge of our discombobulated shifts.

Ideas flow fast and easy and it's hard to say who has the copyright on any one concept or detail. But the core foundation is secured early and we all shared a sense that the world game needs to be taken out of the hands of the suits, petty overseers of the game in various far-flung corners, and the corporate fat cats, and given back, allowed back to the people that make the game.

The World Cup had become a political and monied feast for an elite few - elite in position, not in moral standing - and the game is being mugged into submission, while those that play it and watch it, despite sneaking feelings of something not being quite right, look on and keep turning up.

A Better World Cup. What does that mean?

We devise two phases.

The first will be to introduce acknowledgements of ethnicity or sub-state identity within national team kits. This will require a change in FIFA regulations around players' uniforms, which are very strict and designed to keep any political statements - unless FIFA endorses them - out of games.

It is impossible that FIFA will change the rules for the upcoming World Cup in South Africa. However, we hope that we might be able to engage FIFA and Flight to work with us on this. Hope without much confidence. Brazil in 2014 and Russia in 2018 are likewise highly unlikely, given the many oppressed nations in those vast lands, and the elites that rule them.

Even so, there are ways around this. Chodak notes that players can choose to wear various personalised additions to their national team kit. Coloured laces on their boots, for instance, certain hair styles, or bandages around knees or wrists, which may even have written messages on them. Will have to be careful, lowkey, but it can be done.

This can be done in South Africa and can be subtle enough for team managers and FIFA to be unaware. But *we* will know. More importantly, their supporters will know.

Such notifications can be significant and compelling and will likely register before anyone had cottoned on to what is actually happening.

We all agree to make contact with various players and their agents. Chodak and Haykel have many contacts here and start putting out the word. We - they - need to select their targets carefully as the wrong character could potentially inform on our plan and blow the whole campaign.

Chodak and Haykel both noted that political statements had been made plenty of times before, via kit additions or alterations, personal signifiers or, most openly, via undershirts beneath the playing kit carrying a message, flipped up on scoring a goal for instance. The method is nothing new. We are just applying it more directly and on a larger scale.

This messaging will have little point or impact if it isn't used to introduce something far more revolutionary. We figure players will be less willing to take a risk unless they feel this is going somewhere. That is Phase 2. The campaign for a Better World Cup; the global FA Cup-style tournament.

I have worked hard on a plan and when I have to present it, I feel light-headed and unready. I am sitting and need to walk, so I start pacing, notes in hand, up and down, up and down, while the others wait online to hear from me. I don't know if I am more scared of doing this, or of the whole plan being shot down, of ultimate success or failure. Both possibilities seem utterly overwhelming.

16
JUNE 2010

Cairo

Gascoigne Rush is shorter than I had thought. Power and profile tend to fill out and elongate a man, but it's generally just the illusion of celebrity. Reddish hair thinning on his head and coiled coppery fuse wires on his arms and in his ears. The patina of an orange complexion, pale and diffuse, consuming light on contact with the skin.

He walks like an important man, tipping forward to build speed into the journey, looking to gain value from every step. Head and shoulders leaning into an imaginary headwind, he seems bulky yet swift. A bull in search of a gate.

I am there early and see him charging through scattered people and obstacles like a pinball.

I have called the meeting in the Egyptian Museum. I already don't recall why. It seems odd and a little dramatic. Like a movie or a thriller novel, and as I am doing it, it felt like I am somehow being watched, or written about. Maybe it has something to do with the fact that it is constantly busy and moving and somehow, I find comfort in that. Whoever calls the meeting always gets home ground advantage, and this is the best I can think of.

I guess it also seems historic – incredibly, and obviously so –

and perhaps a fitting backdrop for a conversation that may well change the world's favourite game. And it is very public. Maybe I am uncomfortable with this most public issue being pored over and decided upon in some air-conditioned sanctuary high above the throng, all shiny and inhuman and, for Rush, completely secure.

For whatever reason, I stand and watch one of the most powerful men in world sport careening through school kids and tourists, searching for the Amenhotep II statue, a keenly sporty Pharoah (how often have those phrases been put together?) and a nice touch I've thought of for our meeting point.

There is nowhere to sit, another strategic element I have introduced, to make Rush feel out of his zone. The meeting will be standing up.

I am leaning on a railing on an upper-level floor, people shuffling by at close quarters and piling about down below. I hoped Rush would feel uncomfortable here, as I certainly am. But at least I knew what the meeting is about.

He approaches the exhibit, stands there. I stare until he sees me. I put up my palm, nod. He approaches.

"Interesting location," he says, after the introductions.

I say nothing and try hard to focus and to click in on the topic and the manner in which I have rehearsed its delivery.

We are both leaning on a railing. I figure, hope, that Rush is confused that we are not sitting, but he says nothing.

"So," I say, drawing a line under the preliminaries and moving into the substance.

I give him a quick run-down of who I am, and how I came to be involved.

"I know all of this," says Rush.

"I thought you might. Did you send us a few signs that you knew:

Parkhead? Nairobi? Your doing?"

"I can neither confirm nor deny," he replies, as he winks.

So, another line, next phase.

"First thing is, we've saved your ass."

He raises his eyebrows. "How so?"

"I'll come back to that. You seem to know all, Mr Rush. So, I assume you've heard of the Better World Cup?"

He pauses for a long moment. "Yes, I understand it is part of the landscape now."

Evasive. Generic. Meaningless.

I guess that he knows nothing about why we were in Nairobi, even if he knew we were there, and I figure I can use the unknown as leverage.

I reply to his dodge by offhandedly suggesting that perhaps he can let me know what he knows then, so we don't waste time. I look away, into the massing throng, then, pointedly, back at him. Pressure. Just as I rehearsed it.

He looks straight back at me. Staring. The crowds around us seems to drop to a dull hum. Background.

"Why don't you put in into your words, Mr Fox, so I can best understand where you are coming from?"

Fox 1, Rush 0.

I tell him about The Better World Cup.

"That's why we were in Nairobi, in case you didn't know. Your thugs certainly didn't know much."

He scoffs. "They didn't hurt you."

"Well, I hope you bought your mate there a new car."

He scowls. Moves on. "What is The Better World Cup to do with me?" he asks.

"Before we get there, let me give you some more news. About

saving your ass. You can have Qatar '22. We will withdraw from trying to block it. No obstacles. Work your corporate bullshit and have it."

His face, eyes, shoots back with an audible grunt. I feel the breeze from his sharply swivelling head. His hair springs with the effort.

He gathers himself, feels he'd given too much away.

"Oh? Giving up?"

"Oh no. Definitely not. We need something from you."

With a snort, he says, "How much?"

I have to laugh.

"Money is not it. We need your infrastructure Mr Rush. That's something we don't have and something we don't think we can build. We are, how can I put it, inhabiting you. We are impregnating Flight."

"You're trying to fuck us? How? What do you mean?"

I smile. "You can have the World Cup as long as it becomes a vehicle to introduce a *better* World Cup. We are now directing you, Mr Rush. In not much time, the people will run the world game. You may have the World Cup, but we will have the world game. Do you understand? You've got the attention-getting ring on a finger, shiny and impressive. But we are the hand."

He is still looking into me, face unmoving.

"First, from the next World Cup after this one, 2014 in Brazil, you, Flight, will begin supporting non-state football-playing nations. You will provide kits and other support for teams from ethnic groups which are not state based. Second, you will support players who have Indigenous or ethnic, roots to non-state nations or communities. Third, in your Qatar World Cup you will encourage all players to express their ethnicity as they play, via the introduction of new team uniform rules which allow for different socks to be worn by players to reflect their ethnic identity and for badges to be worn on their shorts to the same end."

I am paraphrasing from a statement we require Flight to sign, nestled in a folder which I now hand to Rush.

"It's all here," I say as I hand it to him. "Flight will be used to dismantle the politicised, corporatized, nationalised, *bastardised* world game, and to set a new culture for a better World Cup. You will do this quietly, while we build the alternative. And, Mr Rush, you have no choice."

"Oh really? Says who?"

"Says about 3 billion people," I reply, sweeping my hand across the planes of people, surging and bubbling like water around the museum's many obstacles.

He looks away, looks about, then stares back at me.

"I don't get it. Who the fuck do you think you are? Why do I need to listen to you? Let me remind you, Mr Fox, you are representing, if I am correct, a few largely unknown rebels in a flyblown dust bowl in northern Africa. What makes you think you have the means to make demands of me and of Flight?"

He seem calm, but I can tell he is brewing beneath the surface.

"The World Cup is already ours," he adds. "Qatar is already signed, sealed and about to be delivered. I'll give you 30 seconds to stop me just walking away and ignoring the fuck out of you and your grubby, delusional eyes."

I've never liked threats. Like war, it strikes me that victory from such a tactic is Pyrrhic. I know we had some heavy artillery with Ebaa's dirt files, but I want to give him the chance to agree without resorting to it. I hold the threats in my pocket.

"I'm not playing any games, mate," I say. "I will just say, we have here an opportunity to revert the world game to its fundamentals.

The game has been run by elites like you for too long. This is just the beginning to bring our game back to where it belongs. And, as I say at the start, we're doing you a favour. You guys are dying. You can't keep up the market growth, the sales, the brand pressures. It's all coming to an end. Brandism is over. And you know it. This way you get to help us reinvent the future."

I pause for effect before continuing.

"You know, the world can be usefully devolved to 22 people on a rectangle of grass."

He says nothing.

"Every game is just a story," I continue. "It's like watching a movie. And everyone loves a good story. Football, the game, stopped being a story when it became a business. You are like a luxury liner on the ocean. You have everything you need on board and it's all beautiful and shiny and fun and gorgeous. You, floating around out there, you need the ocean. But the ocean doesn't need you. We're giving you the chance to be part of the ocean. Walk away if you want."

"What's your price, Fox?" he asks, his face twisting into a sneer.

I can't say I'm not tempted. I can see that walking away from all this with my pockets filled is not without an upside, and that betraying everyone is not just another tragedy in a universe full of them. What *is* the point in all this? Who *really* cares?

In that point in time, while Rush's eyes bear into mine, the crowds around us are hushed and stilled. It seems the planet is awaiting my reply. I know I am.

"We're not going to do any of this," says Rush, emphatically.

Then he walks away.

I still don't know what I was going to say.

17
JUNE 2010

Gulu, Uganda

Wide streets paved with caked red dirt. Shanty style stores along the sides and an awesome blue and white cotton sky canopied over. Wheel ruts and footprints, undisturbed in the still humid air, the only evidence of human presence. Normally this avenue would be crowded with the African commerce and community surging, shuffling, living, car fumes, and moving bodies. Normally.

Today. No-one. Silence. Almost. In the distance, you can hear it. Like breathing or moaning in sleep. Rising, falling. Silence again. A weak breeze emphasises the quiet. The sound of its ghostly feet on the road.

The late afternoon light is moving quickly. The sky closes in, like a switch has been hit to bring in the curtains. Blue sky becomes a grey dome within minutes and rain scents the rising wind.

We can see them now. A huddle of tightly packed dark bodies reaching across the wide street like a nest of ants, bubbling with movement. A hum of voices punctuated by a roar and a falling away, disappointment quickly replacing joy.

The World Cup has started.

I look up and take in the steely clouds making fists above me. I imagine that I can see a silver thread wrapped around everyone here and disappearing into the TV then upwards to touch the plump sky and then off into the now rumbling distance, wrapping gently around Tamils and Gubi Gubi, Ainu and Sami, Chams and Ogoni, Sahrawi and Mapuche.

Across the plains, the mountains, the waterways, and on and on before plunging downwards into Ellis Park, Johannesburg, circling the stadium and touching everyone in it, swirling amid the blue and white shirts, the green shirts, the sweating faces, the laughter, the anguish. Twining around the strangled notes of the vuvuzelas, and ending on the finger-tips of the yellow-clad Vincent Enyeama as he threw himself like a diving canary to the right to clutch at Lionel Messi's left foot curler to divert it from the top corner.

Back in Gulu, a roar, applause, laughter. A few local hacks mimic the outstretched arm. Africa's World Cup had arrived and it has shut down a continent. This, the first game featuring an African team, clears streets across the fifty-something countries and transfixes its roughly one billion people and closes the massive universe in around every single one.

The Nigeria vs Argentina group game on the second day of the 2010 World Cup is a moment in history, and Gulu, a small TV and a rabble of rapturous Ugandans is as good a lens to view it through as any.

Windsor and I have been here for a few days, as Windsor is setting up a team for the ethnic Acholi people – his people. Already their chocolate brown, jade, and sky-blue colours can be seen dotted among this crowd, a testament to Windsor's marketing skills and reach in his hometown.

While this moment in and of itself is beautiful and memorable, redolent of the connectivity and power of the game and its mostprized product, I know it sits atop a steaming pile of lies and corruption.

Haykel and the Tunisians have tracked the path to Africa's most significant sporting victory. From the heartbreak of being promised the 2006 Mundial, and then having it pulled away from them by the snaky, kill-or-be-killed tactics of the Germans, the South Africans have also become lost in the dark arts of the FIFA voting system. Then they worked out how to play the system and assess the value of pure numbers - both in voting terms and in dollar terms, with help from the same Germans who snatched 2006 from them - to now and the Great Celebration that had descended on the southern tip of the continent.

The Tunisians well know the weight of disappointment. They were bidders for the 2006 World Cup but were obliged, to put it gently, to drop out early on.

South Africa's stadium building program is a racket, rife with collusion and graft amid the big construction companies and officials. The winning pitch to save on costs by refurbishing existing facilities is thrown somewhere into the Cape's bubbling waters and replaced with a manic construction frenzy. It throws up massive white elephant structures which would host just a few games and then be consigned to dusty irrelevance. But not before lining the pockets of the few.

Local communities are pushed to the margins as the bulldozers rumble in. Much-needed local services are pushed down the list of doables in the name of the short-term blood lust that the World Cup had become.

FIFA's president, Horst Leverbruck, oversees it all with the kind of winning stupidity that marks his tenure. The suits at the big corporates, FIFA, and others gather like witches around the boiling pot and concoct one of the great thefts of public assets in sporting history.

In a Skype call with Haykel and Chodak, Windsor and I listen to the stories already known, even before the event has started.

Chodak mentions a former teammate of his, a South African squad member, who spoke of a series of friendly games played by Bafana Bafana as warm-ups for the tournament.

"He is sure," says Chodak, "He says that he would swear on a Bible that the games were fixed. He says the officials in these games make crazy decisions and make Bafana Bafana look good. He says something about it to the team officials and they tell him, don't you mention this. Ever. He says, 'why?' They tell him, you want play in World Cup? You don't mention it."

Chodak shakes his head. Grim.

"He tells me he is claiming an injury and will not play in the World Cup. He cannot. He is religious. He is very upset, very depressed. It was to be the best moment in his career. But, he says, other players know and the World Cup too big for them to refuse."

Over the following weeks, we watch games on TVs in a variety of odd locations. All have the same energy of joy and expectation, connection and celebration. And tiny, abused TV sets bleating in a babel of languages, while the singular language of football plays out with commentary we often can't understand, the game immediately recognisable and articulate, using its own universal vocabulary and expressions.

We have calls from Chodak, saying, "watch the French team, watch the Nigerian team." He says they are trying to adopt an ethnic nationalities code. They have put our idea to their team management: something on the kit to identify who they are, where they are from.

And so we watch. And France and Nigeria implode. "Player unrest" is the reason given for both teams simply falling apart. But we know. And Chodak knows. We understand that the governments and the football associations that sucked up to them, or vice-versa, have asserted their power. We know that Flight, kit sponsors and funders for both teams, have not taken our cue, and have not backed the campaign. Yet.

But Qatar is still twelve years away.

Chodak tells us that France's Anelka, himself French born of Martinican parents, "is pushing on ethnic representation for those such as himself. He is trying."

But he becomes painted as a traitor. There are others. Evra from Senegalese heritage, Abidal also from Martinique. Ribery is pure revolutionary. All became involved.

Both well-fancied teams fall out at the group stage and go home to an ignominious fate. The Nigerian President bans the team from playing for two years. Anelka never plays for France again. The dissenting French players are accused of seeking out child prostitutes.

But something has started. We hoped that come 2014 and 2018, more progress will be made, leading into 'our' World Cup. The Better World Cup in 2022.

I catch up with Chodak on the Burma-Thailand border, after days of driving through the jungle and hiking for hours to arrive at a camp inhabited by Karen refugees from Burma. Chodak is there in his role as the Better World Cup's unofficial ambassador - a function he fulfils tirelessly, as his appearance at this location testifies.

I emerge through the sweat-dripping jungle onto a packed earth field to watch young men and a few young women rushing about with inexplicable energy, chasing an abused, earth-coloured ball between two unnetted, wood-pole goals at either end. Later that night, I stand with Chodak and members of the community huddled around a scratchy TV set, all static and jagged lines, with lights strung across the black sky in a drooping matrix above us, each humming with a halo of insects. Paraguay draws 0-0 with New Zealand, and while the game fails to reach any heights, all are left buzzing at least as much as the balls of jungle life thriving in the orbs of light above.

We sit by a stream the next morning, after a sleepless night in the deathly quiet insect-filled night. Water the colour of ginger beer cascades and bubbles in a froth before tumbling onwards. Submerged rocks like reptile backs push through the water's surface.

Chodak tells me there will be a team from here for the Better World Cup qualifiers.

He holds up the ball from yesterday's game. "I brought them some balls and stuff," he says. "So, they gave me this. They reckon they've had it maybe a year. Look at it!"

It seems of Biblical age, scarred and colourless, grey leather caked in red mud. A thing of beauty.

"I'm getting quite a collection of these," says Chodak. "Why don't you take this one?"

I do.

We sit and hear the wilderness and the chattering stream in our silence. I clutch that ball to my side, allowing its dirt to paste onto my already grubby clothes. I take my finger, wipe it across the ball's knobbly surface, and apply some of the mud to my face, like war paint.

"Suits you," says Chodak, smiling.

Soon after, back in Bangkok, I get a call from Gascoigne Rush. It is not his usual number, and his voice sounds muffled, like he is holding a cloth over his mouth. He identifies himself as Rush, but it really could be anyone. There are no formalities or niceties.

"There's a game coming up on June 28th," he says. "England v Germany. I want you to watch this game. Very closely, Mr Fox.

See what we can do. Then think again about trying to take us on."

Then he hangs up.

And so, while Bangkok traffic rumbles on, I watch as Frank Lampard scores to equalise at 2-2 just before half-time and then watch as play continues. No goal. Everyone in the stadium and on TV can see that it clearly is a goal. I see the England keeper David James missing shots on his near post, getting nutmegged. I see the England defence leaving school boy gaps and playing in slow motion. I see Germany win 4-1 in a game that, in reality, is never a 4-1 game.

I can never be sure if Rush was bluffing, or if anything was behind all this, or whether it was Rush at all. Games are games and anything can happen. But I don't believe I will ever watch a competitive World Cup game the same again, without that nagging sense in the back of my head that some kind of fix is on.

*   *   *

Amsterdam

Back for a few days. Before heading off again to feed what we have started, this thing now living its own life, like a teenager taking steps into the wild world. But, like a teenager, The Better World Cup still looks over its shoulder, still needs us, its parents.

A cafe on Oudebrugsteeg, near the old church there, intimate and cool. The waft of coffee and the odd sensation of hearing a foreign language - Dutch - and being able occasionally to understand it. Muted voices and warm, soft-edge tones.

Windsor is staring into his specifically requested Ugandan coffee, the reason we tend to frequent this cafe when in Amsterdam. "It's like drinking home," he tells me.

There is a renewed vigour in Windsor.

I love him as my brother more than ever in these days. When

we had worked together before, we had been close, but largely workmanlike and oriented towards our common goal. But I have always known his heart beneath the focused mind and burden-ready body. I know his truth that hides behind the laughter and the Shakespeare obsessions. And now I see it all without effort or questioning. This is Windsor in his moment. He becomes more open.

It is hard for a man to admit he loves another man. It is often, in male culture, a sense articulated in extremis - in the hazy fug of alcohol, the intensity of battle, the depths of heartache and human pain. But we do say it. We do even feel it in the small moments we spend with another man, we do feel those yawing feelings of love just behind our solar plexus in normality and amid the mundane detritus of common life, lived in grabs. We just don't admit it.

I have never felt the love for a man I feel for Windsor right now. It is not romantic. It isn't sexual. But it is physical, if platonic. We embrace each other a lot. I want his intimacy, to touch him, to enter his world, to hold him. His enduring humour is like an anchor that brings us back to ourselves, cuts through my overbearing headiness and confused intensity.

Our many differences became points of departure into each others' world, like we are travelling in each other's lives, passing through and observing, taking snaps and writing mental journals. I find his presence a gentle, warm and nourishing place to be. Somehow, he cancels out my many fears and anxieties just by his sense of self. Even the thought of him, when he isn't actually there, is comforting.

Male/female relationships are often founded on mutuality and a search for safety within each other and for a security in likeness. Men and women, when bonded in marriage, for instance, nest and pad the middle ground between them, and tend to conflate their many personal differences so as to nurture that in-between space.

Men in my experience tend to actually inflate the differences in male-to-male relationships. This may not be obvious, but it is palpable, as their individual characteristics, views, histories and choices actually become foundations for an on-going relationship. Men will hold back until they are comfortable enough to speak to their differences. Once that barrier is broken, a friendship evolves that hinges on their admitted, often exalted, differences, both open and implied; in the flaws that each sees and openly articulates in the other. Difference, when admitted to and accepted, can be the ground on which men will die for each other, in defence of their differences and the connection that overrides them.

Perhaps men are wired to understand the dangers of difference, and the deadly consequences of not only creating distances and barriers, but in maintaining them over time. And, because of that, we instinctively seek out those differences, to emphasise them, so that they are known and not hidden. Then we make them into bridges to each other. Our differences become our bond. Keep your friends close and your enemies even closer.

If we weren't acculturated and trained to be violent, to go to war, to fight, to stay alive, then perhaps men would be peacemakers. Perhaps if we didn't hail the psychopaths amongst us that tell us we must fight the enemy - rather than make jokes about his ways and give him permission to do the same to us - and don't fall back on violence as the solution to everything…well, who is to say what our world might be?

18
AUGUST 2010

Amsterdam

Nambour Calling.

A groan from the deep, dark nooks of sub-tropical Queensland. A town near the beach, a hot box, sided by steaming hills that enclose it in a bowl of often airless heat. A formerly thriving sugar town, Nambour now glowers from the margins of the holiday strip known as the Sunshine Coast, a brand name given to the region by property marketers in the 1960's that somehow ended up on the map.

Nambour seems to attract men like my Dad, perhaps because they mirror the place itself: tired and broken, trading on former glory. But not giving up.

Yet, they, and the town, can often affect a raffish charm. Seen on a given day, viewed from a jaunty angle, the life beneath Nambour's asphalt and bricks can be sensed. Life in her yet. Here the analogy with my Dad falls away.

My Dad always feels it is my job to call him. If I don't call, then we don't speak. Nambour Calling is a rare event. Nambour is generally a one-way street. In.

We haven't spoken since he called to tell me he had cancer before almost a year ago. Before I left. Before the call in the middle of the night from Gafsa.

My promises to him and to my sister Tess to visit have gone unfulfilled as this whole shebang had gathered speed and drawn me away. To here. Half a world away and some light-years removed from sleepy Nambour.

"Dad." I'm shocked. "How did you...how've you been Dad? How are you feeling?"

"Ah, y'know. Life. Death. What's the difference, eh?" His words are slurred. He's drunk.

No time for drunk. No space for manufactured sentiment now.

You're dying old man. At least be sober for what might be our last talk.

"Dad, I'm not sure now's the time..."

"Tell me what you're up to. You're always doing something weird, arncha? Always saving someone, or the world, or something. How 'bout saving me?!" Drunken snigger. "Eh, 'Ow 'bout me!?" A cackle.

I close my eyes. "What do you want, Dad?"

Sobering tone. But didn't sober, only quietened. For a moment. Soberer though. "Just wanna talk. Just wanted to see whatcha upta, son. See if I can help."

"I don't think you can help. I can't explain the job I'm doing at the moment. But it's complicated and I'm not sure..."

"Tess says it's about the World Cup and corruption."

"Basically, yes. But it's a lot more complicated than that."

Dad grunts. "I'll tell you something about dying Ash – store it up for when you're looking down the barrel. It frees your mind. You don't bother with all the day to day stuff, not that I ever did anyway, but your mind seems to take its chances a bit, goes where it wants to go, not where you think it should go, if you know what I mean."

I'm silent. I don't know if he even notices me as he continues.

"Anyway, I've been spending a lot of time in my past, especially when I am a kid. Things are stuck in my brain from then that I can't get rid of. Playin' an' stuff. There's a whole lotta memories there I can't stop thinking about. Like playing wogball. As a kid. With my mates."

I need to say something. "In Sydney? This when you were in Sydney, Dad?"

I can hear his wistful smile. "Yeh, when I was a kid in Sydney. In Glebe. There was a park in Ultimo, near the dog track. I used to hang around with this kid whose dad played with some big Greek team, can't remember the name. Pretty legendary lot. Bloody rough-heads, they were. Wharfies and butchers and the like. Hard men. Heads like lumps of rock with leather wrapped around them."

He chuckles. Voice rough.

"So, we used to get down there after school, I was maybe 11 or 12, and play wogball until it got dark. There'd always be brawls start up and you'd often as not come home with a bloody nose or a loose tooth. Some of the kids were bigger than us and they'd aim at us and dive in, y'know, like playin' rugby sometimes they'd just ground us, foody style. They'd rabbit punch us, squirrel grips, gouging at set pieces. Rough as old boots. Beat the shit outta us little kids. We took it for a bit. Then, we thought bugger it and we started working out what we could do about it. Ta get back at 'em."

I don't remember the last time dad spoke like this. It's all I can do to listen.

"So, one day we all headed down there and we told 'em. We said, 'we're not playing with you bastards anymore. You stop using us like target practice or we're not turning up anymore'. There was maybe three or four of them and about eight of us littler kids, so without us they didn't have enough to play a decent game, just two against two or something which is pretty boring. So we threatened to go on strike. They told us to fuck off and get playing. But we said 'Nup' and we walked off."

"Then what?" I'm unexpectedly enthralled.

"Couple of days later we got down there again and there they were sitting under a tree kind of kicking a ball to each other, three of 'em. Looking bored. When they saw us they all got up and looked at us like we were pieces of shit. But they kicked us the ball and one of them, the leader bloke, about 15 years old named Abo 'cause he was Greek and had dark skin y'know, nods at us and kind of sneers. 'Alright you little shits. Let's get a game.' We stood still and looked at him. I remember I could hear the trees swishing about, crows caw, cawing and I could feel the blue sky, it was hot, and we all stood there just looking at them, them looking at us. 'Yeh, yeh alright,' he says. 'Fair enough. Let's get a game'.

He stops. A cough. He starts again.

"So we did, and they never beat us up any more, 'cause they knew they needed us for a game. They rough us up and they get no game. They wanted to play a game.

So, we won. The bigger game, y'know? Us little kids got it over 'em. That moment stayed with me. I can still hear those trees blowing around, feel that hot sun on my arms and on top of my head like it was going to set my hair on fire. Can still smell that summer like it is now. It was a big day for me, for a little kid like me. And I started thinking Ash, that's what you're doing eh?"

I start. *What?*

Staring into the night, sensing the power of that hot day in the little life of a man I'd known always only as big and adult, authoritative and knowing. Little kid standing up to bullies. Hair on fire.

"Yeah, I guess it is Dad. I guess it is."

"I took that all through my life, that feeling of protecting the little ones, the weak ones, you know. Felt it was my job. Nearly lost me my life in Yemen…"

"Huh? Yemen?" I figure maybe this is early dementia, or drugs, or just bullshit. I have never heard of him being in Yemen, or in the Middle East at all for that matter. "Dad, when were you in Yemen?"

"1962 and '63. Was there around nine months during the civil war there. I was hanging out with some ex-ADF army blokes and they said there was fighting in Yemen and that they were looking for fighters, mercenaries, you know, to fight for the royalist side, the buggers the Poms were backing. The Poms already had blokes there, but it was undercover. Australia had no official role there, but because we did whatever the Poms told us, we already had a few blokes there. But it was all undercover."

He sounds more lucid than he has this entire call.

"Nasser in Egypt was backing the Republicans and so were the Russians. If I'd thought about it much, or understood what was actually going on, I probably would have been on their side too. But, what did I know? It was a spot where the Cold War got hot. So, I was offered a gig and off we went, about twelve of us Aussie blokes, on the payroll of an engineering company in the Bahamas. We didn't have a clue about anything, but we weren't dumb enough not to know that company was a front for the Pommy government. But, we just couldn't say it."

I clear my throat. "Doesn't sound much like you were protecting the weak there Dad. Sounds to me like you got into a war you didn't understand and took the side of elites and dictators and lots of ordinary people suffered."

"Yeah, nah, you're right. Going there was a big mistake. Good money and all that, good blokes actually, most of 'em. But I never really wanted ta help the Poms like that and back the royal family who, I now know, were bloody corrupt and heaped shit on ordinary punters. But, that's not the point. I wanted to tell you about how I nearly lost my life there. And it wasn't in combat."

He pauses. Waits to see if I object. I don't.

"I had this run in with a Pommy commander. We were in a village and had captured this poor bloke we were told by someone was a spy for the Republicans. We surrounded his home and got him outside after a while. Early morning it was. It was just a mud hut and first thing that struck me was if he's a spy how come he's not got a better place. Anyway, he's with his three little kids and his missus and everybody's crying and he's shit scared and wondering what the fuck is going on. The missus is trying ta settle the kids down and it's all pretty tense. The commander throws this poor bugger down into the dirt outside his house and starts roughing him up. The bugger is cowering, you know, huddled up like a ball, and the commander starts laying kicks inta him, which just went thud, thud, thud, right inta him."

I can picture the scene. I close my eyes as if it will stop, but of course it doesn't.

"No-one still hadn't said anything ta him and we were all just standing around waiting ta be told what ta do. We all figured, I did and I learned the others did too I later learned, this bloke was not a spy or anything. Just didn't feel right. Just in the wrong place and the wrong time. Anyway, we were supposed ta just take him back to the nobs in intelligence who would sort him and find out if he was who they thought he was. Maybe. Point is, we were just sposed ta take this bloke in. That was the task. So the commander is sinking in the boot and after a while we're all of us gettin' pretty uncomfortable with this. I stepped forward an' grabbed the commander on the shoulder, pulled him away. 'Sir, aren't we just sposed ta take him in?'

I said."

He lets out a breath.

"The commander's face, I'll never forget it, went pale. 'Back in ranks, soldier,' he ends up sayin'. I just stood there and the other blokes were too piss weak ta do anything. And so he lays in a few more kicks and the bloke is just still, covered in dirt, in a little ball. We don't know if he's passed out or dead or what. His missus and the kids have just gone quiet. It feels like that moment before a big storm, you know, where the air just seems full. Then the Commander undoes his dacks, flips out his ol' feller and starts pissing on this poor bastard, He's pissing and looking at us, at the bloke's family and kind of laughing and sneering."

"Shit."

"Worst thing I ever saw, Ash. I'll never forget that. The bloke doesn't move and the piss just showers him and runs inta the dust. We were all just in shock, despite the fact that it's a war and bad things like this are happening all over the place. This just seemed so wrong, like not even war could justify this."

He goes very quiet, for so long I have to check to make sure we're still on a call. "Dad?"

"Then, he lifts his pistol out of his holster and *bang*, shoots him in the head. The bloke's body just kind of lifts when the bullet hits and the blood starts dribbling out of his head, like a little river, pooling in the dirt. The missus and the kids go berserk and they all start wailing and screaming. I was still in shock. I grabbed him and lifted my rifle, said something like, 'I'm gunna put a porthole in you, you slimy bastard!'

He holds up his pistol and puts it to my head. 'You want ta go next?' He says and widens his eyes like it was a joke or something. I felt kind of savage and brave. I was so shocked and angry and my finger was curled around that trigger. But I knew I couldn't do it. I never killed anyone there or anywhere else that I know of – shot at blokes over there but can't say if I got anyone – and I just couldn't do it. Wish I had, you know, Ash."

Feel sick. Don't speak. Dad goes on.

"But, when I looked into his face, his eyes. I looked into his eyes and I saw nothing there, nothing human. This guy was gone. Something had broken up there in his nut, wires shorted out or something. I figured he would shoot me, even if I shot him first. His finger was on the trigger. I remember thinking, this is it. Coulda done it if he wanted. We stood and looked at each other while the family rushed up and tried to bring the bloke back ta life. One of the kids, a boy maybe 10, rushed up to the Commander and started throwing punches an' that. The Commander pointed his pistol at him and then the other blokes moved in and pulled the kid away. Saved his life 'cause that Commander would'a shot him for chips. One of the other blokes separated us and we settled down. But I was still pretty fired up. And we just left that poor bloke and his family there. Just walked off. Never even found out if he was guilty or what and there was no point trying to report anything 'cause we were mercenaries, you know, no rules. We weren't even really there, if you know what I mean."

"Dad…"

"I tried ta track down his family afterwards, asked a few questions. But the up-tops told me ta drop it. And it wasn't a request, you know. I said 'fuck you,' and kept trying though. Even went back to that village but no-one would look at me, let alone talk or anything. I couldn't even speak the lingo. And then they told me if I kept looking they would have ta 'deal with me', which wasn't something I wanted. I had really pissed them off and I had challenged the command structure and so I was on the nose. I started hearing I was in trouble. That commander wanted me done in. So I did a runner. Got out of there. That's another story, Ash. Me and a mate, going commando, off the radar. Took us three months and I lost count how many times I nearly died, from hunger, from thirst, from heat stroke, from bandits, whatever."

He breathes out. I can hear his shrug.

"Ended up in Khartoum, then South Africa, then home. Everyone thought I was working with an export firm in South Africa and, back in those days communications were so shit that no-one really questioned if I wasn't heard from for weeks or even months. Long as I kept writing letters, which I did, and which were fake postmarked Cape Town."

"I remember," I said. "I remember you telling me about being in South Africa. There's some pictures too, aren't there? Seemed so exotic. I had no idea, Dad."

"Yep. All a lie to cover the truth. Sorry, mate."

I have nothing to say. The images I conjure from his story hang in the air and hold my tongue in the back of my mouth. I feel light-headed.

The things that a father doesn't tell his children could fill a library. There are narratives, big, dark, important stories that remain within the chests, behind the eyes, of how many billions of men? How much that our species might learn from? How many lessons wrapped in life journeys and behind the words of the follies and triumphs of men through the generations?

"Jeez Dad," I finally manage. "I don't know what to say. I can't believe you went through something like that. Why didn't you ever talk about it?"

He is calm with his answer. "Because it didn't happen, Ash. Well, you know what I mean? It has no form, it's not solid. History says it never happened. And anyway, what was I going to say? Was I going ta tell a kid that? It just gets lost. Mum didn't even know until later. It's too big ta just throw into a conversation in the bedroom or in the shower or whatever. Mums and Dads don't get much quality time together. I just never found the right time ta tell her, or anyone for ages. Just never felt right."

He clears his throat. A wet cough.

"And if I did tell you and Tess, what would you have done with that? You wouldn't even have understood."

"It would have helped me understand you, Dad. I wish you had told me."

He chuckles without humour. "Well, I'm telling you now, aren't I? I'm a bit pissed, so I feel like laying it out. I reckon you can deal with it now anyway."

I wait. But he is done.

As he always does when he is finished with a subject, he just moves on, starts talking about something else. "Never thought you were much like me, Ash," he says. "But you're just like me. You and me coulda been mates I reckon, you know, if we met at the pub like, same age as each other. I think we woulda been good mates."

A lump in my throat. "You only have to look Dad. I reckon you could have seen that long ago."

Silence.

"Dad?"

"Nah, you're not like me. You're not dying." Rough laugh. "Would love to know more about what you're doing, son."

"Sure, Dad. I'll get it down in a letter. That'll be ok?"

"That'd be better than ok."

I grip the phone tight. "Ok."

"Great. Seeya mate. Proud of ya, son."

In almost a whisper, I say, "Love you, Dad."

A dial tone from Nambour. Already gone. Dying more.

Part II

19

AUGUST 2010

Beijing

Tiananmen Square is a vast open space of concrete and paving stones, held together by historical power and modern pollution - perhaps the same thing. An inhuman expanse given definition only by street lamps fluttering national flags and the buildings and the car-clogged roads that ring it. The few people who cross it are tiny dots against the harsh surfaces. Police patrol it like it is a fortress. Which it is. Open air prison.

This is the spiritual and political heart of the world's most populous nation and its most ascendant economy.

Xu Daixing hasn't gotten where he is by fucking with the system, at least not the one that offers him a path to luxury and heady power. As he skirts the square in the back seat of his government-issue Hongqi V12 Limo, he casts a glance over the flat space and ponders his rise through the Department of Foreign Affairs. He is second down the pecking order in the glamour wing of European Affairs.

At just 42, Xu Daixing is among the youngest in such a position. His unusually laconic command of English and French, and an ability to get by in German and even hammy Dutch, make him the envy of many of his doltish department colleagues. His Eurasian good looks, a genetic product of probably Dutch blood impregnated into good Han stock in China's not so distant past, and his ready smile probably don't hurt in asserting his unofficial position as one of the most charismatic suits in the massive bureaucratic complex in the capital's Chaoyang District.

His endless travelling in the last ten years, first as an advisor to department bigwigs, then as a big name himself, has allowed Daixing to construct for himself a massive portfolio of high level and influential contacts. He is on first-name terms with department heads, business leaders, and political movers and shakers. That vast yet largely hidden and thinly populated highway network that runs between the elite power bases of every nation and every multinational corporation is one he traverses easily and often.

It is here, on this circuit, that he first hears of the shimmering politics of change within the global football movement. He is particularly close to the inside circle of FIFA, largely through his friendship with the President of China's Football Association.

Next to him now as he is being driven to this most significant moment in his career, is a leather satchel, bound by a silk cord, containing briefing documents that pertain to these same developments. Arriving at the back entrance to the Politburo Standing Committee, the highest decision-making body in this vast country, Daixing sits still in the now stationary and silent limo. He stares out of the window at the dark, nondescript surroundings. Political power pulses through the air. He feels the frisson of it curling in his stomach.

He breathes in. Breathes out and allows the out-breath to continue until his lungs are searching for air. When there is no more, he holds, stops breathing altogether, and stills himself for some minutes.

Anti-anxiety technique. He picks up the satchel, opens the door, and strides into the building.

Inside, seven men await his arrival.

The seven members of the Changwu Weiyuanhui are hard to get together in one room at one time. These men run a country of some 1.3 billion people, one of the world's oldest civilisations, an armed force with more troops than most countries have people, as well as $9 trillion of GDP at their disposal. The heads of the numerous cells that hold China together, these men never stop moving, never stop administering, never stop exercising extraordinary, incomprehensible power.

Daixing has a mere fifteen minutes. His briefing paper had been handed out two weeks before. He hopes they have read it. Or maybe it is best if they haven't. In it, he outlined the benefits of hosting the World Cup. This was measured less in hard, quantifiable, monetary terms and more in ill-defined areas like national pride, sovereign power, domestic distraction, and international reputation.

All so predictable and likely to receive the requisite nods of approval he has been told are all he is likely to get from his presentation.

But he has a trump. He is rehearsing it in his mind as he waits for the biggest meeting of his life. He has plenty of time to go over it. Two hours and twenty minutes after the appointed time, he still sits in the massive anteroom outside the boardroom. He is entirely alone here, the space populated only by massive pot plants and dramatic, floor to ceiling landscapes heavy with brown and black, done by Zhang Zeduan, the Song Dynasty master painter. No sound and all was still. The tension in Diaxing was immense. The time only inflated his sense of growing panic. Power needed no tricks to assert itself, only passing time. Like water drops. Drip. Drip. Drip.

Over three hours now, 6:12pm, and a small man in a blue suit padded quietly in behind Diaxing.

"They are waiting," he whispers.

Seven men seated around a table made for 20. One or two note-takers and advisors sitting against the walls.

Daixing is motioned to sit at the far end of the shiny table, which bounces sharp light from the ceiling into his eyes. Perhaps the table slopes slightly to have this effect on visitors. Isn't unlikely.

He squints a little as he sits. The men stare. One smiles. A few grimace. Good cops. Bad cops.

He has been instructed not to speak until he is addressed. He attempts to read the room, feel its veins and assess his strategies. But he knows it is probably too late for that now. It is a noose or a wreath that he is about to be fitted with, and it is too late in the game to change much about how he manufactures the outcome. Too late to get out of the whole thing and just go home.

The thought sits with him and he wonders what the hell he was thinking coming here. Panic ripples his soul. A trickle of sweat runs down the base of his spine. The Seven shuffled some papers and stayed excruciatingly silent.

One of the Seven looked closely at him. "A World Cup for our glorious country," says the mouth. The eyes say nothing.

"It is time," Daixing replies. "The Olympics were central to our moving to the centre of the world stage. But the World Cup is more, bigger, better. And even more so than the Olympics, we will become a global sports power by our successes."

Silence.

"You have no disagreement, Mr Xu."

Diaxing feels his world spin a little. Feels a bit dizzy.

"But whose World Cup are we to conduct?" Another of The Seven looks at his sheaf of notes as he speaks. "Mr Xu, the World Cup is currently mired in a political war, is it not? Two competing backers of the World Cup, FIFA and Flight. Whose World Cup are we to hold? Whom should we back for this project?"

This is what Diaxing has rehearsed. *Time to go*, he thinks. *Don't forget your lines.*

"Exalted leader," he starts, "We understand that Flight has effectively staged a successful takeover of the World Cup and taken it from FIFA. The 2022 World Cup will be the first non-FIFA World Cup, although only a few will be privy to this. FIFA will maintain a public charade of ownership until at least then, possibly even after. The 2022 World Cup, which we believe will be run by Flight openly or otherwise, will be held in Qatar. The vote in December will confirm this. Similarly, the 2026 World Cup in the USA will go ahead as planned, likely under Flight's direction but under the FIFA brand and imprimatur."

He takes a breath. Pauses. Continues. "Our opportunity is for 2030. This will be known to you, as I understand the honourable here have already considered a bid for the 2030 World Cup. While a FIFA World Cup, under the previous model, may well have been likely for our country, the take-over by Flight obviously changes everything. There's now a fluidity in world football that we can exploit."

He stops for a moment, both for dramatic effect and simply because his nerves have robbed him temporarily of his breath. He feels his body burning beneath his suit, sure the sweat on his face is casting a tell-tale sheen under the burning lights. So hot, these lights.

The room stills.

The man to his left looks over his glasses at Xu. He sounds a little gruff, but more with impatience than anger or ridicule. Hopefully.

"Go on. How so?"

"The involvement of the Tunisian rebels has added further opportunity. The rebels there have been very active in this space. They have some money. We understand they have begun something of a revolution of world football from the grassroots. They are proposing a very different World Cup to the one we have known. Actually, their concept is very different to any other major international sporting event we've ever seen. They want to run an event including non-state participants. This concept is gaining ground."

This is the moment Xu has been most afraid of. He waits for the dreaded words to dissipate and settle.

Non-states. Like a hand grenade into the room. Every one of the Super Seven is looking at him. Fourteen eyes bore into him.

Non-states. May as well have said it will be a World Cup of pornography, or murder, or cocaine. The spectres of Tibet and Xinzang hang over the room.

He feels his moment may have gone. That this explosive word has killed his chance. And his career will be a likely casualty.

But no one speaks. No one stops him. So, he keeps talking. *It gets worse*, is all he can think.

He goes on. "Our best player is Chodak Lampa. He may become the best player from Asia. Maybe the best in the world. But he has so far refused to play for our national team as he considers himself Tibetan, not Chinese.

"This has caused the leader great dismay," comments one of the Seven.

"Lampa has dishonoured himself, his family and his country." says another.

Xu allows the patronising political commentary, seemingly for the purposes of oiling some internal cogs among those seated here, to pass. "Yes. Yes indeed," he continues, soberly responding to the anti-Chodak outburst. "But we have a means of getting Lampa into our national team. We can use this non-state World Cup as the vehicle."

He has their interest. He can feel it. He thinks.

"Exalted leaders, I am suggesting we, the great Chinese nation, host a non-state World Cup in 2030, taking it away from Flight and FIFA, and gain Chodak Lampa as a member of the Chinese national team effective immediately. By 2030, China can own this new World Cup. With Chodak Lampa, although he will be quite old by then, we might win it."

Xu had hoped this line would have an impact. He gets nothing. He presses on, hoping they have not already bailed on him, and aware his time is almost up. His voice quickened.

"Our bid, esteemed gentlemen, will be the balm to salve the tensions in global football. We will offer both Flight and FIFA a bail-out. We will fund it entirely ourselves. We will hold the rights, but we will not sell any rights. In-house. We will use the event to publicise our own good work. Our own companies will be promoted."

Another pause.

"We will run events and conferences around the World Cup to make it something beyond a sporting competition, something which it has been for many decades, a point which has been ignore by its administrators. We will develop a football academy for players from all over the world, especially those from under-developed countries. We will use the share space the World Cup creates to advocate for an end to world poverty, to end war, to develop security across the planet, to inculcate a sense of harmony in our world. We will lead this and control it because we will own the World Cup."

He leans forward.

"It will be a PR coup, a Chinese narrative that takes over the world. This will be our superpower trump card, our soft power missile. Our Hollywood. Then, when the event is complete, we will give it back to the people."

A few faces look up at this, shaping question marks. One speaks, and the utterance is like a whip crack. "How!?"

"It will be owned and run by the people, not governments or corporations. The people will be the new owners of the game internationally. This will be our gift to the world, and we will be loved for it."

He takes out seven copies of a print-out, each with a burgundy cover with gold embossed writing across it. *The People's Football Forum.* The booklets are handed out wordlessly by staffers to each of The Seven.

One of the Seven frowns. "This will cost us, financially and politically. How can we be sure this will be well spent?"

"We already have One Belt One Road," says one of the men speaking for the first time with a surprisingly gentle voice. "Belt and Road."

"But more people oriented," adds another. "No-one cares about infrastructure, really. But football…"

All nod.

Xu doesn't know what One Belt One Road is. It doesn't matter now.

"Will we not be abrogating hard-won powers for no reason?" another asks. "How sure are you the world will respect and appreciate our generosity?"

"How can they forget we gave them the world game?" he replies.

The questioner nods. "We would be foolish to let them."

20
SEPTEMBER 2010

Dubai

She strides through the street like she knows everyone is turning behind her, that she is a channel through the banality, a finger running through sand on a table. Shop windows she passes flash her explosive image, like a quick-edit commercial, each moment held for a second and gathering in the air around her. Shimmering faces catch in mid-stare, cars freeze, all in a custom backdrop made for her.

It is not her eyes that grab the stare. It isn't the tight Western dress that pockets in a suggestive triangle of shadow at her groin with every step. It is the air of power, of access. This is one who lives high and who accesses the upper echelons of rich and powerful society. She moves like the street is her backyard, like she can arrange to buy anything you can see.

She is on a mission, and everyone wants to be on that trip.

Her apartment in the Burj al Arab Jumeirah is an outward expression of the outrageous wealth she commands. Entering the lavish foyer, she feels the heads turn, the eyes swivel, the men shift in their seats. She pretends it means nothing to her, that this opulence is her destiny. She never forgets the reality. The doorman sees it in her eyes as she passes: a shock that she is here, a fear that she may yet lose her place in this tiny bubble that floats high above humanity, among the gods here in the Burj.

Dubai has been good to her. Its boom has been hers too. Someone who had once been a gaunt waif, with eyes staring from deep pockets of poverty, teeth rotting in her face from malnourishment, stumbling out from the back streets of Beirut never should have been here, never should have has a shot at perfection. But a body and a willingness to use it has been her currency. And many were keen to trade it.

She learned fast that sex could open doors and wallets. She discovered the secrets of the world at fifteen and never looked back. The world waved her goodbye.

As she swishes by, a hotel cleaner emerges, absently sweeping, from behind a fat golden pillar. They almost bump together. The cleaner drops her broom with a clatter. Ebaa flinches, and for a moment, she goes to pick up the broom, as she would have for her mother in the old days.

She catches the rouge flush of the cleaner's face as she realises what she has done, and the discomfort she may have caused one of the Burj's vaunted guests.

Ebaa instinctively reaches out her arm and touches the woman on the shoulder, winking as she does. Her mouth hints at upward movement and her eyes smile and touch. The cleaner's eyes drops, and her head bows before her eyes dart up again to acknowledge the split second of kindness given to one for whom such moments are like rubies found in the mud. Warmth is exchanged and humanity breathed for a moment.

They part and life goes on.

The world has waved goodbye to Ebaa, but she can never leave it behind. Because it was where her mother and father live, her brother

Rafiq, her uncles and aunties, the rabble of extended family, all bony limbs and hollow eyes, still festering in Beirut, awaiting her payments.

This is why, as she goes to run her key card down the reader near the door to her apartment and see the light already green, she is not surprised. Her Fall is always only a shadow shift away. Who is waiting for her inside she cannot know, but she knows that she may soon be back in Beirut. She has always known.

She see the guns first. Then their eyes which run up and down her body as she has seen so many do before. Their smirks try to relay their power, but they only confirm that she was in control here.

"You're trespassing," she tells them as she walks to the cabinet and pours herself a whisky.

These are flunkies. They are only here because someone ordered them to be. They aren't the story, just the messengers.

"Ms. Keterah, we have been issued with a warrant for your arrest."

She smiles. "On what charges?"

"These will be outlined to you when you speak to our commissioner." This is how police business is done here in Dubai. No questions. No answers. Only made-up rules.

"So, you don't even know?" She peer at them. Her turn to smirk.

"No, lady. We are not told."

Folding her arms, she asks, "Then how do you know the law is being served here, with my arrest? Are you so trusting in the system you serve?"

There's no pause. "You should just come with us." The one who speaks has green eyes, like balls of jade in his coffee face. White teeth with a chip in front. Cute.

She gestures to a fat little Paul Masson brandy bottle. "If you drink one with me now, I won't mention it to my friends."

They look at each other like two little boys.

She clutches out three brandy balloons upside down by their stems. Walks past the two men. The glasses clink convivially and she stands looking out across the Gulf, her back to them where they stand like monuments in the centre of the room.

"Give me the bottle," she says, reaching behind her, back to them. They did. Now part of the conspiracy. "Come, let's relax a moment before we get this over with." She throws a packet of peppermint lollies over her head, and they land with a soft thud and low bounce on the heavily carpeted floor. "For your breath. When you get back."

Some time passes.

The men's brandy balloons show various levels, like a transparent cross-section of earth. Each widening wet line is an indication that their words are flowing freer and freer.

Ebaa's first drink remains largely undiminished, One of her mentors once told her, "Just take in enough to give you courage, but not enough to remove your fear."

It is a trick of the companion girl, look like you're drinking when you're not. Give the image but not the reality. The glass touches the lips, the liquid swirls and shifts, but none passes the barrier. Only occasionally is any drunk, just to keep the night interesting and to give the client the taste of the bottle he paid for when the real work comes later.

"Ms. Keterah," one says, "We must get going." He puts down his glass.

Ebaa flicks her legs up onto the wide seat of the armchair. At 38, she still has the moves. Knees parted slightly, one for each of the men. She hitches her dress along her thigh maybe a centimetre. "You still haven't told me why I should come with you."

"We can't say, Miss. As I said."

A slightly suggestive smile. "Do you like football?"

"Yes, Ma'am."

"Someone who knows a lot about football once told me that the rules only define where the physical game ends and the mind game starts. It's outside the rules where all matches are won. Or lost. All games are mental, wouldn't you say?"

One of them shifted in his seat. "I think you may know why you are being called in."

"No, I don't. If I did, I wouldn't have walked in the door when I saw it was unlocked." She swirls the brandy in her glass. "I'm like an animal, you see? Curious even if it may kill me."

One of them shudders a little at the suggestiveness in her words. She pretends not to notice. "You know people in high places," he admits. "You have information that can help us. That's all I know"

Eyes. Legs. Thighs. The brandy starting to loosen tongues.

"So, it's about the men I know, not me?"

A cleared throat. "That may or may not be so, Ma'am. I truly do not know."

Ebaa gets up, brilliantly, lusciously, and walks to the liquor cabinet. She pours and gestures to the men. Both demur. She leans into the furniture, her arm extended along its surface, fingers moving while her other hand toys with her hair, brush her face, her eyes sweeping out to the view over the Gulf.

Until now, the other man, larger and a little older, has stayed quiet. Maybe he is drunk. Maybe he is shy. Maybe none of this.

Now he speaks. "You need our protection, Ma'am. That's the truth."

She arches an eyebrow. "From what? Whom?"

"From superior forces. Big people. Powerful people."

A strand of hair, twirled around her finger. "I am already all of those things myself. Why should I be afraid?"

"The Americans are looking for you. Others too. They want your information. They will do anything to get it. We want to protect you."

She made a deliberate pause. "Information about what?"

"You mentioned you know people in world football, Madam. Let's just say that we know that too. You know the top FIFA people. Intimately, shall we say. And we know them. We know what they are up to, and we know what they want. You are in danger."

After a moment to digest this, Ebaa says, "We'd best be going then."

"Thank you," says one. "Shall we?"

"Oh, no. I didn't mean with you."

Amsterdam

The sun smells sweet on her skin, holding there under the covers since the sunrise. Warm waft from a slept-in body, curling in unseen aromatic breaths from the folds of her night dress. Hair in disarray, like straw strewn on a stable floor. Bed framed by a parallelogram of feeble, early daylight, shifting listlessly as the morning lengthens. Orchestra of birds in the street-lining trees rehearsing notes in the early morning's quiet theatre.

She turns, and an eye opens, consciousness peering around the edges of her lids. Bed marks make a dry alluvial delta across her cheek.

"Welcome to Amsterdam," I greet.

She yawns and huffs. Turns away. "Early," she says to the window.

"Early for what?"

"Early after the night before."

I chuckle. "I would have thought last night filled you with joy and light, unable to resist the dawn..."

With a snort, she says, "Resist is not a word I need to ponder right now."

Destiny ripples the air. Silence on the shifting light. Sigh of bed clothes being coiled as she seeks to dive back into the dark pool of sleep and irresponsibility.

"No-one forced you. Did I?" I face the mound of back she presents like a shield.

She sighs, like the wind. "No, that's just it. Too easy, for you damn it."

"Didn't feel easy from my point of view."

Her shoulders lift. Drop. She still doesn't look at me. "Ok. Whatever. Can't go back, can we? You can help me over the hump of remorse..."

Another time, I might have been hurt. Now, I'm flying high. "Wow. Have you been taking romance lessons?"

"...By making me a cup of cha. Smart-arse!" She turns back to me, and her eyes are bright. A beautiful smile dawns her face. "Lackey, pour my tea! Curses upon you!"

A pillow launches from the heap and lands with a padded whisper on the floor.

"An ineffectual raid, madam. But may tea be upon you."

Bed clothes rearranged and she appears, sitting up straight and, with wild hair and with the soft patina of light on her face, the day begins.

The grumble of electrically agitated water disallows comment. Face in half sun, half dark. Her eyes following the steam rising. At me now. Beautiful, delightful, smirky smile setting sail straight to the core of me. Blood flooding behind my cheeks. Following. Looking with knowing. A conversation across the spaces of our small room while clouds rolled from the vowel-mouthing kettle, singing like a child soprano. Tea. Making tea. Making love.

Perfect.

"Tea, m'lady.".

"Team Lady? Ha!"

*   *   *

Just one day like this. Cal leaves the next day, back to London.

We're sitting in a sterile airport cafe, looking out across the gloomy expanse of a northern winter, tarmac and buildings through the obligatory picture windows. Silence. A bubble of two. The planes outside shifting ponderously, like things we want to say, thoughts that want to fly, but are somehow grounded. Taxiing crafts, about to take off or having landed and now seeking a dock, dancing a silent waltz of unspoken emotion, shifting through our minds.

In the movement around us, outside, we allow ourselves to be expressed. We wore the place like an ill-fitting coat, flapping about us with the shifts of the aircon, the scuffle of feet and staccato bursts of the PA. Movement through space is what we want, a feeling of motion. Shiny surfaces. Lights.

We know we can't rest here, can't wallow.

The energy of airports is not conducive to intimacy. The rush of bodies, the constant emphasis of time ever approaching and passing, of distance and aloneness, even of the privacy of death, of dying by numbers, in your allocated space and seat, a data item, like every flight is fate's meal and you are simply on the menu.

There are things humanity can't manufacture in such surroundings.

"It's lonely here," I say.

Our eyes meet, maybe for the first time.

"Maybe it just is." She says it to my eyes. Into my eyes.

"What?"

"Lonely, I mean. Maybe life is just lonely. Doesn't matter who you're with. We come in alone. We go out alone."

Empty coffee cups got colder on the table.

"Nothing to be said, then."

She shakes her head. "Doesn't look like it."

No eyes now. Both looking away, around. At nothing. Midspace view so as to not tax the brain, allow some free movement, for emotions to expand and be lost in the empty universe of rational thought. Airport thought.

Time passing but honouring no timeline. Only giving us a line to follow, thinking it makes sense to do so, thinking validity comes with a chronological view, straight edges and clean endings. No skipping heart beats, no jumbled words, no dribbling thoughts. All hard and slick.

An airport is no place for goodbyes.

"Call me when you arrive," I says as we hug, while bodies move around us – human inertia activated by the false hope of movement for movement's sake.

"Why? You think that will make a difference?"

She walks smoothly through the gate and turns the corner. Is digested. Without turning. Already gone, even as I watch her back receding.

I love you, I don't say.

And neither does she.

21
SEPTEMBER 2010

Lhasa, Tibet

Chodak rarely makes it home these days. It is hard enough getting into Tibet without being one of its most famous faces and most prominent supporters of the independence campaign.

He has already spent days in Dharamshala, seeking audiences in hovels and ramshackle rooms among the ancient, winding streets where Tibetan nationalism has come to dwell, in exile.

He has spoken with the Dalai Lama and his people, as well as the hotheads who feel peace was a losing game and wanted war.

He is always struck by how unlike the Dalai Lama is compared to the image presented to the West. His is a highly educated, skilled, and insightful mind, unlike the beaming, benevolent, proverb-quoting movie monk he often acts out in the mainstream media. There are no giggles. No aphorisms. Just hard politics and strategy. That famous face never once cracks into a smile.

He takes some convincing that this is the way to go.

"This is a peaceful way of making war," argues Chodak, knowing this is a line dear to the Dalai Lama's heart.

"But it is a great, great risk," he responds. "If you play for China, it will severely disappoint many of our people. It will be a PR victory for the Chinese."

"But they will need to agree to our, my, demands," says Chodak. And he repeats them. "One, I will never call myself Chinese. Two, I will wear a small Tibetan flag on my kit somewhere. Three, I will not overly celebrate goals or wins. Four, I will choose which games I play. Five, I will freely make statements on Tibetan issues and openly back our independence cause."

"The last one. They will not agree," says the leader.

Chodak shrugs. "Well, this whole plan will not go ahead then. That's a promise."

Ponders. Responds. "I have to trust you," he says, looking pointedly at Chodak. He calls over a few advisors and asked Chodak to wait outside.

After around 20 minutes, Chodak is ushered back in.

"I trust you," agrees the Tibetan leader finally with a sweep of his hand.

Later, the militarists are harder to convince. But the reality is that Chodak's is a more advanced plan than anything they have. They don't agree with the idea so much as agree not to block the China play.

Getting to Lhasa from India, he is wrapped up in a blanket under the floor of a cargo of live goats, where he can hardly breath, let alone move, for five and a half hours. He has to run the gauntlet of checkpoints and borders and makes it into Lhasa feeling half alive. No wonder he can't tell the Celtic staff where is was going, telling them he is off to see family in China. Officially, in the world of geopolitics, it isn't a lie.

He knows his parents and community need to see him. He needs to see them more. He doesn't know who is still alive, dead, sick, in prison. Doesn't know if his village is still there or has been flattened to make a bridge or a mine or a Han settlement. If his world has ended, it seems of use to know that, even given his reflexive Buddhist acceptance.

In the pre-dawn darkness in a shed full of watching, tongue-flicking, ear-twitching goats, he tries to stretch his body back into life, coax the blood to move again. Morning cold doesn't help. A window's dark, pitted sheen makes a mirror and reveals to him a dishevelled, scrubby-bearded Tibetan youth. Darkened skin prone to leatheriness fashioned by the harsh air and light, the sandpaper winds and metal twisting cold, just like any other hapless Tibetan wandering the streets of the capital. No great footballer here. No dream maker. No piece of footballing flesh worth a King's fortune. Just a nice, quiet everyday Tibetan. Exactly how he wants to look.

His family don't even know he's here.

But there is one person who does know. A Chinese man of great importance. And that meeting is today, in around six hours.

Better get some food, thinks Chodak. Better *get warm. Better get ready for this, because this could change everything.*

*   *   *

Lhasa is like a desert. Dry air and September sunshine, held by the surrounding mountains, latched onto the pollution that creates a harsh, toxic brew. Eye ducts and mouth corners gum up and their moisture crystallises into a yellowy honey crumble substance. Raspy air. Throats filled with sand.

Like a metal bowl under a griller, thinks Xu Diaxing as his limo cuts through the streets. Interior aircon offers a respite. Beijing too, could be like this in the summer, and the pollution there is even worse.

But in Lhasa, everything is designed to discomfort people like him. In this Wild West, there are always threats to the Chinese government's people, maybe just the elements or maybe via disgruntled Tibetans, seeking some simple revenge on the pampered Han colonialists.

Nothing here is easy. *Las sla po. 'Easy' in Tibetan. Don't hear that very much here.*

Soon he will have to get out and into the punishing air. A short ride from the Chinese government precinct near Potala Palace. Xu wishes the car ride was longer. But this is important business. The children, he knows, are waiting. And so is his contact.

*   *   *

Chodak is at this time on a red-and-white striped bus that funnels fumes in through the windows and has to be ridden on the clutch every time it stops as it is without fully functioning brakes. Could only hope, in an idle moment staring out the patina window, that someone somewhere had the foresight not to assign this vehicle to any hilly routes, of which, fortunately, there are few in this city.

Accompanied by hacking gears, like a man trying to bring up phlegm, a hot, rumbling drive shaft beneath his feet and headache inducing air, Chodak has no complaints. He is happy to be home. In Tibet anyway, if not in his village. The fact he is surrounded by the same wide, etched and earthy faces as his, and with the language with which he grew up, easily overwhelms whatever disturbance the elements may have posed.

The bus chugs to a dyspeptic halt near a rare expanse of parklands on Lingkor East. He gets off with a few other locals, embracing the fresher air and wearing the harsh light like a coat of nails.

He walks the short distance through air that is already filled with the chattering excitement of gathered children. A curtain of dusty air veils upwards from the unseen space, as small feet shuffle in between the sorry tufts and patches of sick-looking grass broken into desolate islands by dry, hard ground. Beneath a roof of trees, Chodak sees, at a distance, maybe a hundred children of varying ages milling about. The boys dressed in grey trousers and maroon sweaters, with dusty black shoes like punctuations at the end of their feet. A few girls wearing maroon skirts and grey tops. The heavy, battered shoes they wear. Each step raises a pillow of dust.

A few adults, teachers, stand by and wait in the sun as the kids push and laugh, waiting for something to happen or to be told why they are here.

As he turns through the scant forest, Chodak sees the other kids – the Chinese kids. These are wearing oddly unseasonal blue nylon tracksuits and backpacks, all of which seem hot and unnecessary. They wear caps and sneakers. They look like cartoon characters. All were covered by a jostling, multi-coloured sky of umbrellas being held by teachers.

Chodak spots Norbu, despite his disguise. They know each other from childhood, and Norbu has helped get the Tibetan kids here. As they meet, their faces crinkle, setting off earthquakes of smile lines and they unfurl their tongues through snow white teeth to each other in traditional Tibetan greeting.

Norbu teaches at one of the few remaining Tibetan schools in the capital. Somehow, by luck and advocacy, it has avoided being swept into the Chinese educational system's giant maw. While facilities are down-market and poor, the language is Tibetan and the teachers are hardy souls who battle with the Chinese curriculum every day. Norbu is one such teacher and he has devoted his life to ensuring this small school remains obscure from the seemingly-omniscient Chinese regional administrators. Hence his disguise now.

Around forty Tibetan children were here now, waiting to help

Chodak. In return, Chodak assures him, the school will remain outside the clutches of the Chinese for ever more. Norbu clearly didn't really trust that proclamation, despite his closeness to, and trust of, Chodak.

Norbu eyed the suited Chinese officials gathering at the other end of the field, wary. This is certainly a gamble, but the school's Tibetan administrators thought it worth taking if the eventual pay-off is that the system leaves them alone. And Chodak is trusted, as are his connections.

When this event was being set up between Chodak and Xu, on secure lines and hack-free servers, it was on Chodak's initiative. They agreed it was important the kids involved were not "Sinicised". It is getting harder to find Tibetan kids in Lhasa who haven't been made half-Chinese through the school system and via other forms of soft and hard power Beijing exercises in its Xizang province. Norbu's school subverts the issue.

Xu approaches the field. He sees the children and the teachers. He watches as a Tibetan man approaches them. He walked to join roughly half of the Chinese school kids, all chattering and wondering about why they are here. Wearing sports outfits and being in a field gives them a clue but no-one has filled them in.

That is kind of the point. By agreement, none of the kids have been told anything.

It becomes clearer when some Chinese officials take some plastic poles and nets from the back of a van and quickly construct two soccer goals. One is carried to the far end, where the Tibetan kids are gathered. The other is shifted to be roughly opposite, a hundred metres away, near the Chinese children.

Another official carries a sports bag to the centre point between the two goals as a group of others began setting up two camera positions, one along the place where a half-way line might have been and another at the Chinese end.

The official with the bag stops and removes a soccer ball, a shiny, new silver and black Flight Condor. He places it on the ground and walked away. The cameras start rolling.

The ball shifts a little as a strong breeze flies off the mountains and scurries over the patchy grass and dry earth, raising dust and litter. Nature has kicked off.

The children have for the most part stopped talking. The adults they are with have explained nothing. *Why are we here?* Each kid seems to be engaging in an internal dialogue, as their small world becomes just a little more confusing. It doesn't feel tense as much as perplexing and uneasy.

The ball.

It is quiet now as the wind sighs away, quiet enough to hear the faint digital blip of one of the cameras as an official adjusts its controls. The kids eye each other. Tibetan. Chinese. Lhasa expands and contracts around them. No speaking now. No movement. Staring, eyes searching for guidance. None.

The ball.

Two Tibetan boys whisper to each other, pointing. Looking about them, seeking the eyes of adults and the admonishments they expect, they step nervously forward. Three, four steps, then a trot. Running on clouds of dust.

The ball.

They reach the centre and start kicking the ball to each other. Free now, uncaring of adult discipline or consequence. The visceral soft thud of foot on ball touches every ear, its beat like a meditation.

A Chinese boy emerges from the pack. Walks tentatively, looking behind him but not being stopped. He reaches the centre and stands, bold in his shyness, arms limp at his sides and eyes on the ball, near the two boys kicking. A comma approaching a sentence, searching for a gap in the conversation. After a maybe a minute, without taking in who the new boy is, a Tibetan boy kicks the ball to the Chinese boy, who shifts it to the other Tibetan boy, setting up a triangle.

A new conversation. Grammatically perfect.

Xu and Chodak both sit in silence. The only sound is that of the game. The two cameras set up at the field have captured the scene as the three boys, two Tibetan, one Chinese, were joined by two lines of children, trailing in towards the centre – to the ball – from either end of the field, growing a conversation, creating a moment.

They watch on the monitor in the darkened room while Lhasa's night blares and buzzes outside in the streets, as on-screen-Chodak approaches the children, now more or less arranged in a large circle, passing the ball between themselves.

"I didn't recognise you at first," says Xu in Mandarin.

"No point dressing like a rich footballer," replies Chodak.

"Well, you sure smell like a Tibetan." Xu smiles, and Chodak recalls he hasn't actually managed to get washed after spending time as a carpet for goats.

"I'll take that as a compliment." Chodak offers a wry smile, choosing to wear the insult with a dry humour without encouraging its assumption. He says it in English, dispensing with the language of the latest colonisers, replacing it with that of earlier ones.

On the screen, Chodak is organising some training drills in mixed Tibetan/Chinese groups, using emptied bags of more balls brought in by the Chinese officials who have accompanied Xu.

The hazy daylight of the city casts a cloak over the scene as the cameras zoom in to capture the details obliterated by the flying earth. Earnest effort charge the space as young minds drive lithe bodies to greater effort. Faces wear concentration and the grim effort of exertion. But what they don't wear is trepidation. There is no discomfort. No wariness. No anxiety. No fear. They could have been brothers and sisters from some massive, fecund family.

Which, of course, they are. That's the point.

As the DVD player hums and the cameras shift through the gathered moments, Chodak looks to Xu, shiftily, so he won't be noticed. Xu is grinning, not a happy, laughing grin, but one of satisfaction, confirmation. His face carries a look of fascination, transfixed. His eyes are sparkling. Grateful.

Chodak knows then he has succeeded.

He returns his view to the screen to watch himself remove a mixed group of Chinese and Tibetan girls and boys. Motion for them to stand to the side as the drills go on, picking out the better players as they train.

When he has enough players, he gradually slows and halted the training, his mouth moving but the sound beyond the camera mics, and the action dies down and ceases. Soon, all stand and the dust is all that moves, wafting like a ghost across the screen. Chodak speaks and the larger group moves away, Chinese and Tibetan now mingle as they leave, some chatting, all sweating, exerted, some laughter, not heard but seen as bursts of white teeth and rocking heads.

Two boys talking, one Tibetan, one Chinese. The Chinese boy lifts his arm and dropped it across the Tibetan boy's shoulders. The Tibetan boy does the same.

All the children head to the halfway point of the quickly established pitch, away from the adults, and sit as a group.

Those selected are divided by Chodak into teams. Each team stands and waits as Chodak explains something. They all look intently. He waves his hands, points, acts out scenarios, holds a ball under his drooping arm propped on his waist. He drops the ball, leaves it bouncing as he goes up to the players, shifting them into shapes they may encounter in the game to come. He turns shoulders and acts movements, seeking their repeat.

Xu speaks. "You are a natural coach."

"We all need a retirement plan."

The game commences, hastily edited down to around a ten minute highlight package now as they watch. It flows and ebbs. There are moments of outrage, of victory and defeat, of frustration and breakthrough.

The players raise the earth and it holds them, in a breath of grit that lifts from their heels like the wings of Mercury. It holds that moment, the game, the watchers, all embraced by the very earth that bore them and to where each will eventually return. In that room, Chodak recalls the sweet, loamy haze that enfolded them, recalled the breathing in of tiny pieces of his homeland and how in its cloud, the sound of the ball moving, being moved, of voices and effort seemed intensified, transcendent. It made a heartbeat, oddly timed and off beat, that joined him to those there in a universe of connections.

He knows that language on a football field counts for less. The commands to pass, or hold, or man-on, are more tone than words, more body language than speech. The lexicon of football is one we all speak.

Chodak sees himself reflected in the screen, a light smile creased across his face like a bird rippling a pond. And Xu, caught surreptitiously watching him, sideways glance, unaware his reflection gave him away.

Screen blackens. It's over.

Xu and Chodak breathe together. Two. Three. Only the sound

of them living.

"We should never see game as being just contest. The space is shared, not fought over," says Chodak, in English still, to ensure they could each talk freely. "Many see the game as something that must be won or lost, about team A and team B. But it's actually about the whole, both teams, merged in shared space, competing but not... contesting. Maybe my English is not good enough to find the words, but the point is...it's a game."

"Competing, but not at war, perhaps," offers Xu, in his measured English.

"Yes. Is not war."

"You know, Chodak, the stakes we are dealing with are high indeed."

"I am very aware. It can be done."

Again, a pause. Time to ruminate and ponder the bigger game.

"I will tell you something about the game, even the game I play at the highest level," continues Chodak. "This explains what it means to those who understand it. And at the biggest games, among the biggest players."

He looks into Xu's eyes.

"When we finish the game, we shake hands. Do you know what is the most common thing that is said at this moment, when opponents shake hands, even the world's best players?"

"No," says Xu.

"We say, 'Thank you for game.' All players know that without opponents, we have no game."

Another long pause.

"I will go back to Beijing tomorrow," says Xu. He looks sincerely at Chodak. "Thank you for the game."

22
OCTOBER 2010

Amsterdam

Nambour calling. But no gruff, pissed voice. This time it's my sister.

"Tess?"

"Ash, he's gone."

A chill in my bones. Is he…

"Dad? Gone?"

"Not dead. Gone. Don't know where. Don't know." She is in tears. "I haven't seen him in a couple days, so I went round. The house is empty, stuff everywhere like he just walked out. Food and beers in the fridge. Monday paper on the table. So, he's been gone since Monday, maybe Tuesday."

It's Thursday.

"Shit, Tess. He could be anywhere. You told the police?"

She has told the police. And asked around, neighbours, friends, the pub. No-one's seen him since Monday afternoon. He was at the pub, went home and then…

Tess isn't the type to say, "What are we going to do?"

But we both thought it, and we has no answer.

"You need me there?"

"Nothing you can do, Ash. He could be anywhere."

Dead man walking.

*   *   *

Ankara, Turkey

"You know they'll be looking for me?" Cal asks. Her room was comfortable and clean. She is well fed and not molested or abused in any way. She has a fleeting thought that this kidnapping game isn't so bad.

But they say she wasn't kidnapped, only asked to visit them and stay a while. A victim of overwhelming Turkish hospitality. Except they weren't Turkish. These were Saudis. She knew that by the way they spoke with the high, flowery Arabic of the Gulf, rather than Turkish or the street slangs and swipes of Egyptian Arabic. Then, the references to Medina, families, Saudi football.

Saudis for sure.

It happened at the airport, in transit to Yerevan. Dressed as local officials, they approached her, asked for her ID, ushered her away and out through an exit that avoided customs, into a waiting van on the tarmac. It all took around five minutes.

Now, they ignore her question.

She asks a few more. Still, there is no reply from the two men who are serving her some bread and hummus, a cold, but fresh lahmajoun, some fruit. One pours steaming coffee from a delicate silver jug and the aroma fills her nostrils. Placed the full cup before her. Very polite.

But silent.

Neither looks at her or offer any acknowledgement of her presence. *We don't care. They won't find you.*

Cal's Arabic is passable and she considers trying again in Arabic, rather than English, just to see if they flinch. But it is best to conceal her ability to understand them - assuming they don't already know that - so she may catch some information.

She sits, mute, and considers her food. Looks good.

The men leave without looking at her.

So, another adventure, thinks Cal. *Another bloody adventure. Why can't I just do normal?*

Cal is indeed immune to banality. Her upbringing certainly should have funnelled her towards a bland, staid life. Her southern English family, upper middle class and a happy, prosperous and healthy childhood. Should have been a big city lawyer or accountant, sit on a few boards, marry late-twenties, kids after 30, and so on.

But Cal swims in deeper waters, is driven by forces no-one else can see. Her actions are always driven by the unfathomable emotions that they stir.

The food is good, sitting alone in a quiet third storey room, even if she ate it in a room with a padlock on the door and a sealed window. Even if unknown, possibly deadly Saudi men could be heard walking about outside.

*   *   *

Two other Saudis. Two Bilaals. Bearded neatly in the urbane, civil, Saudi style. Facial hair edged like a lawn, populated with trained and cultivated whiskers, lying down to attention. Western dress as befitting the post-Ataturk era here in modernist-Islamist Turkey, still prevalent some one hundred years after the Young Turks.

The Bilaals like to see themselves as new era Saudis. Sweet smelling male bodies of rose water, Turkish rosa damascena, and Omani frankincense. Delicate Semitic aromas to quell and subdue the odorous tides of Ankara, as much as for their own bodily smells.

They both head quickly upstairs.

Moments later, Bilaal Two open Cal's door and politely asks her to quickly gather her things and to leave with him. He holds her gently by the forearm as she exits through the door, and though he tries not to let her see them, Cal is confronted with the sight of the two Saudis who kidnapped her and have fed her so politely.

They look asleep, gently and endearingly seated like kids passed out from too much play, slumped against the wall. She starts to smile reflexively to herself at a simple human moment amid her life's complexity, pondering the small moments that make history both grand and personal.

Then she sees the patches of blood on the floor and signs on their clothes of them being dragged.

Her smile vanishes.

She doesn't have time to see if they are still breathing as Bilaal Two ushers her firmly down the stairs.

*   *   *

Amsterdam

Nambour is calling again, but this time from a hotel in Brooklyn, to tell me he is on the move. What is it about men, about the relationships between fathers and sons? Here, a father calls a son. A simple act, happens everyday. But the politics! The oceans that they must swim in to reach even a point to begin the performance that every conversation is.

Why does he call? Surely it is to extend a hand, to reach out. But what kind of hand?

Phone ring tone like a whip crack across physical distance, the aural power play that has acted out for generations of men and their male offspring.

Him.

And yet, how much of that anxiety is mine? How much of the relationship do I, as the pretender, the son, the perennial loser and victim to a father's will, create? How much of this reality do I set in the sky, the same sky that we both know?

How much of this fear and wariness, the smallness, the quick dialogue I undergo within myself every time he calls, about whether I can take the call, whether I am grounded enough to hear him and to try, in that doomed struggle, to be heard by him?

He is me. He made me. So how much of me is me? Has anyone ever read Frankenstein as a tale of a father and son, ironically, or perhaps fittingly, written by a woman?

As the phone rings, I am reminded he is dying, and I realise again that such news brings both relief and sorrow to me. How can I measure these emotions, so I can tell where the moral scale rests? Am I more happy or more sad about my father's imminent demise? Ashamed of the question.

He greets me with, "Guess where I am?" Before I can answer, "New York! Wow. The Big Apple! You should see this place!"

"Dad, what are you doing in New York?!"

He answers my question, "Well, I always wanted to come. I've seen it before and thought, yeah, love to go and check it out. Now I'm dying. I figure it's now or never."

I wait, feel he is scratching for more to say, finding words. And courage. Allow it. Ten seconds, eleven, twelve…

Softly, emerging from the silence like he needs its permission to break it: "And I want to help you out, son. I want to go out in a blaze of glory and do what I can for you. I haven't done much, I know and, well, going to fix that now."

"But Dad, what can you do? You don't really know what I am actually doing. I don't know that you can help. This is really complicated…"

"Well, It's just. I just…"

I hear, feel the void in the gaps between the words. Full stops like tiny portals into his mind and its restless struggle for purpose and meaning.

I have seen it in him since Mum died. She passed from leukaemia at just 46, when Dad was 48. Such a horrible time for us all, and he has managed to drag its residue into every moment of his life ever since. That sense of loss and emptiness. A blank look in the eyes at times, no expression on his face as the mind freezes it and collapses inside his skull. The random reminder of age and mortality that can visit men at this time, and stop them dead, suck the air away, hold them in a cold grip of fear and confusion.

I ask him if he has let Tess know where he is.

"I have," he said. "She's not happy but she understands."

More silence.

"I don't know what to do," he says finally.

"You don't have to do anything Dad. Just be Dad. That's all."

"I know. I know. But. I'm not really sure how to do that now. You're all away and doing your thing. What do you need me for? Anything?"

I smile. "Only one thing, Dad. Just wake up every morning and say to yourself, 'I'm Asher's Dad'. That's all I need. Just that you're there."

The Void rests between us in chapters of silence. I hear muffled movement, clicks, like he is toying with cables, a pen, seeking to animate his thoughts, direct them somehow. It seems a long time, but I sense my role was to wait.

"I'm your dad, Asher."

"I know, Dad. And I'm your son."

23
OCTOBER 2010

New York

Gascoigne Rush looks at his black bed, like a small imploded planet, and he falls into it as his mind tumbles and spirals, searches and reaches for colour, for a palette that can paint a living picture of his deep, personal darkness.

It comes to him in that pre-dawn hour, when fears and anxieties seem to awaken within, imploring poor souls to follow them. Like jolts of errant electricity, these demons fill his head and send shivers through his stomach, clench his arse and grind his jaw like a mule chewing chaff.

As he lays in his fancy bed in his re-brick Federal near Hudson Square, Gascoigne is well aware that the risks that generate such stresses are precisely the kind of actions that underpin all that surrounded him, and all that he has achieved. Risk is wealth, if you're prepared to put up with the unending toll it takes on mind and body, and if you are prepare to never, ever, admit defeat or tell anyone you are wrong.

He has been here many times before and he has beaten it, or, at least, he has found ways to ignore it.

But this time. No.

Defeat sits on the end of his bed. He can feel it. He knows it isn't going away.

He recalls the moment it was delivered a few days before, as he has done countless times since then.

It was late afternoon, and the New York skyline was filling the floor to ceiling window in his office, and he was reflecting on the last few months. Ninety, a hundred countries? He'd lost count. His fat, corporate passport has been replaced twice, stamps and visas weighing down the old ones. Each trip's time and effort added to what has become the small books of his life, tiny burgundy biographies called British Passport - United Kingdom of Great Britain and Northern Ireland.

The interior of his private jet has become threadbare with use as the planet slipped by under the wings in a succession of window-shaped tableaux, moving past and beyond, always out of reach and untouchable, a world he could never catch, a ground he could only ever briefly find.

He signed them. The national federations within FIFA. He won them. And he paid them. How? A lazy few million here, a spot for a dictator's doltish daughter at Harvard there, a place on Lamborghini's new model list, a board post in Geneva, an inside run on a Lake Como house, a mine lease there, a government position over here… it was a sea of phone calls and meetings, pitches and pleadings. It has been brutal, unending and enervating.

And it worked. Most are on board with Flight's Qatar World Cup bid. Those that aren't already would have to follow. Flight has won. It is something of a miracle, a cold, hard miracle bought with mountains of cash and laced with the dreams of psychopaths. Votes have been pledged. Heads have nodded. Hands have reached across and been shaken. Rush and his team have bought the impossible.

Yes.

Yes.

Yes.

Until it was No.

His PA put the call through that day. "It's the Tunisians, about the World Cup," she said.

He picked up, intrigued. It was no Tunisian. She was Lebanese. Ebaa was her name. She said she knew him. He knew her. He might remember her. She purred that she has some information he would likely find interesting. Her voice was like whisky. He knew that voice.

"I have your cell number," she says. "I have just messaged you. Take a look."

He looked.

Ebaa's voice spiked into him as he looked at his cell phone. "Not sure you've ever seen Mr Aronsen's ass, although maybe you've has to kiss it a few times to keep your job. You guys sure know how to party."

He paled. He got up from his desk. Sank to the floor, holding the cell phone out like it was poison, his heart pooling with dread, his stomach left on the seat.

The phone felt hot in his hand, the glow of the horrible lascivious pictures it held - he stopped looking after five or six, even though he could see there were more - could not let him deny their content, even as he held it away from his eyes. He had seen enough to know who was there. Flight people, football people, businesspeople, all high enough, recognisable enough to kill their reputation. Flesh and bodies, wound together, some clearly underage. Really bad stuff. He remembered the night, the Flight founder's 60th birthday in London, and the feeling that, even for his compromised soul, this was borderline.

"It's not just this, Mr Rush." The toxic phone was squawking at him.

"What?!"

"We have more. We have witness statements. This is watertight."

He forces the words out. "What do you want?"

"You can have your Qatar World Cup. So, don't panic. But you will relinquish at a date yet to be set, after 2022."

He gripped the phone tight. "Relinquish? To whom?! You? Who are you?"

"No. Not to me. To parties you will discover in due course. This call. These lovely pictures are just so you know. Any attempt to shut this down, and we all know there are many ways to do this, the pictures will be released. Some can hide. Some can be fired. Some can retire with a gold watch. But there are too many faces here Mr Rush. Too many. Your class has been exposed. Now you must pay the price. You understand the concept of price, don't you? Of cost? That's the only language you know."

His breathing was shaky. "How can I contact you?"

But the phone was already dead.

Now days later, Rush sits on his expensive bed, black quilt cover, steel grey sheets; empty, functional and dark, a little like the man himself. He considers his moves and ponders his errors. He holds the phone and feels unmoved to give it up.

He walks to the second-floor window where his bedroom is and lifts it open. Street smells and sounds play over the curtains, billowing them inwards. He looks again at the small phone in his hand, draws back and throws it hard onto the lamp-lit street below. It smashes satisfyingly, shattering across the road, one large piece skittering and sliding into a gutter inlet where it disappears into oblivion.

Tears well in his eyes. He sobs as a lonely car drives by and *puk-puk, puk-puk*s over the remnants of his phone, made louder by the pre-dawn silence.

A breeze breathes through the open window, lifting the lace curtain. A gust shakes the walls, rattles the hanging pictures. One shifts on its hook, almost falls.

Rush glances, uninterested, barely noted the photograph of his father, Cecil, in uniform in a Middle East village, with a number of other men. Next to Cecil Rush, a tall, thin man, stands with boiling hair, stretching across stories, no idea of the future.

*　　*　　*

Amsterdam

The phone rings as I am emerging from the shower, as calls often do. The unseasonal European sun barely registers across the Amsterdam sky through the glass doors. I throw a towel around my waist and drip all over the phone. Sit. Wet through the towel already.

It is Chodak. He sounds like he was on the moon, distant and spacy. He tells me he is in Tibet.

He speaks. I react.

"She did what?!" I yell.

Ebaa has called Gascoigne Rush. This was unplanned, off the radar. We were hoping to work with Flight, to use their weight and size, their power and networks to run the Better World Cup idea through. I has told him we were getting somewhere by appealing to the weight of numbers our approach represented.

Now, this.

We, Windsor, Chodak, and I, has discussed Rush's cool response to our pitch. But we still have time—*had* time—twelve years in fact. Twelve years to convince him of the value of our concept and the need to work with us towards the goal of a more open and democratic World Cup format.

Now we've either lost him for sure or we've blackmailed him into submission, which, in my view is almost as bad - a blackmailed partner is never worth the effort in the long run, especially one as linked and as powerful as Gascoigne Rush. This is going to bite us in the arse either way.

"I really wish she hadn't done this, Chodak. I didn't give the go ahead. Did you?"

"We discussed it, of course. But Ebaa, she, well, she is Ebaa. She has pictures and videos. Hers, not ours. She can do what she wants. If she wants to support our campaign, then we cannot stop her can we? It's free will."

"Did you tell her it was ok?"

"I say she must do what her heart tells her."

Fuck. *Fuck.* "Why didn't you tell me?!"

"I did not know would do it. Until now. Now it's done. Now I tell you."

How is he so calm?

"This won't work, Chodak. I reckon we could have got Rush and Flight on side without this. We could have kept this in our back pocket until we might really need it. We didn't need it yet. I would have convinced Rush eventually. The force of the Better World Cup would have ensure he has to get behind us."

He replies, "The Buddha says, 'If you do not change direction, you may end up where you are heading.'"

My cheek twitches. "Oh, don't you start! Does everyone I work with have to have a fucking quote for every occasion?"

A Buddhist silence replies.

"Look," I continued, trying to be calmer, "It's a nice quote. But it doesn't help much, you know. What does this tell me? You think we were heading in the wrong direction?"

"No. I think we were heading in one direction. Now we are heading in another direction. Maybe. That's what I know."

I am silent for a moment while the cogs spin around in my head. Chodak breathing.

"What was Rush's response?"

"He's not happy."

"Sure. I can guess that. But what did he say to Ebaa? Has he made any commitment to the Better World Cup?"

"He did not say. Ebaa did not wait."

"Well, what was the point of it then?"

I can hear his calm smile. "Maybe there is no point. But it is done. That point."

I shake my head. I want to shake him too. And Her. All of them. "What are we supposed to do now, with Rush? I now don't know where it's at with him."

"Yes. We do not know. Yes."

My heart keeps sinking towards my stomach.

"Ebaa is very good. She will help."

24
NOVEMBER 2010

Kuala Lumpur, Malaysia

Asian humidity is like a living thing. It fills the air, licks at you incessantly with its sweaty tongue and reaches down into your lungs and coils around them like a fist. In its embrace, and under a sky weighted with smog, the sounds of a football game were sharp and loud, bouncing around in the heavy atmosphere beneath a low cloud ceiling. Shouts cut the air, hold, and then fall away, consumed in the city's funk.

The small field is tightly ringed by houses, a few gigantic tropical trees and a towering wire fence which is breached by a small high gate, which swings open and closed, as on a moving ship in this breezeless and oppressive space, with occasional rusty squeals. It is ignored by all, squawking away like an old uncle in the corner at a family gathering.

Those there have reason to ignore the messages of a talking gate. These are some of the most oppressed people on earth and their faces, all male, carry the burden of untold horrors. Their eyes, re-rimmed and mottled, tell of dark tragedies and betrayals, even as they focus on the ragtag game playing out before them.

In the middle, surrounded by respectful space, a face like history. Skin stretches across it like wet sheets over the furniture of his skull, dull sun glinting off it in flares of white from dark leather. Wrinkles implied as the dryness and malnutrition eat up every fold in an effort to sustain life just one more day, one more minute. Opens his mouth to reveal tombstone teeth, stranded in a gummy cemetery, betel-stained and ruined.

"Ah, good," thinks Xu, spotting him. "The Imam is here."

He grabs his attaché case from the seat pocket in front. His car hums to a gentle halt, and he alights from the back doors while the driver, an embassy man trained to kill, waits at the wheel.

Car doors close.

Kuala Lumpur breathes feebly in the drowsy air. The hum of a city stilled for a moment in this corner of it, a rare patch of green and a moving tableau of football, colours bright in the grey air. Screeching gate.

Xu takes in the scene. Some eighty men, all Rohingya from the crisis-ravaged north-west of Myanmar. Dark brown skin and longhis, lank black hair and eyes that stare. Quiet despite the game. Supporting and watching in a numb silence. Eyes seeing but not, seeing beyond. No camaraderie or chat. Just unblinking eyes, arms down at their sides, and the pervading sense of shock and disbelief hanging over them all.

Balls thud and cries from the field animate the scene. Without them and the movement of the players, this might look like a funeral. Or perhaps a still picture of something imagined or remembered. Unmoving bodies take in the action. Eyes stare and tell silent, inarticulate stories.

Living but not alive, thinks Xu as he makes his way over to them.

As he arrives, he is greeted with *Salam Aleykums*, hands on hearts, and those eyes staring out from the depths of the human universe.

Xu seeks the Imam, who stands looking purposefully away from them. Xu mangled the few Rohingya words he has learned. The Imam looks at him, perplexed, as he clearly doesn't understand Xu's accent, or he has uttered the wrong words, the wrong way. But the Imam's eyes carry some life at least, a light behind the irises. An awkward silence is assuaged somewhat by that light, which shimmers between the two men for a moment.

The approach of the black Mercedes carrying the Chinese Ambassador and the man they have all really been waiting for provides a moment for them both to lift their heads. A distraction.

Across the field from where Xu has just walked, the car stops. Two men alight, followed by two other men, holding folders and talking quietly behind the two central figures. A second identical car soon pulls up and four or five other Chinese men in suits are soon mingling on the grubby pavement. They all, in their incongruous suits and their impressive gravitas, head over to where Xu and the Imam now stand watching the movement.

The game goes on, moving shapes between Xu and the collection of Chinese government officials that now, as Xu himself has just done, walk through the squeaky gate and head over through the ankle length grass.

Xu looks at his watch. *Media should be here. Goddamn KL traffic.*

He sluices air through his teeth and informs the bigwigs that things are delayed. All nod merrily and sling him the surreptitious deadeye look of VIPs held up. After maybe fifteen uncomfortable minutes, it is decided they can't wait. The Chinese Embassy's own media unit will record the event and the international media will have to use that.

The game before them winds down. Players start wandering from the field, questioning faces asking about the 'big event' that isn't happening.

Xu spoke to the Imam, to the coach. "They've got to keep playing," he says.

The players drink some water, mingled a little in that odd half-time-ish kind of limbo. They troop back onto the field, almost pushed by Xu.

Before he can turn back to the VIPs who were about to depart, Xu is bumped by one of them. The Vice Foreign Minister, Wang Zichang. He has flipped off his shoes, thrown off his jacket and tie, rolled up his suit pants and is hurtling on the field with a ball under his arm like a five year old trying to beat his mum's dinner calls.

Xu looks on, stunned. The VIP group is stunned too. Wang's shoes and clothes sit in a small untidy heap, like a dead body he will need to get rid of.

What the hell's going on. Has he gone mad?!

Xu is seared by the VIP's stern unwavering looks that say '*Do something*'. Wang is his superior. He can hardly tell him to come back. But it would be undignified for any of his peers to react or to rein him in.

What's going to happen here? Media might see this. This could be horrible.

Xu feels the breeze of fear circling his gut, clutching at his heart, his throat. He thinks he might pass out. This is a very bad face.

And now, in the corner of his eye, he see the white media van they have hired for today pulling up across the other side of the field. He can see the squeaking gate, but not hear it over the city's incessant hum. Or is it just his pounding heart that is filling his ears? This is all happening too quick.

Between Xu and the approaching media, the Rohingya players, wandering into their positions, turn and see the odd sight of one of the senior figures in Chinese foreign policy bouncing towards them, beaming, ball now at his feet.

The ball. It rolls from the Vice Minister's foot like it is seeking a friend. Closest to it was a young man of twenty-one who has tried four times to leave Myanmar after his village was sacked by army troops and most of his family either killed or missing. Now he is on this field with a half-dressed Chinese government high-up with a football. And the world's media.

His name is Farouk and he used to play left back on weekends in Kyaukpyu before his life became a nightmare.

Xu holds his breath.

Farouk passes the ball back. Wang passes it to him. Others gather and join in. No one speaks - no Rohingya spoke Mandarin, and Wang has no Rohingya - but the ball communicates in its own tempoed language: *thump, thump, thump, thump.*

Connection.

The journos were on their way. They might see what was going on out on the field, even if most probably won't recognise the Vice Foreign Minister. They will be taking photos, videos and whipping out notepads. Xu won't be able to stop it.

Then, within an hour, maybe two, these pictures and videos and words will likely be online for all to see.

Xu stands, feeling the hot glare from the important people behind him, watching as the ball passed between the booted feet of the Rohingya and the bare foot of the Chinese minister. The Vice Minister now looks a little dishevelled and sweaty as the heavy day bears down on him.

Xu's career is over. He knows it. No-one will blame the Vice Minister. In the Byzantine world of Chinese politics, this train wreck will be Xu's fault.

The Minister is dripping sweat and his shirt is pasted to his body like cling wrap.

Executive decision. Xu calls the driver of the media bus and tells him to drive around some more. "Buy time, say you're lost. I don't care but keep them away until I tell you."

He hangs up on the bleating driver and hopes his seniority and the don't-fuck-with-me tone of his voice will do the trick.

The bus lurches off again and Xu can almost hear the complaints from those inside despite the distance.

He approaches the VIPs, hoping none have seen the bus, and tells them it is delayed. "There's been an accident. They may be hours yet. You know KL traffic…"

The Vice Minister's assistants rushed over to the still active man and ply him fussily with tissues and towels to freshen him up. They tell him the news. Still sweating, he throws on his suit jacket and with one last tired kick, he trudges off the pitch, high fiving players as he leaves. He looks dishevelled and disappointed. No way he can front press in this condition.

Within minutes, the VIPs are leaving. No one thinks to tell Xu as he is too far down the pecking order and should just deal with it. These people don't wait for anyone other than the one or two people in the world who out-rank them.

Into their limos and with a series of gunshot door slams, they are gone.

Silent.

The players stand quietly, confused, in the middle of the pitch. The trees susurrate and Xu's heart lifts back up into his chest. He could breathe again.

Xu rings the driver. The bus returns and the press is delivered. When they are all assembled, grumpy and indignant before him, Xu thanks everyone for coming.

He tells them that China understands perhaps better than anybody the power of sport to unite people across political and cultural borders. He reveals, or rather confirms, something that many have suspected for many years: that the Chinese government had in fact orchestrated what famously looked like a spontaneous interaction between Chinese table tennis player Zhuang Zedong and his American counterpart Glenn Cowan in Japan in 1971, an act that led to rapprochement between the USA and China and paved the way for Communist China's entry into global affairs.

"We invented ping pong diplomacy," he tells them. "We know how sport works. To this end, we launch our support of the Rohingya Football Club in the interests of global sporting harmony." Xu knows he has to get that word in as often as possible. *Harmony.* "And in the interests of finding the expression of rights through the beautiful game."

He quickly ad-libs, emphasising the persecution of the Rohingya people and the support such a program would provide. He speaks about the value of football as a bridge and all that stuff that Chodak had emphasised over and over.

The journos all shuffle about and look impatient. This is not the major announcement they has been led to believe would be delivered. But Xu knows he can't make the announcement, so he has to swallow the big story and try to talk up what he can talk about. That's only the Rohingya team. Nice story, but hardly worth the effort for most of those that turned up.

Xu walks away from some bemused and mildly pissed off reporters with the undelivered speech in his pocket; the one the Vice Minister was supposed to give.

Ladies and Gentlemen, we welcome you today to this simple field in the beautiful city of Kuala Lumpur. We are here to show our commitment to a very important cause; the cause of sporting equality.

Today, we announce our program to fund grassroots football all over the world, in the name of the Chinese Communist Party and the people of China. Here, we begin the first in a long march towards ensuring that everyone, every man, woman and child has access to the beautiful game, a game we in China love as much as anywhere in the world.

Today we are launching a series of initiatives to create a better world through active participation and support of the game we feel holds the future of our world in its grasp.

We propose to spend 70 billion yuan over the next 10 years to football clubs and communities to help them establish and secure a future in which all members of that community can engage and interact via the beautiful game.

This program is not for elite football, but for areas we consider under funded, marginalised or ignore. We will focus particularly on areas where we feel football can be a means of peaceful reconciliation between groups, and where communities are in need of development and encouragement, such as these Rohingya players here.

The Great Harmonious World Football Program, is our gift to the world.

That unspoken transcript ended up in Xu's office drawer, and to my knowledge, remains there to this day.

*   *   *

I sit and watch it all from a park bench in an adjoining field. The Rohingya players, Xu and the Chinese VIPs, the Vice Foreign Minister – whatever that had been - and the media. I only arrived from Amsterdam this morning, early, and am struggling with the humidity after Amsterdam's cool Autumnal air and roughly a day in air-conditioned fake air. Chodak instructed me to come here, to sit on this very bench, under the big tree with the yellow paint around the trunk.

I waited on him, but only a text. *Please meet me at Dharma Realm restaurant in 1 hour.*

I set out.

Downtown KL and a garish Buddhist temple with the usual golds and reds, wooden dragon heads and serpent bodies as stair rails. Western-looking tourists wandering about like ghosts, their heavy somnolent energies removed from life, as the temple buzzes and frenzies with day to day action, seemingly never resting.

Sounds of pots and pans from inside, gushes of water, blue smoke carrying spices or burnt oil pluming through the vented walls.

A vast shared space inside, a mottle of odds and ends tables and chairs on a much-walked concrete floor, scattered and grimy in the cloying air of food and people, smog, and the pungent waft from open drains channelling along the floors. A few people hunch and hurry, piling in their lunch as the city outside rushes by them, refusing to wait.

In the recesses, shiny-skinned cooks in abused t-shirts and shorts sweat over bubbling vats and sizzling woks. They dramatically bang ladles and spoons, weaving away from brief bursts of fire from the cooking, sinews rippling like those serpents at the entrance have come to life under their skin. Clouds hang there like it is a battleground.

In front of the kitchen, a series of rickety wooden tables, laid out with rice and stir fried this and that, fishy things floating in brown liquid, oily sauces coagulating on piles of meat, and flies like scattered condiments peppering the food in unending waves.

Chodak sits, not seeing me, curved over a bowl of rice and two plates of vegetables. Where does he put it all?

I sit opposite. "Fancy spot," I say.

He looks up. Smiles his youthful smile. "Ah, Mr Asher, thank you for coming. Yes, fancy. Please get something."

He motions to the food table. Self serve. I get up, load up a little dubiously and return to our table.

"I'm guessing trying out the food here is not the reason you asked me to come to KL.

A nod. Barely. We eat in silence for a while, like it is a sacred act, which I guess it is.

"So, you observed the, er, event today, in the park?" Chodak finally asks.

"I did. Why was it so important to see it? Who are those people? I couldn't hear what was happening."

He leans forward. "Ok, the players, they are Rohingya refugees. You have hear of what is happening to them?"

"Yes."

"The Chinese men in suits are members of the Chinese government. Big men, Vice Foreign Affairs Minister, high officials." He stops for a second. Eats. Continues. "And there is one man there, a Chinese man, you need to know about. You will meet him. His name - Xu. He is the man who is behind China's World Cup bid, he is risking a lot for this because China is risking a lot. He is a good man. Name is Xu."

"So why are they here?" I am curious. "I could see what I guessed was the media. What was the reason? An announcement? I couldn't hear."

"Yes, announcement. A 'presser', it's called. Announcement to media. Big announcement. Announcement about the Chinese starting a new world football charity, to support grassroots football, not elite level like me, but kids in slums or in the desert or in places no famous people go, or where there's no money. They will support them. Give teams money, make fields, give kit, balls, make leagues, make training and clinics. All sort of stuff for kids and grassroots. Only for poor kids, communities with no money or power people. Very big it is."

What? "That's what we're doing already. With The Better World Cup."

"Yes. It is called the Great Harmonious People's Football Program."

This…isn't right. Is it? "So, they're taking our idea?"

"They working with us. I speak with them already. They know about Tunisians. They know about you and BWC."

"But we've already done a lot of work on this, Chodak. This sounds like the Chinese think they can just take it over. Where are the Tunisians on this?"

"Tunisians have not agreed yet. Haykel. He says he needs to talk to you and Windsor."

There's a nervous pit in my stomach. "But the Chinese are going ahead with it anyway?"

"They do what they want. They take your idea, Better World Cup idea, and make it their idea. Better World Cup is like computer software. They very good at copying good idea."

No. This can't be happening. "Did you try and stop them? You know all the work we've done, the effort the Tunisians have put into this? Why didn't you say something, Chodak?!"

He holds up his hands. "Asher. I understand you may be angry and confused about what I am doing. But let me try to explain. China, you see, wants me to play for them, for China. China very much wants to be a good football team, and make the World Cup. It is not enough good to be a big economy. They want everyone to love them too. It is very important for Chinese."

"And?"

"So, they make me an offer. You play for us and we will make this program real. We will develop non-national teams all over the world. We will give opportunities to people like you who are not recognised by FIFA a chance to represent your country. We will even support a Tibetan national team. Maybe they call it Chinese Tibet. Not perfect. But this is very big for Tibetan people, Asher. You must understand this."

I can't answer.

"But, they will only do it if I agree. They will make $5 billion available for the first phase of the program. But, only if I agree to play for China. Now."

I stop eating. "Lot of money, alright," I say, cautious.

"Yes, lots of money. Ha ha. But, there's a problem."

"Yes?"

Chodak explains. "Problem is China is no good at grassroots. Government is only good at government. Don't know about grassroots. Only can be in big office and big building and nice car and old men in new suits. Don't know fuck about poor people. China not democracy, you see. No-one in government understands poor people, because they don't have to. No votes, no care. Maybe *you* can help with this."

He has been looking down at his food as he speaks, but now he looks up, hits my eyes with his eyes. The clatter and din, the shapes and smells fade a little into the margins of my life. His eyes hold me.

"Maybe you and Tunisians can help with this. Is important. I need your help." Chodak starts cleaning up the dirty plates. "I pay," he says, walking away with the plates. "Is ok."

He dumps the plates and paid. I see him reach into his back

pocket and pull out a crumpled $100 greenback and leave it in the honour box.

He returns and sits down. "I like fuck," he says. "Is good word."

It is quieter now. Most people have left to go back to work. The noise of clashing dishes and pots grow louder as the clean up begins.

"Why is China doing this?" I ask.

"Strategy," answers Chodak.

He looks out the front doorway, into the clogged streets of KL.

"Power is about telling a good story," he continues. "China is 1.3 billion people. Very smart people. Leaders need to have a good story so people don't go crazy, start a revolution. First was nationalism, end of dynasties. Then was Mao and reforms - cultural, industrial - then was private enterprise, opening to West. Now they are trying to reach out, make bridges and roads for everybody, other countries. Soon this will become a more serious program. They are using big money to buy influence and position around world."

I frown. Wait for him to go on.

"Very easy to start a revolution in China, people need to be kept moving, don't stop and think for themselves. There is a story all time to think about, already made, no hard work. Chinese state very good at making story. A football program says to people around world, 'see, we nice people. We can help.' And Chinese people say, oh that is nice! Everyone around world likes us and think we do good thing! You know China tell many stories."

He stops. Looks at me. I nod.

"Many Chinese people today hear stories from grandparents and passed down from ancestors about a century of shame, when Europeans and Americans came and stole China from Chinese people, making them opium addicts, taking away Hong Kong. Chinese people remember this time when they were lowest of low, ass-hole of world. But also Chinese people think it their duty to bring their culture to the world. They think we are all poor because we are not Chinese."

"Yes, but…"

"Better World Cup and bringing the World Cup to China is the story they want to make now. One story, and everybody likes China. Second story China makes sure everyone understands China great and good culture. Strong and smart. This makes good balance. Fix bad feelings for Chinese. Good stories. Everybody is hearing, you see?"

"I understand," I finally say, "But if you know it's just geopolitics, just PR and spin so the Communist Party stays in power, I don't understand why you are supporting this."

Chodak sits forward. "You know football, yes? You know every season we play home and away games against every other team. Have to. That's the league."

I nod.

"Well, when you play an away game, you have many fans against you, maybe even the referee against you. You play a good team at their home ground, it is a very hard game. Everything harder. But, when you play same team, at your home ground, you get support, everyone calls your name, happy, singing, good atmosphere for you. Best thing when you have already played that team in away game, at their ground. Then you already know them, know their game, can play to their weaknesses and away from their strengths. You know tactics."

"Right…"

"So, this program is our away game, against China. Maybe they score many goals because they have better situation, much money, much power. We help China make a Better World Cup, let it look like China is very good. They make big world cup for all countries and take away from FIFA and Flight. Everybody happy."

I'm beginning to see more clearly, but I let him go on.

"This is just the China home game. Maybe they score some goals and we score none. But, we watch them, see what they do, we watch every player and every move. And we analyse. We get ready for the home game. And we let them play, we sit deep, defence line very deep, so we can watch them. League competition goes for a long time. There must be a long term strategy. You understand?"

He doesn't wait for me to answer.

"China is too big to refuse," he continues. "We have to play the game and hope. I am a big player for China. If I refuse, I maybe have a problem. Tibetan people have a problem. Have to play game and hope."

I wait until I'm sure he's done. "Chodak, all this game theory stuff. This is not a game of football. This is life and death."

"You're wrong, Asher. Everything is game. Me. You. Power. Money. Life. Death. All this. Game. Is all game."

I ponder that for a moment. "And so, what is the longer term strategy?"

"We can use Chinese money, but no-one cares about the money. Everyone forgets about that. Need heart. Money from rich man is like water from the ocean."

"And that's where you come in?"

Nods. "We bring the connection. Chinese can't do that. They are shit at connection. We bring human...context? Yes, context. We make a better story, the better world cup story. Money from a rich man means nothing. Everyone forgets very quick. Even rich man. But, the heart of any man looks for human connection, souls making conversation, that is worth more than anything. Give someone that and they never forget."

We are the only ones here now. The vast space that not so long ago was bubbling with humanity and action, is deserted. The kitchens are abandoned, benches and tables empty. The fans above circle like slow, crazy birds, their rhythmic whisper hovering just above the city hum outside.

"You're taking a pretty big risk," I say, prodding for a little more clarity.

He is looking down at his hands, clasped before him in a knuckled knot. "Yes, I am taking a risk. But everything is illusion Asher. There are no risks really. Just choices. All lead to the same outcome. What's important for me is The Thing." He stops, still looking down. "Thing is very powerful."

I wait for him to continue. But he remains silent.

"The Thing?" I prompt.

"The Thing. Yes. I have this with me since I was little boy. I don't remember not having Thing. Thing is, how you say...a sense, a feeling, a force. I know I have responsibility. Even before I became rich and famous, big star, when I was a little boy, I knew I have a job to do. The Thing means I must serve. But, not always know how. How can I use my wealth and fame to help my people, help justice and peace, help humanity? Sometimes I don't know. And when I don't know, I get...scared, get anxious because I think I am time wasting, opportunity disappearing."

I don't interrupt.

"When I don't work for bigger cause, I feel like I am a selfish and bad person. I feel I am wasting my gift. Very depressing." He looks further into his hands, almost like he is praying. Head bowed. Talking quietly now.

"That's quite a burden to carry, Chodak." I speak gently.

"That's my gift. I can carry much burden so other people don't have to. That's The Thing."

"Do you feel guilty?"

"No. Never. It's not my fault. I am who I am. I do not control destiny."

*　　*　　*

I sense no arrogance or patronising attitude from Chodak. While I feel betrayed by this development, I find it easy not to take it personally. I can safely conclude that Chodak is working on bigger issues, on planes I may never reach or understand. He may be barely out of childhood, but he is already working way above my level.

Nevertheless, while I don't feel any personal affront at Chodak's lurch in this new direction, seemingly coupled with Ebaa's similarly unitary decision-making, I am acutely aware that both moves potentially lay waste all our work and could destroy the dedicated, visionary commitment of Haykel and his courageous Tunisian colleagues.

At the very least, we are apparently now required to undermine what we have built and to immobilise our efforts beneath the unbearable weight of an unchallengeable power, volunteering, like a butterfly, to be made still by a collector's quivering pin.

But it never actually happens.

It takes us all a week or so to work out that the big launch of the China initiative goes nowhere. We later learn it has been kyboshed because of one Chinese leader's spontaneous act. Before that, though, when nothing appears in the media and there is no mention of it anywhere, we already know that Chodak's plans had gone awry.

*　　*　　*

A New York accent echoes over the phone.

"Mr Asher Fox? You the son of Mr Raymond Fox?"

I hesitate for a split second before I answer. "Yes, I am."

"My name is Officer Something from the New York Police Department," – his name is unintelligible to me – "And we are holding your father under arrest on charges of carrying an unlicensed weapon and acting with intent."

I blink a few times as if it will wake me from a very strange dream. *Acting with intent? Weapon? Dad?*

"Is he ok?"

"He's well, Mr Fox."

I can picture him, sitting in a cell in some New York Precinct while charges are processed, and the squeaking wheels of justice gear up to roll over his name.

What the hell is going on? Instead, I ask, "Can I talk to him?"

"Yes, sir."

Sounds of a busy station, muffled voices, movement, keys and desks, the hubbub of activity. Five minutes.

"Hello, son."

"Dad, what happened? Are you ok?"

He sounds almost relaxed. "Yeah, I'm fine."

I take a moment to gather myself before I speak. "What's going on? They tell me you have been carrying a weapon and looking suspicious?" I guess that's what 'acting with intent' means, anyway.

His reply sounds so earnest. "I wanted to help you Ash. I was just going to scare him, and let him know not to fuck with my son."

"Scare who, Dad?" Alarm bells are ringing in my mind.

"Rush. That wanker Rush's ranga boy."

The words hang in the air. Crystalline. Fragile. Sharp.

"Gascoigne? Why?"

He snorts. "You remember the story about Yemen? That commander, the one who killed that bloke. It was Cecil Rush."

It's like I have whiplash. "Eh?! Cecil Ru...the same one that went on to run FIFA?"

"The same. Fuckin' arsehole."

Which would mean that my dad was once under the command of...

"Gascoigne Rush's dad," we both say in unison.

I don't even know how to begin processing this. "Holy shit Dad.

"Yeah. Holy shit, eh?"

A beat of silence. "How do you know I'm tied up with the son, Dad?"

"Put a few things together, from what you told me, letters, Tess, the papers. I'm not an idiot."

"This changes everything. For me anyhow." Am I impressed? Angry? I don't know. "Kind of wish you hadn't told me now." More questions are piling up on a clogged conveyor belt of emotions and confusion. "Where'd you get the gun? How were you going to scare him?"

Many questions and frustratingly short answers later, I am able to piece together the strategy Dad cooked up to haze Gascoigne Rush. He located the Flight corporate offices in Manhattan, stalked Rush to confirm he was there, and got a gun online within twenty-four hours of searching.

He had wanted to confront him on the street. Let him see the gun in his jacket pocket to get his attention and then get him into a cafe to, as he put it, "Give him heaps."

"The coppers are cool, Ash. They're looking after me. No rough stuff." I can almost hear his shrug. "I'm fine. Just sorry I didn't get a chance to put it to that little dickhead."

"You don't even know him, Dad."

"Yeah, but his Dad…he owes me. If you can't get the father, you get the son. Rules of the jungle. And New York. "'Cause you're *my* son Ash. His Dad, you know, well, he caused me a lot of strain in my life. I can't forget what he did, what I saw. And I figure I just saw one example. He woulda done that all over the place, I reckon. It's just wrong. I still wake up at night thinking about it."

A pause.

"I'm not going to allow his kid to cause my boy the same anxiety. Nup. Nup. Not going to. Whatever it takes. I'm not risking much."

Despite myself, I chuckle. "Well, he is a bit of a dickhead. And I *do* know him."

He laughs too, sounding like a clogged machine gun down the line. Ends with a hearty cough.

"Did you tell the cops what you were intending?" I ask.

"Na. That would just complicate things, wouldn't it? Na. They just reckon I was a bit confused. Y'know, old man, etcetera. I told them the gun was for protection 'cause I got scared in the big city."

"So what happens now?"

"Dunno. Not sure if they're pressing charges or not. Pretty interesting here. Feels like I'm in a TV cop show."

I smile. "As an extra, maybe…"

Another bubbly, lung-cracking laugh.

I ask him if he needs anything and he says no. He puts me back on with the copper, who tells me he will probably be held for the next twenty-four hours, minimum, until they work out what to do next.

I'm given back to Dad to say bye.

"Listen, Dad, I love that you've done this. I don't agree with it, but I love what you were thinking, looking after me I mean."

His voice softens. "I'm your Dad, Ash."

"And I'm your son, Ray," calling him by his first name as a mate would.

Sun Ray. Never thought of that before.

*   *   *

I call my sister immediately after I finish with Dad. She's surprised, but not shocked. All seems part of a logical course, we both realise.

Then I sit and wonder whether I should call *him*.

I have to.

He answers on the third ring. "Fox. Escaped from the museum?"

Maybe Dad *should* have shot him. "Hello, Gascoigne."

I tell him what my dad had planned to do. I expanded, talking about the combined history of our fathers. It took a while to get through all this, him just listening.

"I had no idea of the details about Yemen," Gascoigne says.

There is silence. But it seems weighted and filled with something I can't identify.

Finally, he says, "Your Dad did this to protect you, to look after you?" His voice was noticeably softer, compared to the bluster of the previous statement. Quieter.

He's vulnerable.

"Yeah. That's what he told me," I reply.

More packed silence. It seems the lack of words is conveying something. Gascoigne is telling me something in his silence.

I wait.

"That's a good dad."

I can barely hear him, like the phone is a long way from his mouth.

"Gascoigne?"

Silence.

Waiting.

Then, slow and quiet, "I'll call you back."

And he hangs up.

*   *   *

He rings the next day. His voice seems fresher, as if some burr has been removed.

"Fox."

"Rush."

"I'll get to the point. I won't be pressing charges. Your father will be released soon."

I don't know how to react.

"Listen, Fox, I don't know your dad, but I think I like him," he finally says after another pause.

I hesitate slightly, then say, "Maybe you should meet him one day."

He doesn't answer directly. Instead: "You like your dad, Ash?"

Ash. Almost friendly. Surreal.

"Sure. He reckons we would have been mates, if we'd met at the same age. He's probably right. Not to say our relationship has been perfect..."

He cuts in before I can begin to tell my father-son stories, the ones we all have, ferreted away in the drawers of our conscious and subconscious minds. "Me and my dad never really worked out. He never would have done what your Dad did. It got me thinking about stuff. Not that I haven't thought about it before, but..."

"Thinking about what?"

"Stories. How we all have our stories and, for us men, stories about our dads are pretty central. How we use those stories to blame our dads, or to make ourselves victims. I am who I am because of the stories I tell myself." He swallows. "I don't like myself, Fox, and it's not my Dad's fault."

"So what do you do about it?"

He is silent for just a moment. "I just need to change my story about him and accept I made my own choices, all the way."

"Was just thinking about that myself."

He either doesn't hear or isn't listening. "That's a really interesting thing you just said, about liking your dad if you were the same age. That's a nice way of approaching your relationship. I'm going to need to think about that."

Once again, I have no idea how to respond.

His voice gets more crisp, business-like. "Anyway, I wanted to call you to find out more about your little World Cup plans."

I blink at the change of track. "I already told you about them."

He chuckles. "I know. Tell me again. I wasn't really paying much attention. I was thinking you guys were just blow-throughs, no balls, no longevity, you know. Didn't think you were important. Bit of fun for a while, but a waste of time."

"But you think we're important now?"

"Not sure. Just feels different."

I nod, almost absently. "What changed?"

He rattles a breath. "Maybe I did."

25
DECEMBER 2010
Al Khobar, Saudi Arabia

She can never really be held. The car trip with the two Bilaals takes three days from Ankara, stopping in Beirut, through Jordan, and then a long haul across the expanses of the Arabian Peninsula skirting the Iraqi border. If they stop at any borders, she doesn't notice. They just keep driving.

In Beirut, they stayed at a low-key three-star, two separate rooms, with each Bilaal taking turns through the night to stand outside her door.

Cal figures early on she can get rather used to being a hostage.

The two Bilaals bicker and fuss over the slightest things. One misunderstands the other or some other detail, and the other has to correct, with an air of indignation and affront. For instance, checking into the hotel in Beirut. They stand with Cal between them and Bilaal One speaks to the receptionist in English.

He says, "Room for two please."

"No, two rooms for three", says the other Bilaal, also in English.

"Yes, but this good woman," gesturing to the receptionist, "knows we have two rooms...when I give her the name under which it is booked."

"Are booked," says the other. "That's just poor grammar."

They fall into Arabic. "Grammar or not, the case here is that we are booking a room and…"

"Well, rooms and actually the rooms are already booked. You did that last week. You are now checking-in. Actually."

The receptionist looks at them both like watching a tennis game, then they look at Cal. Bilaal Two says, "You understand that the checking-in process is where you actually provide your details and you take possession of the room for the period of your stay?"

"Yes, yes. What of it?!" demands Bilaal One. "The process is not important, nor is the name we call it. We are simply doing it. Doing it now. And we are conducting ourselves civilly, are we not?"

"Indeed we are. Civilly."

"We are Thompson," says Bilaal One, turning back to the desk.

"Booking under the name of Thompson," says the receptionist. Professional. No disbelief. "Could I have your ID please?"

So Bilaal Two hands over three forged passports. Bilaal One, sees the passports, kind of blanches, and pulls Bilaal Two away by his shirt sleeve. They walk off, away from the desk, with Cal in tow. She's keen to see what's coming next.

"These are the wrong passports," hisses Bilaal One.

"Why so? These are in the name of Thompson. The name you just gave and the name under which you booked the rooms."

"Yes, but we were told not to use these ones. They are no longer valid, I think."

"But. But, you never told me this."

"No, perhaps not. My bad - as they say. But we must use the McTavish passports."

"We are McTavish?!"

"Yes, we are McTavish. Sam and Lachlan. You, Ms Cal, are Sonia."

McTavish?!! Cal has to bite her tongue to keep in a laugh. Swarthy,

Mediterranean types. Arabs for sure. McTavish indeed.

"Indeed. McTavish," says the protesting one.

"But," says the other, "We have already given her those passports. Will this not look suspicious and alert to our dishonesty?"

"No. Of course not. She hasn't even looked at them yet. Watch me, I shall conduct a ruse which will cover our purposes adequately."

The way they speak makes it even harder for Cal not to laugh.

Bilaal Two looks pretty non-plussed as Bilaal One strides off back to the reception desk. As the receptionist approaches, seeing him coming back to the desk, Bilaal 1 reaches out, grabs the passports that he has left lying there. He makes a big effort to drop them and to look embarrassed. For some reason, he's coughing away.

And as he picks them up, he switches between the Thompson passports and the McTavish passports. Cal can't help but note how obvious it is.

The receptionist looks on, deadpan, despite the comedy show unfolding in front of her. She picks up the McTavish passports, opens them and says, "So, different passports?"

Bilaal One's face drops.

"Oh...er...Is that a problem?" he asks.

"This is Beirut," comes the dry reply, with perfect comic timing. The receptionist proceeds to book the McTavish's into the Beirut Lucky 7 Hotel for one night, no breakfast included, no questions asked.

*　　*　　*

Cal tells me the story of her kidnapping in a cafe near the Seafront area of Al Khobar, Saudi Arabia, over strong, sugary coffee and pancakes. Cal laughs that generous, lost-to-the-moment laugh that she keeps nestled behind her chest, never far from the surface. She laughs for the first time for what seemed like years.

Al Khobar is the port city for the unending flood of oil that pours from the giant Dhahran refining facility close by. It feels tense and uneasy here, a seemingly common mood as the Wahabi Sunni regime in Riyadh keeps the whole of the Shia majority across the Eastern Province under its thumb. For all its obvious wealth and shiny streets, Al Khobar is effectively a colonial outpost. And it feels like it.

"Honestly, getting released by them was hardly an event," Cal tells me. "They never really captured me in the first place. In fact, they told me that if I'd walked away, they wouldn't have stopped me."

"So…who kidnapped you? Why?"

She shrugs. "No idea. These things aren't that rare, not here."

She's right. In these times, in the moving shadowland that was the Middle East, you learn to accept such incomprehensibles.

"But the guys who took you first. The Bilaals killed them, yes?"

"Ah, a beautiful story of non-violent violence," is her answer. "Actually, what they did was ether them. You know, the old school method of Chloroform on a rag to knock them out. Then, this is perfect, they put fake blood on them and scattered it about to make it look like they had been beaten up. Why? So, whoever found them would be more worried about looking after them than about chasing after whoever did it."

I'm almost impressed.

"Isn't it great? It's kind of nasty, sure. But, it's very cute don't you think? These guys don't really want to hurt anyone. They're really so sweet."

At that, I have to laugh.

As the day's intense heat leaves and early evening falls about us, we feel brave enough to leave the chilly aircon confines of the cafe and walk.

The Khobar area abuts the Red Sea, where the Saudi coastline edges into the water along raked and manicured sand beaches and low pillared walls like teeth in a curvy mouth, smiling endlessly along the coast. Like many places in the Gulf, it seems like the big architecture is looking for a home, settling uncomfortably in the desert light and landscape, seeming a little alien. So many ideas and sizes seem out of place. The word *Ozymandias* came to mind.

Lights on a distant shore flicker and wobble in the remaining daylight heat while the Persian Gulf sloshes gently ashore in saliva froth, reaching like a cool tongue to test land's flavour.

We sit on the wall and we don't speak, hearing our hearts beat and our thoughts entwining.

Her hand on my thigh, my arm around her waist, leaning into each other as the warm fuggy day air struggled with a cool sea breeze to take the night.

There is a lot I still don't understand, a lot she isn't telling me.

"I still don't know why I'm here. Why did you want me to come?" I say at last.

"I'll show you," she says, "Tomorrow." She looks into my eyes and stroked my thigh. "But tomorrow is after tonight."

*   *   *

Al-Dalwah, Saudi Arabia

Just outside Al Khobar is sand. Sand. Sand and more sand. Then you finally get past the sand. And find sand. The efforts at civilisation seem Lilliputian in this vast space. Al Khobar quickly fades behind us as we head west. Desert is all we can see, shaping and shadowing off to the horizon on all sides, bordered in parts by the Red Sea to the east.

It's something about the curve of the earth here, or desert light, or something, but distances seem smaller. Non-desert things, like villages, are unseen and then we're in them. The approach seems somehow compressed.

And so, the small city of Al-Dalwah shocks me after around two hours of nothing. It's simply there, without warning. It seems like it arrived rather than that we did.

A crowd of mud dwellings, a lot of tents, camels, kids, goats. Palm trees dotted about like silent giants with novelty hats, standing at attention. Then, boom, buildings, traffic, urban life.

Cal and I leave early to beat the heat. It is cool, in the car aircon and in the brisk sand dune air. But, now as the sun rises and charges in through the left side window as we drive south, it is already dry enough to parch my throat. The aircon just emphasises the dryness. I brought two two-litre bottles of water and have already emptied one.

We drive through the streets quickly and emerged again in a wasteland of sand and horizon on the other side. A village of sorts is away to the left and we approach it. We stop there and waited for the car cloud of dust that trails us to pass before getting out. Cal greets a few older men and hugs a few women. Some of the kids hang around and the goats bleat.

The sun is fierce, despite the early hour. We are not really doing anything, but our clothes already seem silty and powdered by the grainy air. Standing for just a few minutes there in the morning sun, my skin is burning and it feels like my brains were cooking in the pan of an angry sun. There's sand in the corners of my eyes, gathering at the edges of my mouth.

Cal returns and speaks. "This little place doesn't even have a name, she said. It isn't officially on any map."

"But these people live here."

She puts her hand on my shoulder. "Look this way," she says, pointing out across the dunes.

I can see dim shapes in the distance, like horses' heads atop long necks, still shadowy in the early light, dipping to drink. Can just hear a rumble of mechanic intent rolling up from over the horizon.

"Over that way is Ghawal. Have you heard of Ghawal?"

"Isn't it an oilfield? They're oil derricks?"

She nods. "An oilfield. Yeah. More like The Oilfield. Ghawal is the world's biggest proven reserve of untapped oil. Biggest, think of that. Think of what that's worth. And who gets that money? Well, have a look around. It sure isn't coming here."

She motions for me to come with her, and we walk towards a large tent. There's a hump in the sand, like a snake hiding subsoil. Cal clears away the sand. It's a pipeline. A silver-coloured metal pipe.

"Come over here. Put your hand on it. Can you feel that?"

Through my palm I feel a faint shimmer, like something is moving in there, squirming and wriggling but not stopping. Constant movement.

Cal watches me. "That, sir, is the Saudi Arabian blood stream. That's what makes this pile of sand one of the richest, most powerful nations on earth. Ever."

She points to the horizon. "Oil. Heading for the refineries in Dhahran. Going right through here, where these people have lived, like, forever. Passing them by in every way even as the stand on it. Live on top of it. Why? Because they're the wrong religion. Shias in a Sunni state." She pauses, looking away, then back again. "My friends are from here. Kind of."

She glances away, waiting for me to prompt her for dramatic effect. I comply, and she continues.

"The Bilaals are Saudis from Medina. They are Sunnis, but they sympathise with the Shia people here. They are actually from a security firm aligned with the Saud family—well, pretty much everything that makes money here is— and they are supposed to secure the pipeline here. Full time, like they live here and they have guns and whatever.

But they don't. They let the people here sabotage the pipeline all the time. They just ask them to co-ordinate it so they can balance their own existence, between keeping their jobs and giving the locals some sense of rough political justice."

"If they just keep allowing it, they would just lose their job?" I asked.

"That's it. It's an arrangement. Quite cosy really. They were the ones to get me here as they could easily get about, especially inside the Kingdom."

We fall silent. There seems to be only us here. There is no wind and the morning light etches sharp-edged shadows on the ground. The moment is eerie, like something is happening, a moment building and looming.

Cal appears not to feel it. "The reason they brought me here is the same reason I brought you," she says. "They heard about the Tunisians and what they were doing. They want to do the same. They knew about Flight—they don't have much of a network I guess, so even that longshot was worth something to them—and so they thought, let's get them here somehow. *Voila!* Cal arrives in Al-Dalwah!" She sings the little rhyme at the end like a chant and does a goofy dance, thick with irony.

Her voice trails off into the heavy silence. The sky seems to have fallen and the sun seems closer. I feel slowly crushed. Perhaps it is just Cal's will that is bearing down on me.

It's a feeling I've had before in her presence.

"I'm fucked if I know what I'm doing here," I say at last.

"What do you mean?"

I sigh. "Well, what's the point of me? I don't really know what I'm supposed to do and whether I have really made a contribution. How the hell did the Tunisians find me anyhow? I still don't know why the hell they picked me."

Cal gives me that smirk, like she knows something I didn't.

"What?" I stared into her for an answer.

"Well, you don't reckon those Tunisians ever heard of an Australian dufus who can barely pay his rent, living in a big country town called Brisbane stuck on the arse end of the Pacific, do you?"

"So, they came to *you* and…"

"And you went from the amateur league to the top division. I should be taking agent's fees."

I process this then say, "Wow. Why me?"

She shrugs. "I've never seen anyone get the gaps in the system like you. Everyone else is looking at where things connect and at how to make something of it. But you look at where things don't connect and try to work out how they should. It's a completely different way of thinking. It's a rare, er, characteristic."

"Not a talent?" I ask wryly.

"Sometimes a talent. But talent is something that you work on. This is just you. You are the Great Synthesiser. You pull things together. It's not something you work at or have cultivated. It's just you. It's how you're wired. I don't think most people really understand the value of what you have."

"Clearly. That probably includes me."

She puts a hand on my shoulder. "I knew you could manage something."

"How did you know?"

Another mysterious smile. "Come and talk to the Sheikh."

*   *   *

We approach a rough concrete block dwelling, one storey, with a number of tent annexes jutting out from all sides. Out front is a white Toyota four-wheel drive with its bonnet up like a mouth at the dentist.

Cal speaks in Arabic to one of the women looking after the kids playing. The woman points to the Toyota.

Cal makes a gesture, obviously indicating she can't see him.

The woman sticks two fingers out horizontally and points at the car again.

Then we see the two legs sticking out from under the car.

Cal snorts. "Meet Sheikh al-Husseini," she says, pointing to the jeaned legs ending in two grimy, abused feet. She makes a little flourish. "The man who had me re-kidnapped."

She crouches and speaks in Arabic and then the man emerges, covered in dust, rust and oily stains.

He is probably in his forties, although the desert adds years to his face. His bearded face is etched and harsh looking, with deep cheeks and shadows pooling above his eyes and around his mouth. A sharp, curved nose charges out from the darkened ruins like a brown, fleshy shark's fin cutting through the sea of shadows.

His eyes are shielded and squinting in the sun, but when they focus under his visored hand, as they do when we greet and shake hands, they take us in and held us. Those eyes could easily watch him kill a man, but I still feel safe under his gaze.

When he speaks, his mouth looks like his village; his teeth broken and sparse, his lips like the dry wasteland that surrounded us.

I have always thought of a Sheikh as someone grand and wealthy, the Orientalist narrative of the late 1900s of oil rich families and the vast abundance of black gold. But Sheikh Husseini disavowed me of that ropey misconception.

With Cal translating and prompting, he tells me that he and his people see none of the wealth that swishes through the pipelines and pools beneath our very feet as we talk.

"Even the Two Bilaals," he says, "See the injustice and turn a blind eye to our efforts at sabotage and disruption, despite their government-paid security role. They even sometimes get involved," he said with a gleam in his eyes and a moment of enthusiasm. Then it's gone. "But they can't do much when the goons drop in here from Dhahran from further afield."

I nod. He goes on.

"Occasionally, phalanxes of four-wheel drives arrive here and bloated, over-rich Wahabis pour out into their village and make trouble."

I try to press him more, but the Sheikh is unwilling to go into detail, despite Cal's and my efforts.

"They cause trouble for us," is all he will say. "When we see the dust from a distance, we get out of here. Sometimes we don't have time though, if the wind is blowing the wrong way." And he says no more. His downcast eyes and flexing jaw say enough.

Across the expanse, the horizon wobbles in the heat haze. Plumes of distant clouds could be oil refineries or the next Wahabi raid. When I look back to the Sheikh, he is back under the car, legs out from under. Dirt-rimmed soles of his feet flexing and shifting. I hear his voice from under the car, muffled and metallic.

Cal listens and turns to me. "He says he'll take us on a pipeline raid tonight. Maybe. *Insha'Allah.*"

*   *   *

Desert nights are blacker than black. This night has been picked because of the lack of a moon.

"Lucky us!" says Cal with unbridled keenness. Blackness was surely an insurmountable barrier to our detection.

I am less thrilled than Cal, of course, and wonder what will happen if we are found in the middle of the Arabian desert disrupting the blood flow of our globalised, capitalised, carbon-soaked world.

We are in two Land Rovers, eight of us including Cal, the Sheikh, and me. Lights off, thundering too loudly and too fast for my comfort across the dunes. Up and down. Up and down. In the dark, not knowing when the up and down will be is disorienting. We furrow upwards and slide downwards. It is like a fun park ride in Hell.

Maybe an hour. Maybe ten minutes. It is hard to tell. I just want it to end.

At last, it does.

In the post-engine silence, the dust washes over us, hissing like a voice, heard but not seen.

A torch. Oblong of lit sand held by a shimmering cone of light. A grainy ocean white and yellow in the harsh light. And feet. The Sheikh's feet.

Arabic voices, male. A female voice, but not Cal's. A flash of wire fence, a thick pipeline a few metres on the other side of it. A shovel. Wire-cutters. Scenes blurred and momentary in the torch light. Feet. Voices. *Where's Cal?* I'm reluctant to talk.

What I thought was a woman's voice is actually a boy, maybe twelve or thirteen. He slips under the wire, following a shifting hole. Hands and feet. Mechanical things. Wires and switches.

The boy squeezes under the fence and cuts the wire. Seems odd that such a prized facility is protected only by a rudimentary wire fence, something a pair of corner hardware wire-cutters can easily make short work of. Not even electric.

The torch switches off as the boy makes grunting and shifting sounds getting under the fence. Props up his phone torch and goes to work.

Five minutes. I stand feeling alone and isolated. No other voices and the extreme darkness like a cave, like a home no-one wants to live in.

Muffled voices. Arguing? The Sheikh's voice speaks, two words, probably something like, *Shut the fuck up!*

"Two Bilaals," says Cal. I could hear her grimacing in the dark.

"What the fuck are they doing here?" I reply.

"They directed us to the spot we could hit," says Cal. "And anyway, if they're here they don't have to come back on their own and report on where the incident is. They can phone it in from the village."

"Incident?"

Ten minutes and done. The boy shuffles back, no light this time. The darkness wraps around us. Silence.

"They say these Land Rovers are like good she-camels," says Cal as we squeeze back into the bench seats.

With a snort, I say, "Don't know why they have to be Land Rovers. Crap cars, in my book. No-one buys them anymore. And the irony is they need the very stuff, that stuff," I point to the pipeline, "To make them go."

She shakes her head. "Actually no, these ones are juiced up on alcohol fuel. Make it themselves. They're not supposed to drink it so…"

"I feel like I'm in a scene from Seven Pillars of Wisdom."

She's about to reply, and then—

The boom rattles the doors and wobbles the glass in the windows. A flash of light like lightning fills the Land Rover cabin, etching faces and bodies in a strobe-light photograph. A rumble rolls on and shakes the car as we drive.

The boy, who is driving, says something to the Sheikh. The Sheikh replies.

Cal says something in Arabic that must have been, *what is it?*, because the Sheikh holds up the boy's phone towards us. There is a picture of the tangle of wires and electronics the boy built back at the pipeline.

The boy speaks as Cal translates.

"We placed the explosive under the join. You see? Where the pipes join together. That way, the rupture is ensured and is often more damaging. We take these pictures to assess our work. We can tell from the sound of the explosion how well it went, we can guess the damage. We will draw a diagram from this picture, make a report which we bury in a box in the sand, and delete the pictures, so there is no evidence."

When she's finished translating, Cal comments, "Pretty bloody organised for desert tribes.

I ask the Sheikh, "What is the damage, do you think?"

The boy answers in quiet English. I'm surprised to hear it from his lips. "Back there is now river of oil, going straight onto sand, thousands barrels until can be fixed."

The mental image holds me as I sit in the darkness, a black waterfall flowing into the black ocean of sand in the moonless night. The sound of it flowing, money gushing away, vomiting back to its subterranean source. No-one around. Darkness. Just happening in the desert.

We stop suddenly as the car in front, the leader in our convoy, shudders to a halt. The door of the front car opens, and two men emerge, slapping at each other in silhouette against the now dawning sky. I can hear them hitting each other.

Cries in Arabic and squeals of anguish, pain, panic. Slapping.

We sit and watch in the closed cabin of the Rover, hearing ourselves breathing as we watch two grown men, now running in circles, yelping and slapping at themselves and at each other. The scene is made more curious by being etched on the deep blue horizon, like Wayang puppets.

Cal says, "Two Bilaals." She winds down her window and attempted to hear what the commotion was about. "Seems like there was a wasp or hornet or something in the car and they are blaming each other for attracting it or harbouring it somehow."

"While they slap each other," I observe.

"Yep, while they slap each other. Seems it's trying to sting them. Maybe it has stung them."

We all sit and looked in a sort of dumb-struck silence as the two men dance, cavort and writhe in the sand, slapping at each other and at the air. As dawn breaks, crazy shapes against the half-lit sky.

"Classic Two Bilaals," says Cal.

*　　*　　*

The Sheik says, "We are different."

It is early the next morning, that desert sunrise piercing the blackness and heating the air and earth in degrees by the minute. The night chill has been burned away by the deep orange light from the east that cloaks our bodies. We're hunched over steaming, sweet-smelling coffee and bread.

The Sheik, Cal, and I—with the boy who was also a translator—sit on ratty carpets in the Sheikh's grimy tent. It is set up right next to a dwelling made of adobe and besser blocks, but they don't really like it in there, according to the Sheik, so they mainly live here.

He is telling us about Twelver Islam, the Shia roots of his people in a Sunni country.

"We are Bahrani, descended from the Banu Abd Qays," he said. "We were mainly Christian and then converted."

His hands widen to depict the expanse of time. They are thrown wide, arms stretched, and I get lost, in between the translating and the historic markers and names in the narrative that add up like grains of sand on a dune.

"We've been here almost as long as the oil has," he says, eyes twinkling. "And, while we live here in poverty, the Wahabis in Riyadh and Mecca and Medina live, well, like kings. But they are not our kings. And we are not their subjects."

Stateless. Like so many. Given state status, a flimsy citizenship perhaps, but no real access and no real rights. And here, no oil money.

The day wobbles by on a haze of heat and mirages and now the sun is setting as the dunes rise to meet it to the west, towards Riyadh. Cal's phone has a satellite hook-up—

of course it does—and so we tune in to watch the FIFA vote for Qatar being announced in Zurich.

On the phone screen, Leverbruck looks a little stunned as he holds the envelope in his trembling hand. The World Cup trophy glitters to his right and no-one, it seems, thinks to question what it is doing there, given this is not actually a football game. No-one here is winning the title.

He thanks the Russians and the camera pans. There's Rush. There's Aronsen. And there's Ebaa, just a few rows behind the sickly, grinning maw of the Russian bid leader, also the head of the Russian sovereign wealth fund..

"And the winner," Leverbruck pulls the card from the envelope, "is Qatar."

The reaction is underwhelming. As the camera falls on the celebrating Qatari delegation, the audience offers desultory applause, almost a slow hand clap, and sour faces. Everyone knew beforehand, of course.

Cal and I sit, leaning into each other in the cooling desert air as the last vestiges of the day falling beneath the horizon. A gang of kids, oblivious to the World Cup vote, emerge to kick a ball against the brick wall of an empty, dilapidated government storage building near us.

One of the kids kicks the ball hard against the wall, spraying sand, and when it hits the wall, it makes a kind of boom that resonates through the structure's vacuous interior and coughs bits of brick and mortar into the air. It bounces back and it is kicked again. And again. And while the doomed Horst Leverbruck and the exalted Qataris fill the FIFA stage, speechifying and mugging for the cameras, the thumping ball drowns them out, shuddering the wall and widening the cracks.

Boom. Boom. Boom...

Cal snuggles in and says knowingly, "See? You're making connections again."

Part III

26

DECEMBER 2021

Brisbane, Australia

Now, it seems like that was all a very long time ago. As I write, the 2022 World Cup is scheduled to start in under one year's time.

The world now is a very different place. The Covid-19 pandemic has threatened what is already a highly fraught and controversial event, one which is likely to be boycotted by players and perhaps whole countries already. Our campaign has been building all this time in the background.

Qualifying tournaments for the event in each of FIFA's geographical regions have been delayed. It is difficult to see how some regions can even finish the qualifications, given the lockdowns and travel bans.

Now, the World Cup may not go ahead at all. Right now, no one really knows. Some, more importantly, don't care. Once an inexorable quadrennial force, rolling forward without interruption since 1950, now 70 years non-stop, the World Cup event has become just another seemingly meaningless date among many, written with an uncertain finger on a calendar made of sand. And the winds of 2021 are blowing endlessly.

But, if it does go ahead, what will it be? The twelve years between the events here and 2022 have seen so many shifts in this world and our efforts, while still relevant and evolving, have been subsumed by other more pivotal developments.

What can we expect? The answer may well lie in what's happened in these last twelve years.

Many threads. Many stories.

*   *   *

The Tunisians

Almost synchronised to the FIFA vote on the 2022 venue, Tunisia reached headlines for reasons that had nothing to do with football. What became known as the Arab Spring rose in a fist of ghastly smoke in the Tunisian town of Sidi Bouzid.

A man, a simple man, a fruit and vegetable vendor who pulled his cart to and fro around the streets, took his own life. After yet another humiliating confrontation with authorities, he self-immolated in a stark and violent protest, in an embodiment of honest human toil meeting systemic cruelty just once too often.

As this man's, Mohammed Bouazizi's, flesh barbecued on a street in Sidi Bouzid, not more than an hour and a half drive from Gafsa where rebels sat and pondered the Qatar World Cup, the cinders that were once human took flight and lit a raging inferno across the region.

From there, the Arab world itself set on fire, too. While some gains were made, many were lost. Today, many in North Africa and the Middle East are as oppressed beneath the dubious jewels of money and power as they have ever been.

In 2010 and 2011, the term Arab Spring was uttered with a mix of awe and hope by most. But by now, the ideal it generates has taken on the feel of an empty stadium, a vacant space, resonating with human energy but bereft of life.

The Arab Spring is like a muscular tendril reaching out from the systemic failure of the 2008 financial crisis, the Occupy movement, and a sense that the global system was and is failing most people. By 2019, the world was consumed by what could only be called a welling up of street activism. Cities all over the world have experienced uprisings, the majority of which, while differing in detail, have been embodiments of whole populations identifying a broken system and seeking to replace it.

Then Covid. And the protests stopped. The system re-asserted itself.

As a result of the tsunami of revolt that ravaged Tunisia, the money that had been made available, that which was liberated from the robbers in the Gafsa phosphate facility, was soon withdrawn from us. It was diverted to more localised agendas. We were therefore unable to finance our work as we had done, or to carry out our agenda for football democracy along that channel.

But we found ways.

Haykel is now on the coaching staff of the Tunisian club known as EGS Gafsa. He still limps from that shattered hip. But he always looks so smooth and is still an important planet in my universe.

Many of those we knew in Gafsa, during those dark days in that city, have gone from this world, or their whereabouts are unknown. Most of the living have likely fallen back into civilian life, exhausted by their efforts and motivated now by the concerns of older men and women: family, work, money.

But their job has been done. They started a bigger revolution, one which goes on despite the breakdown in the Arab Spring itself.

From the depths of their own struggle, they have been able to build a structure which, while incomplete and unfinishable, has empowered so many. While now consumed, understandably, by their own more immediate and local concerns, they laid a higher platform for something wonderful, forged in the heat of their pain and frustration.

It is a truth of human history that many must sacrifice in the present for unknowable gains in the future. The narrative of our species is thick with the corpses of such individuals as those in Tunisia, in Gafsa.

It is a noble field in which to lay.

*　　*　　*

FIFA

Yes, FIFA has changed since 2010. Hasn't it?

Horst Leverbruck was deposed in a polluted haze of corruption and is now a lost old man, broken and ridiculed. Many of those involved in FIFA's horrible era, starting with Cardoso in the mid-1970s, have been removed. Some are in jail. Others are dead.

Luigi Managetti is now at the head of the organization. Qatar is his second World Cup. Russia in 2018 was his first and, well, Russia…I can't help my eyebrows arching whenever the words "Russia" and "World Cup" are mentioned.

To be fair to Managetti, Russia and Qatar were awarded before he was on watch. But, he was the UEFA boss before he was the FIFA President. Russia is part of UEFA. I think I should leave it there. I'm sure there are complexities there as elsewhere. If my experience has taught me anything, it is that there is generally more to the picture than the image you see.

Also, more pointedly, Mr Managetti was investigated in 2016 for claims that he had broken the FIFA Code of Ethics. To be honest, the claims made were pretty light, certainly in comparison to what FIFA bosses had been up to before.

But I'm not convinced.

It's a deeply questionable proposition that so vast a family that is football should be administered by such an elite rabble and owned by small hands clutching at vast sums of money on the inside, while those of the vast football family are fidgeting hopelessly with the locks that have been set to deny them access, trying desperately to enter.

It is clear that Gascoigne Rush, at the very least, saw the implosion of FIFA coming.

For all that, FIFA returned to business as usual. The Brazil and Russia World Cups were run as per normal by FIFA, with the sniff that term deserves. Of course, we expected this as Flight, with our interests in mind, is not meant to stage its ultimate takeover until Qatar '22. But, all the signs are that FIFA has circled the wagons, and turned ever further inwards.

How FIFA won back its power and regained its central position says a great deal – everything, you could say – about world football and the corporate abuse it has knowingly endured and welcomed over the last few decades. It's a story for another time—one with no ending.

The truth, as I see it, at least, is that FIFA is too powerful an agency for many to let go. The power of the FIFA business model is that it offers itself to be manipulated by various corporate interests who can then hide behind the football body and carry on with some degree of impunity. It's always FIFA's fault and FIFA seems willing to take the fall. As long as it keeps its grip on the World Cup. That's the trade-off.

To me FIFA is like those baffles you see that trap rubbish on waterways, allowing the water to flow on but holding the crap.

Corruption is a complex beast, and I am not here to explain the forms it takes across the landscape of world football beyond what I have already detailed in my story. But I will ask—how can it be otherwise? How can a single body wield such power, size, impact and influence and not be somehow unfair, unrepresentative and ultimately unfair? To see the corruption you need go no further than the fact that the most important and popular sport across the globe is run entirely by a single organization and a handful of individuals. It's a medieval model that survives only by a suspension of credulity and common logic into the contemporary era.

No official move has been made to broaden the World Cup as we campaigned for and as we thought Flight committed to. Many of those on whom we—or at least, Ebaa— have such incriminating evidence are no longer there. It rather removes the weight of the dark matter we hold.

How and when—and, indeed, if—Flight's move will take place, we do not know. Time is running out. Perhaps they are waiting for the moment, a chance accepted when, say, big clubs or FIFA tries something that even they can't sell. Perhaps the European Premier League, now a defunct and ridiculed concept, will be the trigger. In the reaction to this, perhaps the movement will be underway. Now, as I write, we wait.

But, the fans, the weekend players, the progressive clubs, the communities and a growing number of professional players and administrators are getting the picture. The fix has been on for decades. Now the shift is on.

In the years covered in this account, it seemed obvious that FIFA was heading towards disaster. By 2015, it got there. The leadership of Leverbruck was clearly untenable and he was quickly gone. The many spotlights on corruption at the highest levels involving leading figures and dealing with vast amounts of money should really have ended FIFA.

Important heads rolled for sure. But the body, like a monster from a B-grade horror movie, remained. Within a few years, despite some crushing headlines and revelations, everything for FIFA remained largely the same.

The Game was still, and remains today, FIFA's plaything.

The Better World Cup is taking on FIFA at the World Cup level. But, clubland is changing too. Qatar may yet be a watershed moment in FIFA's history, and not for the reasons it would hope. What happens there and after may change the face of football.

*　　*　　*

Gascoigne Rush and Flight

Gascoigne Rush departed Flight soon after the Brazil World Cup in 2014. Why he did this is not entirely clear. Flight looked to have manoeuvred FIFA so that it was set up to conduct a takeover of the World Cup in 2022. Flight had won. The world was laid out for him.

Maybe it was what Ebaa had on him, and he panicked. Or maybe he saw something coming that none of us saw.

Either way, when he left, it helped FIFA in asserting its dominance of the game again.

We have stayed in inconsistent contact. I expect some inexplicable truth hit him hard; one he had no choice but to accept. As I say, it may have been Ebaa's pictures. It may have been something to do with his dad, following the conversation with me. Maybe all of this. Maybe something completely different. He has never told me his reasoning.

The fact that Rush left Flight probably had something to do with

FIFA's swift recovery. But it can't be as simple as that. I do believe that many will choose an uncomfortable comfort zone over a comfortable one, simply because it is known. My feeling is the major powers in world football have their comfort zone and they choose to stay there, even as the fires burn all around them.

Soon, the money channelled back in, big media stopped investigating, governments walked away from the carnage and, with the spotlights switched off and the focus turned elsewhere, the pieces fell back into place. And so, FIFA remains as big and as powerful as ever. And Qatar goes ahead in its name.

The Frankenstein built by Jorge Cardoso may have died, but its progeny was looking not much different. The names at the top may have changed but the organisation and its corporate tentacles seemed only to gain strength.

What Gascoigne Rush has been doing in the years since 2014 is perhaps worth another book. He may end up writing it one day. Or maybe I will.

Gascoigne—Gaz—has certainly changed. Of that there is no doubt. Something has moved him to work to *our* agenda. And it isn't just the blackmail factor of Ebaa's pictures. While we have never been close, it's clear to me he has transformed. There's something else I've noticed, we've all noticed. I think Gaz Rush is slowly but surely becoming one of us.

Flight since Gaz's departure in 2014 has continued to campaign to undermine the FIFA World Cup. Also, Flight has been leading a campaign to discredit the Qatar World Cup and is actively seeking to convince various companies and countries to pull out of the event. This is not done openly, but behind the scenes. Their action is significant, and many are reconsidering their involvement. It's known by most in football where Flight sits and that it is gunning for FIFA, even if they didn't know about all the rest of that story—until this book.

Flight has also ramped up its support of non-state teams. While Flight have not allied with the Better World Cup officially, the company has been openly sponsoring many non-state teams, mainly through kit sponsorships, and through campaigns to gain recognition for non-state or post-colonial identities. This has largely been conducted off the books.

It is possible that Qatar '22 will be a clear moment of positive social justice activism in football. It is clear many players and even whole teams and associations are scheduled to use Qatar to make a point and to lay the ground for a Better World Cup model. Human rights are a major issue.

So, given all this, will Qatar be FIFA's World Cup or the people's World Cup? Will there be a World Cup at all?

Right now, there are no answers.

*   *   *

Cal

Cal is like liquid. Always has been, and I fear, always will be.

She remains on the board of the charity she founded in her father's name.

Nothing to do with what I was working on. But Cal, while she champions my ability to synthesise and to connect, finds links where even I would hesitate to consider.

Her role with Retero-Varsey and China was, and is, troubling. But, oddly, and typically, it led to opportunities for Cal—or at least allow her to manufacture them.

China, as we know and as I will detail a little more later, launched an initiative known as Belt and Road. For Cal, this program was something of a lottery win. She had developed a high-level relationship as a result of her work with Retero-Varsey thanks to some extent to her involvement with the Better World Cup.

Retero-Varsey already had strong Chinese connections and their widespread links into Africa and the Middle East had them well-placed to become brokers for the Chinese in the early stages of the initiative. Cal was very much involved in this phase.

She has done very well.

Cal is not directly connected to the BWC. But we remain in contact. Intermittently.

Of course, Cal and I have a connection that reaches beyond this story in both time and space, and reaches into personal territory. I have tried to be open and honest about us, but I have sought to focus on how she impacted on the core story.

In the interests of closure, I will make some attempt to draw this out.

This is difficult as our relationship is hard to articulate in mere words. It is perhaps why I have struggled at times in this story to really express her character. That is partly because her character is so indefinable. But it is also because finding the words to describe what we are, and what we have, is often beyond me.

Perhaps the best way of suggesting what Cal means to me would be to note that I often talk to her when I am on my own. She remains my default interlocutor in life, even if we are at either ends of the planet and completely out of contact. I run things past an etheric version of her, or test ideas with her, and, in the anticipation of her response which I can confidently predict, those thoughts, positions, arguments evolve and sharpen in focus. Or are discarded as absurd or inappropriate.

These ghost-conversations are a central chamber of my inner

dialogue, opened more or less on a daily basis.

I say inner dialogue. But these interactions are often out loud. I sometimes catch myself mumbling to myself in public—less so lately of course as Covid has pushed us all into isolated corners of ourselves—and chatting with her in absentia. I even make jokes I think she will like and imagine her eyes brightening and her mouth reflexively broadening. I hear music and think 'she would like this'. I see movies and think 'must tell Cal about this one.' I think of moments we shared and relive them.

The worst part of separation is the memories.

I have never actually told her any of this, of course.

I think of her at odd moments, in both pain and joy. I share my life with her regardless of our proximity or status.

As such, I am constantly reminded of her presence, her existence, multiple times each day.

What does this mean? I don't know. I only know that it is there.

She broke my heart. More than once. I am not one to invite a lot of people into my inner world, into that little home we all carry inside us. She was one of those and she entered, stayed a while and then smashed all the windows, broke the furniture, tore up the garden and shat on the floor. And each time I felt I was tidying it up, she came back - and I let her - to destroy everything again.

There's a lot I still don't understand about Cal and me.

When I wrote about us in the desert in eastern Saudi to finish this story, we were in a moment of connection. These moments have been few since then. But those that have been, shall I say, have been well-rounded and memorable.

Our last meeting was in 2019. Our worlds collided in Berlin, a city that held some weighted moments for us, as for history, and we arranged to meet. She was distant and cold, and I reacted to that, pulling away and offering little of myself.

She said, "I have to go now."

And I said, "Sure, bye."

And that was that.

*　　*　　*

China and Xu

In 2010, the Chinese Government was prepared to rush headlong into leveraging football to put the country on the world's 'good guys' map. China has always had a bit of a chip on its shoulder since it was humiliated by the English in the nineteenth century. And so, starting with the Olympics in 2008, the country's leaders were looking to sport to be what I would call, its soft power wedge.

Xu, whom I never actually met, was well aware of this. His foresight and energy, and his position within the Party, added up to a lot. He identified the weather patterns in Beijing and saw that moving towards hosting a World Cup was a means of channelling the prevailing winds.

There was even, by all accounts, significant support for the Better World Cup idea and for incorporating ethnic groups into the World Cup model. I'm not really sure how genuine this commitment was, and I remain sceptical it was ever a sincere strategy. I believe China's support may even have extended to include Uighurs and Tibetans. I am not sure — in fact I don't really believe—that the Chinese leadership equated this apparent openness with any increase in political freedom. I am firm in my belief that the Chinese were simply seeking the kudos this move would generate to be the world's nice guys. To lay down cards for all to see and then withdraw them when no-one was looking.

It had to be a trick.

The rise of Xi Jinping—he became the Chinese Communist Party General Secretary in 2012—brought a shifting of the skies in China and changed the weather in big ways. He started quickly by getting rid of most of his rivals and built a cult of personality around himself, based on fear. It's been done plenty of times before, hasn't it?

I have a strong feeling that China's poor performance in international football was a major factor in this shift away from football and the Better World Cup, as tacit as that may have been anyway. I can imagine there may have been a decision that, even with Chodak in their team, and with various naturalised international ring-ins, the Chinese might still be struggling to qualify for World Cups or to get very far if they did. It may have seemed that the risk of bringing shame to the leadership, and the price they were expected to pay for his participation, a murky deal at best, was probably not worth the effort.

The Belt and Road Initiative, formally started in 2013, soon replaced any thoughts of football outreach anyway. By now, some 70+ countries and countless carpet bags full of Chinese money, some of it passing through Cal's delicate hands, have zinged around the world backing numerous half-baked infrastructure ideas which have been used to leverage China's physical presence in every one of those countries, building everything, using Chinese workers and companies, staffing it with Chinese when its complete, and owning every screw and light bulb.

Xu has largely disappeared. No-one we know has had contact with him for some years, although Chodak tells me he has a channel to him. But he says little more. I expect he has been swallowed up by that vast bureaucratic beast in China. It's a shame, but I expect his career has well and truly peaked.

If he's still there, maybe he still has some influence and he still has some belief for what we were working on. It was an imperfect model for sure. But there was potential in it.

*   *   *

The Better World Cup

You remember that our initial idea was to convince the investors in Flight to see the ethical minefield—the Qatar World Cup—into which their money had led them? Clearly this was an error. You might say it was naïve. You'd be correct.

I was, and am, a little embarrassed about it. Either way, it was a big moment. I was worried we had blown it, that we had wasted the Tunisians' money and efforts. Maybe we were the wrong people for this.

It's still painful to think of it now.

I doubted us. I doubted myself. I was right to do so, I guess. But I have learned to doubt the world, and me in it, every step of the way. It seems more realistic and less ensnared with the traps of entitlement and expectation. Doubt is like a hat I put on every day before walking into the world, occasionally set raffishly, but always firmly placed.

Certainly, I carried a trust in humankind that was misguided. It is perhaps an indication of my foolish faith that, while Windsor and I had been victims of human folly, and seen enough evidence of it, suffering at the presence of it, we could still muster some belief that money might buy the freedom to be wise or compassionate or generous. But we were wrong, weren't we?

This troubles me still.

The Better World Cup must be understood, therefore, to have been born in adversity. It was not a pure idea, complete and whole from conception. It was an idea developed in a scramble. A bastard idea, conceived in panic and born in a raging storm of anxiety.

Which point, I think, makes it more authentic and more pure. It came not from reasoned thought, but from raw emotion and passion. It was not a plan, but a constantly moving series of actions and reactions, random and hurried, fraught and tense in all ways.

Like the game itself, the sum of movement and effort, of attempts to control what we could not, led to shapes and results we could not have anticipated. The best footballers are those that adapt quickly to changed circumstances, who can play different and even dampen their own strengths to fit the landscape the game creates around them, in real time, and to take their team-mates with them.

We at least did this and the Better World Cup is our answer, our plea, from within the cages we found ourselves in.

From 2010, from building the grassroots organisation, reaching from Kayole outwards, to the Association of Progressive Professional Football Clubs, through Brazil in 2014 and Russia in 2018 to here, will take some explaining. Too much. The last 12 years is again, another story.

From the start, we sought out the disadvantaged and disenfranchised all over the world, to be the basis of the Better World Cup. Non-violent humanism was the capstone of our structure, holding everything together.

It is always important, in this logical and spreadsheeted world, to find ways to define and to strategize a campaign such as this. So, the aim for the most alienated in the world often led us to those who were stateless. Our core group are those who lost in the lottery of statism; those who have found themselves, despite their centuries of culture and history, without the right to place a border between them and others and to define themselves in terms of formally mandated nationalistic expressions.

From the population of maybe 80 million Kurds scattered over numerous countries to a few thousand Rapa Nui, clinging to a sense of country and tradition, here were the people who lost categorically, without blame, without agency. They were people in the margins of a world many falsely believe is a seamless fabric of nations and cultures, woven together by something we call the international community.

The stateless are stuck in the corridors. The doors are closed to them. Many don't really even exist, in terms of global political reality.

They are Tamils and Kurds, the Catalans and Mthwakazi, Mapuche and Gubi Gubi, who may have nominal statehood or some recognition in an artificial situation which does not encourage or recognise – or may even actively suppress – their own national identity.

There are a lot of people crowding into that corridor. Windsor, as a member of the Acholi people in Northern Uganda, tells me that tightly packed hallway is a dark and uncomfortable place.

But this is about even more than the lives of these people and of the generations of those that have been denied before, and of those yet to come.

It is the value of these peoples in our collective human story. Can you read a book if some chapters are missing? Can you follow a movie which has whole sections not there? Of course not. Yet, this is what FIFA has done, and is still doing.

And so, the Better World Cup now has some 2000+ members, on all settled continents and from maybe 150 countries. There are no fees. No restrictions. Only that each team or club signs a pledge to act exclusively in the interests of social justice, human rights, non-violence and non-discrimination. That's our Holy Quartet. Our SHRINNe, as Windsor puts it. Maybe that acronym may need some work. Let's go with Holy Quartet. Windsor is no brand merchant.

Breaking the pledge to these things is instant exclusion.

We have some women-only teams. We have some mixed gender teams. We have ethnic and issue-oriented teams. All are equal. All can compete in the Better World Cup on the same footing, as long as they pledge to keep to the Holy Quartet. You don't have to be a country, just an identity.

Among our first teams was the Acholi Chargers drawn from the ethnic groups based in northern Uganda and southern Sudan. As an Acholi, this is Windsor's team and he is, in his own words, the Founding President and official Worst Player.

We have not yet started to roll out a Better World Cup proper yet. Our plan is to wait until after the 2022 World Cup, to lay foundations among the football establishment, to ensure the longevity and sustainability of the project.

We have struggled at times to do that. But the structure is largely in place. Truth is, we didn't bet on FIFA surviving this far.

I have mentioned the cases of the French team and the Nigerian team at the 2010 event.

In 2014, there were more examples. Players wore socks down, maybe just one, or got new tattoos—a popular form of personal expression for this generation—or wore their hair in a certain way to signify a message to their supporters, backing issues or peoples. Some feigned injury to sit out the event in protest at the corruption in their federations and in FIFA, and to highlight the lack of representation for their people in the event. While FIFA or the vested interests may have been ignorant to these statements, we knew about them and, more importantly, their people knew about them.

The case of the Brazilians in 2014 is one I cannot confirm. But I have had word that the 7-1 defeat by Germany on July 8 in Mineirão to lose the semi-final was not all that it seems. I have been told the Brazilians fell out with management and wanted to make a political statement against the incumbent President, Dilma Rousseff. While Rousseff had left-wing grounding, and had been imprisoned for her Marxist views, she had shifted to the right and was losing ground on the street. A movement known as the *Movimento Passe Livre* – Free Fare Movement – had developed which was intended to highlight the struggle of poor workers having to pay expensive fares on public transport. But, it became, of course, more than that. A broader campaign focusing on numerous social inequalities.

Given the game against Germany was in Belo Horizonte, Rousseff's hometown, it was seen as a strong statement against her and her apparently anti-social policies. She was to extend her presidency after the national elections later that year. So, it didn't really work.

But it went wrong in the execution before then, I am told. The Brazilians thought they could lose by just a few goals, or even just by one. Be competitive but remove any kudos the Brazilian government might get from a Brazil win. Then, after the game, they were supposed to make it clear they felt unmotivated to win when so many people in Brazil were suffering via a public announcement. But, with such an unexpected defeat, they kept their mouths shut. Not even popular politics could explain that debacle. Demoralised and broken by the Germany game, the team then lost lamely to The Netherlands in the third-place play-off, 3-0. That's 10-1 in two games. Brazil? In Brazil? World Cup? Doesn't sit right somehow.

Many of the members of the Mineirão Massacre team didn't play for Brazil again. Most saw their careers languish in the years ahead. It was some sacrifice, especially given it went wrong.

If the story is true, that is.

Since 2010, there have been some attempts to give a space for non-state teams, for instance, to play international games. The Confederation of Independent Football Associations was established in 2013 for instance.

The 2018 World Cup was won by largely ethnic African players. The common 'joke' is that 2018 is the first World Cup won by an African team. They just happened to play for France.

If the campaign takes at Qatar '22 there as planned, then you will be aware of the consequences. The Better World Cup will come into its own. If it does not, well, there is much that could happen. The next World Cup after Qatar is in the USA, Canada and Mexico Will the campaign for a better world game continue?

*　　*　　*

Chodak

In 2010, Chodak was an up-and-coming young player at Celtic. He was then just 19 and the first Tibetan footballer to have risen so high. It was all at his feet.

But things went very wrong in Chodak's promising career.

In mid-2012, while he was on another of his clandestine returns home to Tibet, he was struck by a car on a street in Lhasa. At this time, he was a permanent starter in the team. Talk was of him being scouted by numerous top tier European clubs.

He had told me before then that the Chinese were still pressuring him to play for the national team. He continually refused, arguing that he had agreed to play for them on the basis that China backed the Better World Cup. Until there was evidence of that—and, as it turned out, there wouldn't ever be—he stood his ground.

Clearly the Chinese government thought he would boost their chances of making Brazil in 2014.

But Chodak kept saying no.

His club backed him. Celtic FC has never been a club to shy away from nailing its politics to the mast and it didn't hesitate to defend their young player and his decision.

Around this time too, the politics of Tibetan Buddhism were prominent. Whether it was the work of the current Chinese leader or his predecessor, I can't be sure. But, by now, the Chinese were seeking to divide the Tibetan resistance to Beijing's colonial rule by cultivating a dissenting Buddhist sect known as Shugden.

But the cut-to-the-chase line is that Chodak believes the car was no accident and that he was taken out either by the Shugden or the Chinese, or maybe even both.

The results for him were devastating. He suffered a serious spinal cord injury and spent the best part of six months in a hospital.

He medically retired and has never played professionally again.

The driver of the car was never found.

Fortunately, he can walk now, sometimes with a cane.

He remains very much a part of the Better World Cup and now lives in Goa, India with Ebaa. They never married, nor do they have children.

Ebaa retired from her former career and now runs a number of orphanages, which she started with Chodak. She too retains a high level of involvement with the Better World Cup.

*　　*　　*

Windsor

Windsor and I are the major directors of The Better World Cup.

In the years since 2010 to now, we have had a multitude of journeys, physical and mental, as we have sought to hold onto ourselves and our vision in the tempests of life.

We have shared a great deal, travelling, initiating, creating, failing. We have fallen into each other's arms and high-fived to the sky in victory.

Often, we were obliged to put the Better World Cup on hold. More than once in fact. During these times, our friendship deepened. There are those relationships which are cultivated by contact - indeed, some rely upon it. Windsor and I have something different, something I have not known with anyone else, possibly only with Cal and, as I've explained, that is a unique relationship.

As with Cal, Windsor and I both live in an ideal of peace, love, respect and dignity and we don't need to see or speak to each other on the material plane. But, unlike with Cal, this is a mutual space. We communicate regularly in that etheric space we have created, and that we do so in inarticulate, non-verbal, non-corporeal ways. This is soul communication and I sense this is another world where others too may dwell - for I feel them in the breeze, know them as they pass by.

We connect at the oddest times, in a moment of music, a glimpse of an image, a palpable shift in the air as energies slide in and out. We feel each other. These are our portals through which we traverse in our wordless, disembodied connection.

There is such a space for us, as humans, somewhere out there, which is not here in this 3D world, not on the ground. And this is where the connection between Windsor and I lives. We all live out there somewhere, just some are more aware of it.

Windsor married a woman called Dembe in 2016. Their daughter, Afiya, was born in 2017. She has eyes like dinner plates and a look of intelligence when she observes the world that suggests she may have more wisdom than all of us.

Now that she is talking, I often ask her questions on Zoom calls with Windsor about strategy or politics just to see what she answers. She considers, looking straight ahead with those moon-like eyes and generally offers something remarkably oracle-like for a five-year-old.

Capturing life in a few words seems an Obili characteristic. I can't wait for her to start learning Shakespeare. Windsor is already reading - reciting probably - the Sonnets to her before bed.

Windsor and his family still live in Kampala, and he works occasionally at the university, lecturing on English literature and drama, although, he laments, it's not very popular these days. And he runs the Kampala Globe Theatre, putting on a couple of the Bard's best each year amid the grimy, people-teeming streets of the capital, a setting perhaps more like Shakespearean London in both appearance and atmosphere, than London itself.

*　　*　　*

Dad

The old man finally gave up the ghost in May 2011.

He did come home after all his adventures, including his arrest in New York, and passed quietly while I was out buying him a newspaper, as I did everyday. He never read it, but he seemed pleased to have resting on his bedside table. I had finally come home to be with him and Tess and I spent a week or so with him, at home, while he slowly but peacefully—under daily care, thank god— slid away.

In those last few days there was no verbal communication, only a few grunts, sighs, groans, but he had his moments of lucidity. One morning, one of the last, he pointed to a cupboard near his bed, which I opened.

I wasn't sure what he wanted, so I held up what was there— a tennis racket, a cassette deck—and with each, his bony, pallid hand said *no, next*. There were some winter clothes—*no, next*—and under them an old football.

Yes! Thumb up.

I brought it to him, and he reached out his hand, cupped it and held the ball. His hand shook with the effort, and I took it from him. His body still and his face slack and gaunt, but his eyes still alive. Looking at me. Communicating.

I will always hold that moment.

The funeral in Nambour had eight people: Tess and me, some mates from the pub, and an old buddy I didn't know who came up from Brisbane.

When I emerged from the half-hour service and said goodbye to the him that remained in that box, the cool Autumn air seemed to have gone cold. A southerly wind whisked down the street, like it was taking him away. I breathed it in and wondered if it felt, smelled, any different.

Of course, it didn't.

*   *   *

The Ball

It's brown leather, twelve panels.

A Superball Duplo T, official ball for the 1950 World Cup. One of the first laceless balls and the first, and for some time only, World Cup ball to have a logo on it.

Flat now. Hand sewn stitches blown out. Colour of aged flesh.

Lifeless.

But not.

Across one panel, barely visible in some kind of ink or paint: *Raymo d Fox, Ag 10*. His name, his age, his life, battered and almost obliterated by his own foot, and others, rubbed away by grime and dirt and movement and time. Like his life.

It sits on my desk as I write now, full of captured life and memories, of humanity and hope, of past, present and future.

And when I feel low and lost and without solutions, I hold it and feel something bigger than me, bigger than my life.

A connection.

ACKNOWLEDGEMENTS

Thanks to the Sunshine Coast Council for their grant through the Regional Arts Development Fund which helped me complete this book.

Special thanks to Kelly, Bryan and Hari at the Brown Sugar Espresso café in Nambour. I couldn't have finished this book through some difficult times without your dirty chai's and beautiful humanity.

I also would like to acknowledge the work of the late, great Andrew Jennings, who put the wind up FIFA and created the inspiration for this novel.

Finally, thanks to Shirl and Dougie, Steve and Linda and all the "Rose-Downeys" for their enduring support and tolerance of my wild ideas.

More football fiction from Popcorn Press

Introducing – Jarrod Black
Jarrod Black – Hospital Pass
Jarrod Black – Guilty Party
Anna Black – This Girl Can Play
The End of the Game

Coming Soon

The Gaffer
Jarrod Black – Chasing Pack
The Yawning Giant

Also from Fair Play Publishing

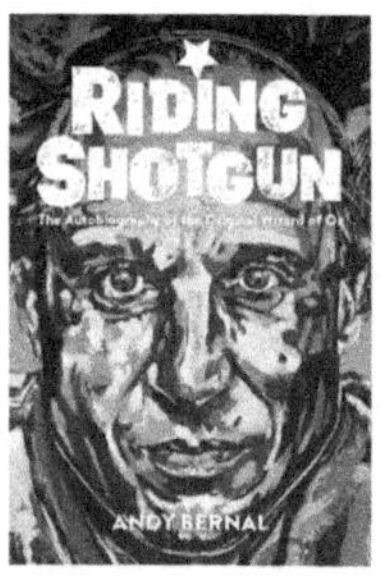

Riding Shotgun

Burning Ambition

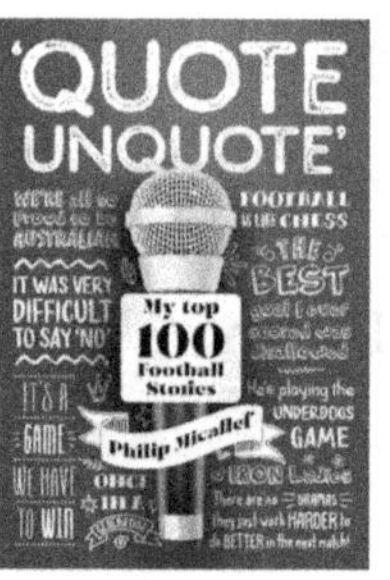

'Quote Unquote'

Be My Guest

Whatever It Takes

www.fairplaypublishing.com.au

ABOUT THE AUTHOR

JJ (James) Rose is a journalist, author, communications and media specialist, academic, and former political advisor who has worked in Asia, Africa, the Middle East, and Australia.

He has written for The Columbia Journalism Review, Nikkei Asia, The Age/Sydney Morning Herald, Al-Jazeera, The Lowy Institute, The New Statesman, The Washington Post, and the South China Morning Post, amongst others.

He has worked as a global media advisor for Morgan Tsvangirai, Aung San Suu Kyi, and the Burmese pro-democracy movement, and was Advisor to the former Special Humanitarian Envoy for the World Food Program, Hon. Abdulaziz bin Mohamed Arrukban.

He has taught Journalism at Brisbane's Griffith University.

As a teenager, James trialed with Wolverhampton Wanderers, Coventry City, and Brentford, and was offered a youth contract with Eddie Thomson's Sydney City Slickers. He's not a fan of the billionaire's club, otherwise known as the EPL, but if pushed he would turn up at a West Ham game, and he occasionally Roars for Brisbane. He still dreams of the '06 Socceroos Golden Generation, Guus, and the lost opportunities.

In 2011, he published his first novel 'Virus', a political thriller, and in 2001 wrote 'Ethical and Active Shareholding – an Australian investor's guide'.

www.popcornpress.com.au

9 781925 914412